THE FASHION COMMITTEE

THE FASHION COMMITTEE

A NOVEL OF ART, CRIME, AND APPLIED DESIGN

Susan Juby

PENGUIN TEEN
an imprint of Penguin Random House Canada Young Readers, a Penguin
Random House Company

Published in hardcover by Penguin Teen, 2017
Simultaneously published in the United States by Viking, an imprint of Penguin
Random House LLC

1 2 3 4 5 6 7 8 9 10 (RRD)

Manufactured in the U.S.A.

Library and Archives Canada Cataloguing in Publication
Juby, Susan, 1969-, author
The fashion committee / Susan Juby.
Issued in print and electronic formats.
ISBN 978-0-670-06760-2 (hardback). —ISBN 978-0-14-319620-4 (epub)

I. Title.
PS8569.U324F37 2017   jC813'.6   C2016-905206-0
                                               C2016-905207-9

Book design by Kate Renner

www.penguinrandomhouse.ca

Penguin
Random House
PENGUIN TEEN CANADA

For Jim, whose sense of style
contains multitudes

The performance
that is fashion
is one road
from the inner to
the outer world.

—Elizabeth Wilson,
Adorned in Dreams

PART ONE

The Fashion Competition

Green Pastures
Emerging Talent Scholarship

This year the Green Pastures Emerging Talent scholarship will be awarded to a student who shows promise in the field of fashion design.

To apply, candidates must submit an application by February 15, detailing their interest in fashion, discussing their inspirations, and describing their approach to designing and constructing garments. The top applicants will be invited to show their work at a fashion show at Green Pastures Academy of Art and Applied Design on Saturday, May 4. Those selected to take part in the fashion show will also be invited to attend an introductory workshop on Saturday, March 2.

The contestants must document their design process by keeping a fashion diary (which the judges may ask to see), and they will be asked to submit drawings, photos, and other research materials, such as mood boards. We will be looking for students who demonstrate ingenuity, creativity, and an ability to be responsive to the needs of their chosen models.

The fashion show will be judged by an elite committee of fashion professionals and artists.

The winner of the fashion show will receive a one-year scholarship to Green Pastures Fashion Program. The competition is open to students entering grades 10 through 12. For full details and the application form, please see: www.fashionscholarship .greenpasturesacademy.com.

KEY DATES

Deadline to apply:
February 15

Workshop for applicants accepted into competition:
March 2

Fashion Show:
May 4

one

ℒCHARLIEℒ
ℒDEANℒ

> **HERE'S AN IDEA** © CHARLIE DEAN DESIGNS:
>
> *Dress for your destiny. Do it now, even if your destiny hasn't happened. If you want to be an astronaut, wear white. Be puffy. Add patches. Want to be a hedge fund manager? Wear a beautifully tailored suit, even if you have to wear a fast-food uniform over it. Dressing for your dreams makes them 75 to 85 percent more likely to come true!*

DATE: FEBRUARY 8

I know I probably don't have to hand this diary in, but if anyone asks for it, I would like it to be wonderfully comprehensive. Who knows! It may end up being part of the Charlie Dean™ archives stored at the FIT fashion museum. I want anyone who reads this to know that life has a way of working out. When things appear bleak and there is no hope on the horizon, you are likely to be surprised by a wonderful turn of events just around the corner.

I will be forever grateful to Mr. Oliver, our guidance counselor, for alerting me to such a life-changing and almost miraculous opportunity. Of course, he didn't *personally and specifically* contact me about the scholarship, but I'm sure he would have eventually. He knows how much I want to go to Green Pastures. I've asked him about how I might get into the school seven times since I arrived at R. S. Jackson Senior High in November of last year. I think he's becoming a little bit afraid of me. That could be why he's so rarely in his office. On the other hand, he could be at one of the other four high schools he covers.

I take my breaks in his empty waiting room. It's a good place to retreat from the noise and many unchic sights at R. S. Jackson, even though the waiting room is also quite unchic. Still, today suggests that it's a place where miracles happen.

I was sketching away in the waiting room at lunchtime when the school secretary came in. He's young and has gorgeous brown skin and marvelous almond eyes. He's also enormous, well over six feet tall and bulky, bulky, bulky in a way that is immensely comforting. Best secretary ever! You just know that if a box needs lifting or a sad feeling needs a sympathetic shoulder to lean on, he'd be absolutely ideal.

We even have similar names. His is Charles. Mine is Charlie, short for Charlene. Isn't that so much fun?

"Charlie, you in here again?"

I smiled. One can do nothing else when confronted with such positivity and warmth. He's like a woodstove! Wrapped in a marvelous snuggly blanket!

"I told you to check out the old art room. That's where all the creative types in this place hang out at lunch."

"I'm fine in here," I said.

"Okay. Well, if you see Mr. Oliver, tell him his mailbox was full. He should really come to work sometime. Santa gets less mail than that guy."

Charles held up a tall stack of mail.

Before I could respond there was a cry and a thud out in the hallway.

"I told you to suck it, loser!" shouted someone. Then there was a crash that sounded like a body being slammed against a locker.

Charles groaned and dumped the mail on the table in front of me.

"Back in a sec," he said. Then he went into the hallway to break up the fight.

Outside the noise level rose, and I was glad to be safely tucked away in the empty waiting room. Then I noticed the envelope peeking out of the pile. It bore the Green Pastures logo.

C'est très interessant!

I slipped the envelope out of the pile and held it in front of me. Then I glanced at the doorway. A face appeared, mouthed the word "freak" at me, then disappeared.

I took a deep breath and slid the envelope into my purse. Then I gathered my things and hurried out of the office, away from the post-fight crowd, and headed into the girls' bathroom.

Inside the bathroom stall I opened the envelope with trembling *mains*, which means "hands" in French, if you don't know. As I'd hoped and prayed, the letter contained the notice about this year's Emerging Talent scholarship competition.

Angels sang and choirs choired when I read that the talent this year was *fashion*. My specialty! Fate was unfolding in front of me like a red carpet, handwoven just for me by a team of exquisitely talented, old-world artisans in perfect white smocks.

When we moved to Nanaimo last year I was partway through tenth grade. The timing of the move wasn't ideal from a schooling-disruption perspective, but my dad's entire parenting style is based on disruption. Then I realized that Nanaimo is the home of Green Pastures Academy of Art and Applied Design, which has *the* best fashion program of any high school in the country. Maybe on the continent. Seriously. It's as good as many of the top fashion colleges, or even better.

I found out that Green Pastures only offers a few general entrance scholarships every year, and only to students *entering* tenth grade. Tragically for the fulfillment of my dreams, I'm in eleventh grade. Last spring, I applied anyway and noted on my application that I'd be willing to go back a year, but my application was rejected. It's basically ageism, which I supposed I'd better get used to if I'm going to be in fashion. The people in charge of giving out general merit scholarships may have been influenced by my grades, which aren't what some would consider scholarship-worthy. My focus is fashion. I can't afford the distractions of things like science and math, except as they pertain to fashion.

I don't mean to brag, but I'm talented enough to be in the fashion program, even though it's so far beyond competitive it's like *etitive* or maybe just *ive*. The problem is the cost of Green Pastures and our current economic status, which is best described as extremely depressed. The place is *très cher*! (Please note that I am currently teaching myself French from Google Translate. I know I make a lot of mistakes, but I also feel it's very French of me to keep trying. French classes were cut back at R. S. Jackson last year, and it's almost impossible to get into the one class that's offered, but I *persister* in learning and growing intellectually. It's crucially important to speak French if you're going to be in fashion. French is basically the *lingua franca* of fashion!)

Because life is good and there is a god and she loves me a lot, there's also a discipline-specific Emerging Talent scholarship each year. Each year it's different. Last year it was pottery. The year before it was fabric arts. In theory, I might have had to wait NINE years for fashion to come around! I'd be twenty-five and look very out of place, even though I take skin care *very* seriously and am one of the top part-time skin care and makeup associates at Shoppers Drug Mart. But *this* is the year they're offering a fashion scholarship. What are the chances? Well, I suppose they're one in ten. But still!

I stood in the bathroom stall and stared down at the pamphlet. It was purest fate that I came upon it just in time to apply. I found the doorway leading directly to my dreams of salvation!

two

FEBRUARY 8

It seems pretty stupid that applicants have to keep a diary that no one is going to read. I hope this one won't get held against me in a court of law aimed at prosecuting scholarship fraud cases. What the hell. I'll tell the truth, get things off my chest, and then I'll burn this.

When I saw that the scholarship to get into Green Pastures was for the fashion program, I wanted to kick someone. I'd hoped it was going to be metal arts this year. Drawing. Carving. ANYTHING ELSE, FFS.

But the scholarship was for fashion, which meant no art school for me.

I got the good news from the girl who sits next to me in the class our teacher calls "Career Trajectories," which is known by those of us learning to lower our expectations as "Career Tragedies." The girl left the scholarship brochure on her desk while she went to the can, probably to tend to her weird makeup or to fix that lumpy-ass hairstyle she wears. I looked at it because I was tired of listening to Ms. Donner drone on about how a job in the oil fields or natural gas or the logging industry or mining was the only responsible choice for a "certain kind of student." Meaning poor and working-class students. Meaning academically average or ungifted students. Meaning me.

Ms. Donner obviously never watched *Dead Poets Society* or *To Sir, with Love* or any of those other movies about inspiring students to do and be more. She didn't say so directly, but Ms. Donner thought the smart thing for us was to check all hopes and dreams at the door. Put that shit away so it wouldn't interfere with being a cog in the economic machine.

Her message of practicality had not gotten through to the girl who sat next to me. Only a mime or a pro unicycle rider could have been less practical than that girl. She dressed up every day like she was going to a costume party where the goal was to look forty years older than you actually are. She was probably ecstatic that the scholarship for Green Pastures this year was for fashion, since she seemed like exactly the kind of person who would want to be in fashion design. Exactly the kind of person who would want to work in the most corrupt, bullshit so-called creative industry there is, an industry entirely aimed at making people crave more than they need and feel bad about how they look.

I read the details. They made me want to set the piece of paper on fire. Or shred it up and put it on the bottom of a rabbit cage.

Granted, it doesn't take much to set me off. My grandparents have this embittered little schnauzer–Jack Russell dog called Bites who is truly the most miserable of animals. After he bit the meter reader, animal control made my Gran take him to something called Reactivity class. I joined them out of interest. The dogs in that class lost their mind at the slightest thing: other dogs, noises, movement, air currents. Dogs barked, snarled, and hurled themselves against the gates of their kennels and their leashes. Bites was the calmest one. He even seemed a little afraid, which isn't like him. I think the class might have scared him temporarily obedient. The thing is that I understood those dogs and had a lot of sympathy for their position. I'd be better off in Reactivity class than high school. John Thomas-Smith, Reactive. If I ever get business cards, I'm getting that printed on them.

But back to the scholarship, Green Pastures, and fashion.

Green Pastures has been my main reactivity trigger ever since I was in ninth grade and our art teacher took us there on a field trip. A field trip! Like we were going overseas!

I clearly remember getting off our crappy yellow school bus and standing in the Green Pastures parking lot. We probably looked like inmates on a work detail.

In keeping with its overwhelming and oppressive specialness, the campus was luxe. The architecture, the interior design, the landscaping, and the furnishings: every detail was designed to nurture creative young people. But only rich ones.

We spent the whole day there. We got to sit in on an oil painting class. We watched a graphic arts lesson. Tried our hand at sculpting and saw the pottery studio. We walked the wide, bright hallways, passed a living wall made of plants for "enhanced air quality" (!), looked into the "dedicated carving shed" (!!), and ate our bag lunches in a huge glass atrium surrounded by semiprivate pod work spaces for seniors (I can't even count how many exclamation points that needs). We walked around a goddamned "atelier" used by the fashion design students. It had a brick feature wall, vintage furniture, fitting rooms, a big dressing room, dedicated classrooms, and a runway. A *runway*.

The school had a room for students who wanted to learn

"small-animal taxidermy." Meanwhile, at our piece of crap school, a mere fifteen-minute drive away, we took half our classes in portable trailers, and there was talk of canceling gym because of the high price of balls.

My girlfriend, Barbra, was on the tour, too. She could tell I was rancid with resentment from the first minute we set foot on the campus. She kept putting a hand on my arm. Not telling me what to do or how to feel but reminding me that I exist, if that makes any sense. There was something about Green Pastures that made me feel invisible and angry. Barbra understood that.

She started making pointed little remarks at each new ultra-excellent detail. When we were shown the dark room she said, "We had one just like it when we were children. This really brings me back." When we saw some kids editing their films in the film suite, she said, "They've really got them packed into that teeny little space. Poor things."

In addition to siphoning off some of my feelings in a way that wouldn't get me thrown off the tour, she also stopped me from getting charged with assault.

"John," she warned, when we saw a kid sauntering down the hallway in a white suit, like he thought he was Tom Wolfe. (For anyone who doesn't know, Wolfe is this writer who is known for dressing in white suits. We were assigned something by him in English. The story made no impression on me whatsoever, but our teacher, who told us on the first day that his undergraduate degree is actually in business, couldn't stop talking about Wolfe's white suits and how they were such a genius way for the guy to brand himself.) Anyway the kid, who had this little mustache, jaunted by us whistling, and it took every bit of dog anti-reactivity training I had and Barbra's good influence to keep me from tripping him, hip-checking him, or otherwise interfering with his excessive well-being.

Back on the bus to go home everyone was quiet. Even our teacher seemed shaken by what we'd just seen. There was no debrief, just a lot of sighing except for one guy who kept talking about how "sweet" it would be to go to Green Pastures.

"You got a winning lotto ticket?" asked Gus Joseph, who is good at drawing cars but not known for his attitude.

"The good news is they offer scholarships," said Mr. Fairfax. I admit that the old sphincter of hope tightened up at those words.

Dare I hope?

Mr. Fairfax checked his phone, then muttered "damn."

"I'm sorry, guys. The deadline for the general merit scholarships was last Friday."

He stared at the screen for a few more minutes.

"But it says here that they hold an Emerging Talent scholarship competition each year for students in grades ten through twelve. You missed it for this year, but you guys could apply for that next year."

We took that tour in February. By the following September, thanks to government cutbacks and a general societal disinterest in lower-income kids, our school no longer had any art or music classes. Our main creative outlet was carving swear words into our desks and, in the most troubled cases, into our arms. A few weeks ago I saw Mr. Fairfax working at Starbucks.

As for the mythical scholarship to Green Pastures, which Mr. Fairfax had breathlessly referred to as "the Sorbonne of Vancouver Island," the following year the Emerging Talent competition was in ceramics. That was a no-go for me. I nurtured my resentment at the unfairness of life, made angry metal art, drew my angry pictures, and was bitter. It might not have been the most productive approach to life, but it was honest, at least.

If the Green Pastures tour sparked smoldering class resentment in me, my job at the Salad Stop turned it into a blaze.

The Salad Stop is located between the Waterfront Pub and the Ocean Breeze Liquor Depot on Hammond Bay Road, not far from Green Pastures. Maybe Steve, the franchisee, who spends most of his time at his other businesses (a CrossFit gym and a weightlifter's "supplement" store), located it there so that drinkers could replenish the vitamins they lost during their boozing.

We serve salads to the ladies whose sole job seems to be doing hot yoga twice a day. They come in between classes to grab a small organic greens or, when they're feeling ready to risk a pot belly the size of an acorn, a half serving of ancient grain salad.

The serious boozers who move between the pub and the liquor store weave past our front window like fronds of kelp swaying on the incoming tide. They don't bother with salads, which I appreciate.

Then there's the youngest part of our customer base: the spoiled shitheads—sorry; reactive—from goddamned Green Pastures. They come in wearing their duck-hunting hats and goddamned mime outfits, carrying tin lunch boxes or those little round plastic buckets construction workers carry on their belts, the ones meant for nails and whatnot. The art kids keep them filled with chalk or paintbrushes or pens or feathers. They are hard to take, but the worst of the worst are the ones in the fashion program.

They're instantly recognizable. They wear all black and have severe blond or severe black hair, severe bangs, or hair pulled severely away from the face. Smiles strictly forbidden! Red lipstick on both males and females. They vary in size from fat to thin, but they're *all* super controlling about what they eat.

Samples of questions I have been asked by Green Pastures fashion students:

"Where do the greens come from? Are they local? How local? Like, do you have mileage you could share with me?"

"Did Chuck Wiggins in Parksville grow these? I'm partial to his produce."

"Are the walnuts on the apple salad non-GMO? What about the apples? And the oil? What can you tell me about the oil?"

"Is this container biodegradable?"

"Did you wash your hands before touching the lettuce? I sort of have this thing about hepatitis. Not saying you have it or anything. I just like to be safe."

Oh yeah. I've been asked these questions and more by the Green Pastures fashion students, who seem to be in training to be pains in the ass for the retail sector, which is probably going to be me and my kind if I don't get a trade after I graduate. *If* I graduate.

So I wasn't surprised that the girl who sat beside me in Career Prep felt she was Green Pastures material. She's intensely precious, patently fake, and basically unbearable, all red-lipped, be-suited ridiculousness. She doodles her way through every single class, same as me, but she does it in an annoying way that causes me to have harsh reactivity.

On the scholarship pamphlet I'd pulled over to read, the girl had written several depressing things in the margins, such as "Me!" and "Destiny calls!" and "Charlie Dean Designs!!™®" There were a lot of exclamation points and sketches of dresses and shoes and patterns.

When she sat back down, I tapped my finger on the brochure.

"So you're ditching this dump and going to Spoiled Brat Academy?"

"I hope so," she said. "They have an amazing fashion program. Going to a school like that would be a life-altering experience." Even though she'd only been out of the bathroom for sixty seconds, she whipped out this little compact and checked her lipstick, presumably to make sure it was still murder red.

She was right, though. Much as I hate to admit it, people who go to schools like Green Pastures have different lives. Better lives.

"Oh yeah?" I said. "I've always been real interested in fashion."

She looked over at me, and her smooth, milk-white brow nearly furrowed.

"Really?" she said in a careful voice.

"I mean, what's not to love? The glamor, the models, the money. That sort of shit."

She looked down at the piece of paper, probably debating whether to get up and go to another seat.

"Is that contest open to anyone?"

Her mouth dropped open half an inch, but she didn't answer.

"Because of how much I like fashion I might enter. Throw a few of my outfits in there for consideration. I might be the next..." For a second, I couldn't think of a designer. "Hasbro," I said, thinking that was probably the name of *some* designer.

"Do you mean Halston?" she asked.

"Him too," I said. "Halston and Hasbro. Jules and Verne. I love all those guys. Their outfits are just, like, glorious to me."

"You sew?"

"Are you kidding? All day, all night, as they say in the song."

"What?" she said, getting a little testy now. "I mean, *what* do you sew?"

The girl was the awkward type. Hardly ever spoke. Just sat looking like she'd break into five sharp pieces if she fell over. But I had her blood up now. My specialty.

"You mean besides the seeds of destruction? Little of this, little of that."

She smoothed her skirt, which looked like it used to belong to Queen Elizabeth. Wool. Pleats. Granny shoes. The whole bit.

"You *should* enter," she said. "I'd like to see what you come up with. Maybe it will be as good as something by Jules and Verne."

The "loser" at the end of the sentence was unspoken, but I heard it loud and clear. And didn't care.

"Mind if I copy down the website address? I don't want to miss the deadline. When is it? Next Friday?"

Wordlessly and maybe a bit reluctantly, she pushed the pamphlet to me. When I'd written down the address, she took it back, folded it neatly, and put it in a leather case the size and shape of a Buick's fender.

"I really, really love fashion," I said to her profile. "It's so *important* and meaningful. I just hope you don't mind some competition—what did you say your name was?"

"Charlie Dean," she said. "And I welcome competition."

three

CHARLIE DEAN

HERE'S AN IDEA © CHARLIE DEAN DESIGNS:

If you are unable to afford beautiful clothes, treat the ones you have as though they are irreplaceable. Fold them neatly. Hang them gently. Wear them with utmost pride. In fact, treat all your personal things with care and deliberation. Love and attention make everything more attractive.

DATE: FEBRUARY 8

Days until application is due: 7

I was so consumed with thoughts of the application that I nearly forgot to be nervous about what I might find at home after school.

Let me explain. *Avec réticence.*

My father got out of drug rehab two days ago. For anyone unfamiliar with the experience, the first few days out are always uncertain for the newly clean addict. Relapse is an ever-present threat. Due to having to attend school, I hadn't been home to monitor my father's behavior. Even though Alateen says it's impossible to try to get or keep an addict clean, he seems to do better if I keep an eye on him.

So it was with some nervousness that I conducted my initial inspection of our unglamorous rental house, located in the unstylish reaches of the poorest part of town. There were no unsavory drug friends hanging around, and when I went inside, I found no high father and, best of all, no dreadful new girlfriend. Great news!

Instead he'd left me a note on the kitchen counter saying that he'd gone to a meeting and would be home around five. It might even be true!

This day was turning out perfectly!

Relieved, I went to my room and opened my laptop, and after luxuriating around the Green Pastures website for fifteen or twenty minutes, I downloaded the application and wondered idly who my competition might be.

It was a surprise to me that the boy from Career Trajectories was interested in entering. Not because he's unattractive or without style. He is actually quite handsome in an athletic but slightly unkempt way. I could see him featured in a Street Style spread about skateboarders or BMX riders. He has bright blue eyes, *très* striking against his dark complexion.

The verbena accents on his shoes were a delightful touch, and I'm almost certain his pullover was vintage Patagonia.

Don't misunderstand me. I'm not interested in him romantically. I have decided that I cannot afford to be distracted by even casual relationships until I am well established in my fashion career. I haven't had a romantic *liaison* yet and have no plans.

But back to the boy. I do hope he enters. The fashion world needs all kinds of people, even ones who make jokes about fake designers, which I could see was quite funny of him. It would be good to know someone else, even if I would wipe the floor with him. I have been making and designing clothes since I was a child. It is my life. He probably made the joke because he couldn't name even one designer. Poor thing.

I read through the many sections of the application and experienced a touch of what the French call the *nerfs* when I saw the section devoted to personal biography.

No one looking at me would think I get nervous, because I am impeccably put together. Carefully dressed people always look unflappable. I know in my bones that I am Green Pastures material. It's just that, well, my personal history is . . . not fashionable.

Here are the facts of my case. As you have already gathered, my dad has a small drug problem. Well, it's a bit bigger than small. He gets periods of sobriety, then, *inévitablement*, he meets a new woman who turns out to be a bad influence. He relapses and goes downhill like a professional bobsledder in a new wind suit. This is followed by breakup with said lady-friend, and a move to a new home or a new town. Repeat, *ad infinitum*. (It's good to throw in a little Latin for variety!)

His latest stay in rehab lasted eight weeks, which meant that I was by myself this past Christmas. I've not told anyone that, of course, and I'm not mentioning it here to gain pity or extra sympathy points from readers or possible biographers. There is nothing less stylish than being an object of pity. Anyway, it wasn't that bad. Being alone was *certainement* preferable to having my father and his druggy friends hanging around the house while I attempted to maintain a chic and festive holiday atmosphere!

I kept so busy that I hardly even noticed I was alone. First, I took extra shifts at the makeup counter at Shoppers Drug

Mart, where, as noted, I am a valued team member. Christmas Eve I walked home from work and spent the evening sewing and reading fashion blogs.

I woke up Christmas Day, put some apple juice from one of those enormous glass jugs—so rustic and reminiscent of yurts!—and mulling spice on the stove to give the house that *It's a Wonderful Life* smell. I spritzed the cedar boughs and made myself a lovely brunch of raisin bread French toast.

In the afternoon I reread part of *D.V.*, the memoir by my idol, Diana Vreeland, a true fashion visionary and a person who understood the critical importance of beauty, and in the afternoon I talked to my dad on the phone at his rehab center. He had just gone in, so he wasn't allowed "outside" visits. He told me he was with a "good group of guys," and they would get a Christmas dinner cooked by people from a local church.

"It's not very attractive here, Charlie," he said.

"Just get better, Jacques. That's all that matters." I sat in my room, which is by far the most stylish space in our house. I was hemming a pair of wide-legged pants in the whitest linen and rawest silk. They were going to be too Jil Sander for words.

"Charlie girl, I'm sorry I've gone down the tubes again. I had such high hopes. But when Leanne ran into trouble, I ran with her. Damn it, I should know better by now."

"It's okay. Recovery is a process."

"God, how did we get so lucky to have such an incredible kid? Your mom would be so proud. You know you remind me of her."

I didn't want to have that conversation on Christmas Day or any day, really. I'm like my mom in that I love fashion, love sewing, and care about beauty. In important other ways, I am not like my mom. For instance, I don't plan to die with a needle in my arm. Oh dear, forgive me. That got dark rather quickly. Back to the heartwarming holiday conversation with my dad.

"We'll do Christmas dinner and presents when I get out," he said.

"Of course we will."

Long pause.

"On that subject . . ."

I waited.

"When you're allowed to visit next week do you think you could bring me a few bucks? And a carton of smokes?"

"I've got money and your cigarettes ready. I can drop them off tonight if you want."

"No, no. It would take you most of the day to get here and back. Holiday transit and all that."

"I don't mind."

"I forbid it, Charlie. It's Christmas Day. You should be enjoying yourself. But maybe you could come tomorrow. I just need money for incidentals. We have enough to give the landlord his rent?"

"Mr. Devlin will have his money on New Year's Eve."

"You really are the greatest. Merry Christmas, Charlie girl."

"Merry Christmas, Dad."

I've been more or less looking after my dad since I was nine. He gives me his disability checks, and I make sure the rent is paid. When he's doing well, he also gives me the money from his DJ gigs. Between that and the money I make at the makeup counter we not only get by, but I manage to keep myself in fabric and notions. This early training in discipline and frugality will pay off when it's time for me to run my own fashion line.

Enough about Christmas past. Purposeful forgetting is something I learned from studying the life and works of Mrs.

Diana Vreeland, who ignored all unpleasantness and focused on taking care of business. That is always the best thing to do.

Back to my contemplation of the application. I wondered what my mother would have said. She would have been so excited. Thinking of her reminded me of the last time my dad and I drove through Edmonton on our way to some dumpy new rental in some dumpy new town. We passed the intersection where everything in our lives had gone so wrong. It had been turned into a construction zone. The mall across the street from the old motel where we'd been staying when it happened was half-demolished, and the motel was boarded up.

As we waited for a construction worker to wave us through the intersection, I wondered if my dad had noticed where we were and if he was thinking about my mom. But he wasn't doing well and was very short-tempered, so I said nothing.

But maybe driving by the scene of the crime made an impression on him, because not long after we drove past the mall, he gave me a book called *Black Friday* that was full of photos of abandoned malls. The images showed how much beauty there was to be found in the most unlikely places.

Now I closed the application and got up from my desk and picked up the copy of *Black Friday* and flipped through it.

Remarkable. Haunting. A bit like our past. But I'd spent too much time there. Now I had to look to the future. I put the book down and continued to sketch ideas for my entry. Whatever it was had to be epic, extravagant, gorgeous.

Days until application is due: 7.

Hopes for fabulous future: high!

four

FEBRUARY 8

I was reading the application and jotting down curse words and offensive comments in the margins when Booker and Barbra came over after their shift slinging baked goods at Crumb.

Bites lost his mind when they knocked, barking and growling and hurling himself against the door. There's no sneaking into this house.

While Barbra got Bites, whose reactivity training never quite took, calmed down, Booker presented my grandparents with his usual offering of baked goods. Booker's my best friend, and he's great with older people. And younger people, too, I guess.

My grandparents are in their late sixties, but they seem about ten years older. They both worked physically hard, unhealthy jobs most of their lives. My grandma spent the last twenty-five years working cleanup at a fish-packing plant. Grandpa was a welder for his whole adult life. They retired with about twelve serious health conditions apiece: bad backs, bum lungs, arthritis, diabetes, allergies. The whole deal.

Neither of them is supposed to eat sugar or flour, but I was not about to interfere with their crush on Booker and his gifts of highly refined carbohydrates.

"Well, Booker!" I heard Gramps say from his easy chair in the living room. "How's life treating you? Baking up a storm?"

"Yes, sir," said Booker.

"Oh, Booker. Cinnamon swirls!" said my grandmother. "And apple Danish. You are a stinker!"

"Damn it," said Grandpa. "Going to make us fat."

My grandparents weigh about eighty-six pounds apiece. They weren't going to get fat at this stage of the game. They go nonstop from about five thirty in the morning. They putter around the house and the yard, meet their friends for coffee at McDonald's or Tim Hortons, golf, curl, attend meat raffles at the Legion, and do a lot of other activities that appeal to the fun-loving senior crowd. By eight p.m., it's like someone took out their batteries. They sit in their chairs in front of the TV and don't move until they go to bed at nine o'clock.

"No, sir," said Booker. "Not you. Or Mrs. Smith."

"Hello, Barbra," said Gramps. "I guess you're here to keep John on the straight and narrow?" This was followed by a hacking cough and some laughter. My grandparents are extremely okay people. They really are.

My mom and I have lived with them for my whole life, so they've basically raised me. In the past seven years my mom has started traveling for her work, which is teaching ESL, so she's hardly ever here. Now she works in Dubai and only comes home once a year, which is fine. We're not super close. There's not a lot of difference between having awkward conversations on Skype and having them in person.

Living with my dad had never been an option. He's a long-haul trucker who lives on the mainland in an undisclosed location. I don't go to visit him. Ever. My dad takes his duty to shirk his paternal responsibilities seriously. From him I got my impressive hyphenated name.

All in all, my situation is fine. My grandparents are the best people I know, except for Barbra and Booker. But they're also sort of tired and let me get away with anything. Which I appreciate.

After the greetings were done, Booker and Barbra slid into my room and closed the door behind them.

Barbra gave me a kiss and then flopped onto my bed.

"I love them," said Booker. "Seriously. Your grandparents are like the salt and pepper shakers of the earth."

Booker's home situation is lousy, and he never misses a chance to admire my grandparents.

"So stay here. They've invited you enough times."

"No can do. My sister left last year. The position of Target-in-Chief falls to me now. My little brother is too young for the job." He glanced at the paperwork on my desk. "What are you doing?" he asked. "Don't tell me it's time for college applications already." He took the extra chair, turning around in it so he could prop his legs on my bed. He pulled a can of beer and a bag of Doritos out of his knapsack. "I thought we decided to stay working-class heroes forever."

"I'm not even sure the Salad Stop qualifies as a working-class job."

"Yeah, it occupies a strange middle ground. All that kale. It's not right."

He offered us chips. We both said no.

Booker's the first one to say he's got a bit of an eating problem. It gets worse, then better, then worse, depending on how his mother is doing. If she's stable, he eats like two regular guys. When she's in one of her dark periods, he eats like a powerlifting team. Booker is big and good-looking, with dark hair that reminds me of early Elvis, and he looks like he couldn't give a shit, which is deceiving. He cares so much that it takes about five thousand calories a day to keep himself soothed. At least, that's what he says. His relationships with girls aren't much better than his relationship with food. Either he gets too attached and the girl pulls away, or the girl is completely wild and ditches him for an asshole.

Barbra and I have been together since we were all in eighth grade, so he thinks we know just about everything there is to know about relationships. He says that if he could meet a nice girl, and by that he means a girl like Barbra, he would settle down. It's probably true. Barbra has a way of making you feel like the world makes sense. She's really grounded. If I ever forget how lucky I am to be with her, Booker reminds me, pronto. Actually, everyone does. I basically won the girlfriend lottery with Barbra.

"No, it's this application for a contest. I'm just rage reading it."

I sat near the end of the bed, and Barbra wiggled around to rest her feet on my thighs.

"Is it an application to take me on a ten-day cruise to the Bahamas? I think I would enjoy cruising the ocean blue with a few thousand seniors."

I rubbed her feet.

"No, it's for that annual scholarship to get into Green Pastures."

Barbra sat up quickly, jerking her feet out of my hands.

Booker stopped drinking his beer, and his hand froze on its way to deliver a chip to his mouth.

"*What?*" they said together.

"Is it sculpture this year?" asked Barbra.

"Tell me it's metalwork, dude. If it is, you're in like sin!" said Booker.

"Nope. Fashion. And this is the last year I'll be eligible."

"Shit," said Booker.

"Huh," said Barbra. "You in a fashion competition. Now that would be interesting to watch."

"Are you saying you don't find me fashionable?"

"Well, you do have a hate-on for anything that seems trendy, including all stores and most clothes," said Booker.

"There's that," I said.

"Green Fields is a dump," said Barbra, her brown eyes seeing right through my jokes and into the disappointment. "Their facilities are barely even so-so."

"Yeah, well, it was a long shot."

The three of us didn't talk for a while.

"I found out in Career Tragedies," I said finally. "You know that girl who wears the funny suits and has that old-fashioned hair? She had the announcement this afternoon."

"I know that girl," said Booker, who has made a point of knowing every single girl in school, an impressive feat, since there are nearly twelve hundred people in our school and half of them are girls. "She's got some serious style."

Barbra also nodded, recognizing the description.

"I think she looks ridiculous. Well, anyway, she had the flyer." I gave a little laugh. "I told her I was way into fashion. Said I was going to enter. She looked unimpressed."

"You should do it just for the hell of it," said Booker, chugging his beer.

"Please," said Barbra. "He doesn't need that place. Can you imagine listening to him complain about all the spoiled kids up there?"

"True. You've got us. You've got your workshop in the garage. Screw Green Pastures."

"Just imagine what he would make for a fashion show," said Barbra, grinning.

"I'm fashionable," I said, feeling a little stung by their reaction, even though I agreed with them.

"You," said Barbra, giving me a kiss, "are fashionably unfashionable. Just how I like you."

I made a big show of crumpling up the application and throwing it in the garbage. But when they were gone, I pulled it out and started to fill it in. I would strike a pointless blow for the have-nots and those of us who are not going places.

Motto: What's to hate about fashion and fashion people? See quote below.

Never fit a dress to the body, but train the body to fit the dress.

—ELSA SCHIAPARELLI

five

❧CHARLIE❧
❧DEAN❧

HERE'S AN IDEA © CHARLIE DEAN DESIGNS:

The next time you see a fashionable person, don't think: that girl/boy/fascinating mix of both was born with all the advantages. Think: that person has made an effort to make my eyes happy. And be grateful to them for attempting to improve your day with their appearance.

DATE: FEBRUARY 8

Days until application is due: 7

I was in the midst of writing about my creative influences for my application and had mentioned Charles Frederick Worth, Madeleine Vionnet, Charles James, Elsa Schiaparelli, James Galanos, Miuccia Prada, Christian Dior, Claire McCardell, John Galliano, Coco Chanel, Jean Muir, Hardy Amies, Cristóbal Balenciaga, and Valentino and was wondering how many more designers I could include and how much detail I should go into when the front door opened and my father called my name from the kitchen.

I could tell from his voice that he was clean. The child of an addict learns to determine such things at a great distance.

With luck he'd gone to the meeting and found a wonderful, stable, *male* sponsor who would not allow him to be in a relationship for the suggested year or maybe the ten- to twenty-year period I would prefer.

All happy thoughts were banished from my head when I reached the kitchen and saw that my father, Jack, whom I prefer to call Jacques for reasons of Frenchness, was not alone.

He had a ladyfriend with him.

My face may have fallen the tiniest bit. So soon! Couldn't we have at least a month or even a week without having our lives torn apart? Especially with me about to enter the most important project of my life so far.

At risk of sounding overdramatic, which is a tendency Charlie Dean readily admits in herself, I felt like weeping, screaming, crying, and stamping my nicely shod feet. My father has the worst taste in women of any man, living or dead.

I'm proud to say I hid all signs of the turmoil roiling in my breast from my father and the new lady. This is because I learned about manners from Diana Vreeland, who is said to have had fantastic manners, except when she was unhappy about matters pertaining to design.

"Hello," I said. "How do you do?" And while I was speaking, I conducted a lightning survey of the new lady in the same way a paramedic or police officer might assess a dangerous situation that was sure to get worse.

Inappropriately young? Check!

Too much leather and denim and unfortunate tattoo work? Check!

At least one accessory featuring the logo of that great fashion house, Harley-Davidson? Check!

Still and all, Charlie Dean felt a tiny flicker of relief because at least this potential *paramour* did not appear to be actively high. When Charlie Dean's remaining parental unit comes home with a lady who is already under the influence, it's time for Charlie Dean to head for the nearest Super 8 because things are going to get *hors de contrôle*!

Jacques was in high spirits or what passes for high spirits when he is clean. Moderately fine spirits?

"Charlie girl," he said. "I'd like you to meet Mischa."

Mischa, who had surprisingly excellent bone structure and unblemished skin with so little color in it she'd be quite striking in makeup, smiled wanly. My father's women have two smiles: wan and far too wide.

"Doing homework?" she asked, noting the Montblanc in my hand. Points for Mischa! Hardly any of the ladies asked me questions relating to myself. If they asked me anything at all, it was usually the ever-popular "Where's the bathroom?"; the classic "Can you call me a cab?"; or my personal favorite, "Do you got ten bucks you could lend me?" This was the first time I could recall one asking about my health, wellness, and education.

"I'm filling out an application," I said, surprised at myself for revealing that much.

"The worst," said Mischa.

I felt my eyebrows go up. Mischa had filled out an application at some point in the past! I was tempted to glance at Jacques in surprise, but he wouldn't have noticed because he was staring into our empty fridge. Bless his hopeful heart! My dad may be coming up on nine weeks clean, but we weren't yet in the full-fridge phase.

"Where are you applying?" asked Mischa. She gripped a shapeless black slouch purse with both hands, as though it might be torn from her grasp.

Again, I surprised myself with my willingness to answer. I
don't like my father's ladies to know too much about me. When
they show up, I become like a distant, antisocial boarder in my
own home.

"I'm trying to get into this competition. To win a scholarship to a fashion school."

Mischa smiled. Good teeth for one of my father's ladies.

"That's exciting. You want to be a designer?"

"Charlie's got an amazing eye," said my dad.

"Two, actually," I said.

"She can make anything," said my dad, undeterred by my
delightful repartee.

"Other than stones into soup!" I said. "Believe you me, I've
tried!"

He closed the fridge and gave me a look.

It's true that I may carry around the *tiniest* bit of resentment
toward my remaining parent.

I briefly considered offering them some crackers from
the private stash of food I keep in my room, but decided
against it. If experience told me anything, I would soon need
it while my father and Mischa descended giddily into the
chaotic nightmarish lifestyle only the truly drug addicted
can manage.

"That's so neat," said Mischa.

She should probably be in my high school class, not dating
Jacques. She couldn't be more than twenty-five. Oh well. We all
have our life path, and mine involves getting out of my present,
reduced circumstances and into some much more attractive
and fabulous ones. NO MATTER WHAT LIFE THROWS
MY WAY! I don't think it's an exaggeration to say that winning this competition could not only secure my future but also
save my life. I have had the blues once or twice. It was pure No

Fun City. I would never again descend into the depths if I could study fashion at Green Pastures.

My dad and Mischa went into the living room, a tacky man cave featuring faux velvet flocking and a large-screen TV with a crack in one corner making it un-pawnable.

I decided to get back to work.

There was no sense fretting about the new reality: there was a lady. There would soon be a relapse.

I'd survived it before. I would survive it again.

When I sat back down at my desk, I stroked my copy of *D.V.* She is the person to whom I turn when I need inspiration and strength. My "Here's an Idea!" lists are directly inspired by her "Why Don't You" columns, which made her famous. She advised people on how they could make their lives more beautiful. Her suggestions included things like: "Why don't you put all your dogs in bright yellow collars and leads like all the dogs in Paris?" and "Why don't you paint a map of the world on all four walls of your boys' nursery so they won't grow up with a provincial point of view?"

Isn't that wonderful? How mind-expanding! In D.V.'s world, everyone has a lot of dogs and boys and nurseries and pays attention to how things are done in Paris.

At the moment I don't have any dogs, and I'll probably never have boys, because I don't care for children, but that doesn't stop a Charlie Dean from dreaming.

I began to type in the area for personal biography.

Please tell us a little about yourself and your background in fashion.

My name is Charlie Dean (short for Charlene) and I have dreamed of being a designer since I was a tiny child. My father is in the entertainment industry and we moved around a lot for his work.

My mother passed away suddenly when I was nine. Fashion helped me to overcome this early tragedy and has always been my passion, my solace, and my escape. My mother taught me to sew when I was seven and together we made costumes and almost all of my clothes, a practice I continue to this day.

My particular interest is women's formal wear, and when we've stayed in one place for long enough, I have often ended up making prom dresses for girls in my school. My clients have always been very pleased with my work, calling it exceptional.

I have taught myself couture sewing techniques and try to employ them as much as possible. I can drape and make patterns using toiles. I have an insatiable appetite to learn more about all aspects of design and construction, as well as marketing.

I sat back and considered my words. They had to be enough to get me in. After all, I alluded to the loss of my mom without mentioning any of the *désagréables* details, and I talked about the constant moving without getting into the foster homes and the times we've lived in the car. I think it is best not to get too specific about Jacques's career as a lower-echelon DJ and sort-of songwriter. If I get too honest in the application, the organizers might be worried about exposing the other students to me.

I once attended a school near Red Deer that banned a book because one of the characters smoked pot and did acid. *Mon Dieu!* I remember worrying that if they knew how we lived, they'd ban me. After all, I sometimes went home to find strangers shooting up in our living room. I've called the ambulance more than once when somebody's speedball-aganza went wrong. There have been no fewer than three locks on my bedroom doors since I was ten because when my father is using, bad people appear as though by black magic. Also, drug-afflicted individuals tend to wander. I didn't want them disturbing me when I was trying to rest or work. To think that those kids in my old school couldn't even *read* about a little minor drug use. *Incroyable!* Imagine if they had to live with major drug addiction? Who was going to ban that?

With luck, the application readers from Green Pastures will assume Jacques is a high-powered entertainment exec rather than a minor DJ who hates EDM and pawns his equipment at least twice a year. I hope the application is heartwarming but in no way suggests that I might be too far outside the realm of a normal young person's life.

My heart sped and slowed, sped and slowed in spite of the calming breaths I took. This application had to work. Everything was riding on it. My future, my well-being, my dreams. If I could just get in to the competition, I could win. And then everything would be possible.

Calm yourself, Charlie Dean, I coached. Panic isn't chic and neither is desperation.

I dropped it into the mailbox and said the first of countless small prayers.

FEBRUARY 10

Creative writing is another thing they don't offer at our school anymore. It's too bad, because my application to enter the Green Pastures fashion scholarship competition suggests I might be good at it.

I figured most of the applicants would be as eager to please as golden retriever puppies. My application would be the only snarly schnauzer in the bunch. You'd be surprised how many people like that. Schnauzers have their fans. I've always had an ability to withhold things from people in a way that makes them want to find out what I'm keeping back. Until I lose my mystique, that is.

I still remember when Mr. Tanaka, our woodworking teacher (this was back when we still had woodworking), tried to take a special interest in me. He said he thought I had the right temperament to work with wood. After that I tried to be how he saw me: calm, one with the grain and whatnot. He let me stay after class and even gave me a piece of purple heartwood to use as an inlay in the gift box project.

Oh man, nothing went right with that box. Seriously. I sunk a hole into it in the wrong place. Cut a tenon joint that broke off. And about halfway through the project, right in the middle of class, I lost it. I screamed some choice swear words and swept the pieces of the box onto the floor, and then I kicked them for good measure. I yelled a few more swear words before stomping out of the room, out of the school, and out of Mr. Tanaka's special attention pile.

That is just one example of the many times the inner snap show that lies beneath my supposedly mellow exterior has been exposed.

Lucky for me, not long after that Gramps got me going on metalwork. The thing about metal is that it won't put up with your bullshit. If you throw it on the floor, you're going to cut your hand. If you try to stomp it, you're going to hurt your foot. Metal is always the boss. Even a reactive person with low self-control, like me, has to keep a certain respect.

The basic point is that my calm-and-aloof routine is well-known to be bullshit, at least among those who know me, but for the purposes of my application, a little distance seemed like a better strategy than trying too hard.

I wrote all my answers as vaguely as I could get away with. I skimmed a few fashion design books from the library and read some blogs and fashion sites.

Under the section where we were meant to list our technical skills I put:

18" C-Thru transparent inch/metric ruler
hip curve
French curve
tape measure

blue dot paper

I have them and I know how to use them.

All lies. I have no idea what a hip curve and a French curve might be. Ditto blue dot paper.

I wrote that one of my specialties was "fitting shoulders" after reading how hard that is on a clothing design forum.

If I get into the competition, I had better watch a lot of YouTube videos about French curves and shoulder holes so I can find out what they are.

As for the part about my inspirations, I did not paste a photo of the Diabetes Society donation bin, which is where all my clothing inspiration comes from currently, but instead I looked up a bunch of fashion designers who make stuff that looks like rags and said they were my inspirations. I figure that if I get in, no one will be surprised when I make something ugly.

I am not just reactive. I may also be something of an evil genius fashion fraud, if I do say so myself. Now I just have to tell my friends that I actually entered the competition. I'm kind of dreading it, though I couldn't tell you why.

Sardonic Quote for Embarrassing Mood Board

"I never touch sugar, cheese, bread . . . I only like what I'm allowed to like. I'm beyond temptation. There is no weakness. When I see tons of food in the studio, for us and for everybody, for me it's as if this stuff was made out of plastic. The idea doesn't even enter my mind that a human being could put that into their mouth. I'm like the animals in the forest. They don't touch what they cannot eat."

—KARL LAGERFELD

PART TWO

Day at the
Atelier

seven

ℒCHARLIE℘
℘DEAN℘

HERE'S AN IDEA © CHARLIE DEAN DESIGNS:

If you knew today was the last day of your life, how would you dress? Well, today might be the last day of your life. So dress for it. This approach will ensure that you keep your look as profound and authentic as possible. From such beginnings is true style born.

DATE: MARCH 2

Days until fashion show: 63

When I checked the mailbox for the two hundred and twenty-seventh time since I mailed my application, and saw the crisp, white envelope, I turned hot, then cold, then numb. This was it. Would I have a future or would I be sentenced to the slag heap of shattered dreams, never to rise again?

I took the envelope out of the box like I was extracting a bomb and walked on pins-and-needles feet to the house and shut myself in my room.

"Please let it be an acceptance," I whispered. Prayed, really.

"I don't think I can do this," I muttered as my heart smashed around in my chest.

When I finally cut it open, I did so with extreme care. I extracted the thick sheet of paper, and as soon as I read the first word I began to cry. Just a touch. Nothing disfiguring. A few drops of purest joy rolling down my cheeks.

Being accepted into the Green Pastures fashion competition was like being admitted to heaven. Or at least the place you go to be interviewed by God Hermighty before you get into heaven. Not only would I have a chance to show my work in a fashion show judged by a committee of fashion professionals and maybe win a scholarship to the best art high school in Canada *if not the world*, I would be spending a day at a workshop at Green Pastures, soaking up the creativity and knowledge.

X X X

I GOT THAT GOOD NEWS TEN DAYS AGO. TODAY WAS WORKshop day—also known as the best day of my life so far.

So why was I running late, which I never do? Why? *Why?*

To put it simply, Charlie Dean couldn't get into the bathroom.

I awoke at six a.m. My plan was to meditate, which I do to improve my focus; eat a healthy breakfast of fruit and croissant (you-bake, but still: French!); take a shower; and then get dressed.

I'd spent a long time the night before deciding which suit to wear. I have been collecting suits since I reached my full height of five foot ten, which is an ideal height for a lover of clothes. My favorite right now is the one I think of as my Wallis Simpson. It's a wasp-waisted, double-breasted charcoal number with a magnificent collar. I wear it with antique medals pinned to the hip to give it that authentic flare. Wallis was one of Diana Vreeland's most famous clients. She was a forbidding-looking divorcée who lured the King of England away from the throne. The two of them eloped, which created *un scandale majeur*! I think they later became Nazi sympathizers or something equally heinous, so one can't look to her for anything *other* than her taste in suits. Sure, she was somewhat homely and liked Nazis, but all most people remember is her fierce style. Wallis had more edge than a steak knife. She was also the person who said one can never be too rich or too thin, which shows she had sense.

I didn't go with the Wallis for the workshop. I thought a more approachable look would be less intimidating for the other contestants. Instead, I wore a menswear-inspired tweed number that Katharine Hepburn would have been proud to play a round of golf in.

Like Mrs. Vreeland and Wallis Simpson, I have devoted myself to becoming as perfect as possible in order to overcome some of my natural physical and circumstantial limitations. Diana Vreeland had to overcome a critical, attention-seeking mother and unconventional looks. I have to overcome a deceased mother, average looks, and dirt-common beginnings. I believe I can make up for those deficits by being as interesting as possible in my physical aspect and dress, having an excellent vocabulary and a superhuman work ethic, and being a superb designer. Diana Vreeland came from a society family in New York, so in some ways life was probably easier for her than it is for me, but I believe in the power of positive thinking!

Back to trying to get ready in the morning. When I went to the bathroom at 6:03 a.m., it was *occupée*.

I walked down the hallway and peered into my father's *boudoir*. He was in there, sprawled among the sheets and assorted blankets not made of natural fibers.

That meant Mischa, the new girlfriend, was the culprit.

Perhaps she wouldn't be in there for long. After all, she wasn't much older than me, and teenagers need their sleep.

It should be said that my father has been dating Mischa for nearly a month, and neither of them has hit the skids. Yet. Mischa is polite and considerate and, at least so far, drug-free. She gives me my space, and I stay out of her way. She started staying over immediately, but I keep different hours from them. This was the first morning she'd been up before me.

To give Mischa her privacy, I stood behind my half-closed bedroom door and waited for her to emerge. And I waited.

No Mischa.

Charlie Dean is not now and never will be a camper, but she does know how to go outside when the occasion demands! This was a lesson learned during the times Charlie Dean and her father lived in their car. This was before I was put in charge of managing the rent money.

I ducked around the back of our unattractive house and hoped none of our neighbors would see me.

Then, because Charlie Dean has basically parented herself from a very young age and has learned about waiting and waiting and waiting some more when parental persons do not arrive on schedule, or at all, I did my fifteen-minute meditation. Surely Mischa would be done with . . . whatever she was doing in there by the time I was one with the creator and the universe.

But at 6:25 Mischa was still in the bathroom. My clothes

were laid out, freshly ironed, and a starched blouse waited on a wooden hanger. My supplies were stored in my portfolio bag. I was supposed to be at Green Pastures at eight thirty.

I ate my healthy breakfast, enjoying the slices of honeydew, the two strawberries, and, when it was ready, the flaky, warm-from-the-oven croissant, of which I ate only half. Then I went to stand in front of the bathroom door.

Meditation and oneness with the universe or no, Charlie Dean was becoming frustrated.

I debated waking my father and asking him to get Mischa out. But that would mean talking to my father in the morning, which is an unsettling experience because of his extreme lack of vivaciousness.

So I knocked quietly but firmly on the door.

No answer for a beat. Then, "Yes?"

"Are you going to be in there much longer?"

"I'm not sure," came her unsatisfying answer.

I took a deep, steadying breath. If Mischa was using drugs in there, she might not be entirely reasonable. It was important to tread carefully.

"I have to get ready for school," I said, feeling that the bathroom door and I were getting to know each other a little too intimately.

"It's Saturday."

"I got into that fashion competition. We're having a workshop today. This morning, actually."

"Oh my god! That's so great," said Mischa, who is sweet even if she is a bathroom hog.

"I know. I'm really excited."

"Does that mean you won the contest?" she asked, her voice only slightly muffled by the flimsy door.

"No. They're going to tell us what to expect today. Then

we go away and make our designs for the fashion show in May."

"Are you nervous?" asked the voice behind the door.

I'm sad to report this was the best conversation I'd had for weeks. Maybe months.

Normally, I practice optimism because it's supposed to lead to success. But something about talking to my father's girl-friend who had locked herself in the bathroom caused me to de-optimize.

"Yes," I said.

"You are going to do great."

"You think so?"

"Look at you! You've got everything going for you. You're so striking and unique. Your dad says you're really talented. I love the way you dress."

"You do?"

"Totally. It's not like everyone else."

Charlie Dean likes to give as good as she gets, so I said, "You too."

Mischa didn't answer. The door remained a scuffed white.

I considered pulling up a chair and settling in but decided against it. I had places to be.

"Are you okay in there?" I asked.

No answer.

"Do you need help?"

A long pause. "I'm having a panic attack," she said.

"Ah," I said. "They're very common among people who are newly clean and sober."

Charlie Dean knows this for a fact. When her father is not filling the house with active addicts, the house is full of newly clean addicts who are having a lot of panic attacks.

I fought back the drowning feeling I always get when I'm

in danger of being late or, Dior forbid, actually am late. This woman was in trouble. I had to calm her down so I could get ready.

"There are easy and effective ways to get over them. Panic attacks, I mean." I considered all the methods I'd employed while waiting to see if I'd been accepted into the competition. All that self-care would be for nothing if I made a bad first impression by BEING LATE on the first day. Breathe, Charlie Dean. Breathe.

"There are?"

"Absolutely. If you come out, I'll show you."

"I don't think I can move."

I took another deep breath. Charlie Dean does not let down the person in need, even when her entire future is riding on her getting into the bathroom.

So I took Mischa through the breathing and body awareness exercises that I'd learned from a counselor I saw when I lived with one of my foster families. At 7:07 Mischa finally emerged from the bathroom.

"Charlene, I feel much better," she said.

"Please, call me Charlie," I said, fighting back the urge to shove her aside so I could get inside.

Mischa looked younger than me. She had on one of my father's T-shirts and some flannel pajama bottoms, which she'd clearly brought from home, since my father does not own pajamas. I thought of Calvin Klein's basement rec room ads with the waif kids. Panicky Mischa would have fit right in. She really was a cut above most of his ladies. Indeed, she was almost as pretty as my mother had been.

"I really have to get ready now, but I'm happy to tell you what I know about coping with anxiety later," I told her.

She smiled.

"Thanks, Charlie," she said. And she patted my shoulder awkwardly, like she didn't quite know what to do with me, and it was a strange moment indeed.

I sped through my ablutions and raced out the door. And I felt sort of like I'd made a friend, which was a nice surprise.

I also prayed that I hadn't just blown my entire future in the process.

eight

MARCH 2

After I sent in the fairly half-assed application I basically forgot about it, so I was surprised when my grandma handed me
the envelope a week or so later.

"This came for you," she said, handing it over.

"I'll go to my room and open it." I don't know why I felt like
I needed privacy.

My whole body felt strange.

I sat at my desk and used the sickle-shaped letter opener
I'd made to open it.

> **Dear Mr. Thomas-Smith,**
>
> **We are pleased to invite you to take part in the Green
> Pastures Fashion Scholarship Competition.**

It probably took a full minute for me to process that I'd gotten in.

Being accepted confirmed my suspicion that it was a bullshit contest. But it also meant I had a chance of getting into Green Pastures if I could somehow bluff my way through. If I won, I could switch into another program. I might have only a one percent chance, but it was a chance all the same.

"John?" asked my grandmother. She stood in my doorway, holding a covered Tupperware. "Everything okay?"

"Yeah, it's fine."

"Grandpa and I are going to the Legion for Cal Droog's birthday party tonight. We have to make burgers. There's lasagna in here. You just need to heat it up." She gestured the container at me.

"Okay. Have fun."

"You're sure everything's okay?" she asked. My grandma isn't fancy. She never wears makeup, and her hair is short and plain, and I think she's pretty beautiful. Nobody has eyes like my gram.

"For sure."

She was staring at the letter, and I lifted it.

"I just got into this, uh, contest thing."

"Do you need money?"

This is always her first question after she asks whether I need food.

"No, Gram. It's free." And then I told her about the contest and about the workshop.

"Are you sure you don't need money to help you do this? Just ask us if you need some money. You need to save the money you make at the Salad." My grandparents would probably sell their house to send me to Green Pastures if I asked them to. I have to be careful not to let on about wanting expensive stuff.

I love that she always calls it "the Salad."

"I'm fine, Gram. I'm not really that serious about this. Just thought it would be interesting."

"Okay, then, honey," she said, and came over and gave me a kiss on my head the way only a grandma can do, and I felt calmer, somehow.

That night, when Booker and Barbra came over, I told them I'd entered and gotten in.

Booker laughed his ass off, but he sounded happy about it. Barbra did not.

"Really?" she said.

"You never know," I said. "It's worth a shot, right? If nothing else, it'll give you guys something to laugh about. I doubt I'll make it through the workshop where I have to meet the instructors and the other contestants."

Barbra didn't say anything. I guess it hurt her feelings that I didn't tell her I was applying.

"You'll be awesome," said Booker.

But I sure as hell didn't feel awesome when the day of the workshop came and I was sitting there with the other candidates, feeling like a fraud and a person who is the opposite of fashionable. The conversations around me were so bad, I half wished I was at the Salad Stop, texting Barbra and Booker rude comments about my customers. The fashion conversations made me feel like I was being stabbed in the intellect by forty dull butter knives. Allow me to quote a couple of choice samples:

"I considered dying it gray. Silver hair is *huge* right now. But you can only carry off gray if you're not tired. At least, that's what my mom said."

"But you're soooo gorgeous. And didn't you say you just turned sixteen! Are you sure it's time to try silver?"

"Think fairy elf. Then think me."

(Conversation between two candidates. I think about hair.)

"Shut up about that."

"No. You shut up. It's the seaming. So hot for the ass."

"It's doing yoga nine times a week, not seams. Seriously. Learn a thing."

"I'm telling you. I read an article about it. Seams make the ass. And it's not yoga. It's Tracy Anderson."

"Gwyneth's trainer?"

"You'd better have Anderson ass or some major great seams."

(Conversation between a contestant and one of Carmichael's helpers. Not completely sure what it was about. Asses?)

I was on the verge of getting up and leaving due to not being able to stand it, when the guy who was running the show came into the classroom. Mr. Carmichael is a sharp-dressed black guy. He introduced himself and got right to it. It was obvious that he knows his stuff. Hell, he seemed to know everybody's stuff. I guess that's the kind of teacher you get at a fancy private school. For a while I forgot to hate fashion and rich kids and numerous other hateable things.

I even felt sorry for that strange girl from Career Tragedies when she came in late, out of breath and trying to hide it. She nearly fell trying to get into her seat without drawing attention to herself. She was loaded down with a big portfolio case and a purse and about three other bags that made it look like she was running away from home.

Mr. Carmichael paused in his remarks and stared at her. I thought he was going to make a snide comment about her lateness and worried that she might lose it if he did. But all he said was, "You must be Charlie Dean. Welcome. Glad you made it." And then he went back to speaking about how fashion is a mirror of society and people's aspirations.

I looked at her and noticed that her eyes had welled up. The girl is high-strung as shit. I hope she doesn't end up having a breakdown.

He talked to us about the history of fashion and how it's this major signifier of culture and gender and economics and a whole lot of other things. He touched on what he called "the evolving craft of making clothing" and talked about different ways of viewing the industry. He introduced us to "academic perspectives on fashion" and was generally smart and interesting.

Carmichael had two assistants helping him, both fashion students. One was a pale, fine-boned white girl with ultra-straight, ultra-pale blonde hair and a studious expression. He introduced her as Tesla, and I nearly retched. Her parents had probably picked out Quinoa and Beret as their second and third choices. The other helper's name was Bijou. Of course it was. She had perfect olive skin and looked like she'd been put on the planet to sneer at the less fortunate. She also looked like a skunk had designed her hairstyle: all glossy black with a white streak on one side.

There were eleven contestants, including Charlie Dean, who'd worn an old-man suit, complete with these pantaloony-type long shorts and her trademark lumpy hairstyle. There were a few girls—Asian, Hispanic, and maybe regular old white—who looked interchangeable thanks to their long, flat-ironed dark hair and similar makeup and outfits; a girl with long, curly black hair who looked like she'd gotten dressed using only things found on the path in a fairy- and unicorn-infested rain forest; a mixed-race guy with a rad Afro and shredded clothes; a First Nations girl dressed like a heavy metal goddess in studs and denim and leather; a pale, preppy white girl with a precise haircut and a completely blank expression; another girl with dark skin and huge brown eyes wearing a head scarf and a white jumpsuit that made her look like an old-school break-dancer or a stunt woman. And then there was a super-pretty girl with wavy red hair in a wheelchair wearing what looked like a bunch of see-through scarves, as best I could tell. We were like a poster for diversity, with me in the ever-popular role of White Boy. I'd seen quite a few of the other contestants around R. S. Jackson. No surprise that my fellow students would be trying to upgrade educational institutions.

x x x

DURING THE BREAK, WHEN WE WERE TOLD WE COULD EXplore the school and have a snack, the other contestants spread out around the atrium. I hadn't brought anything to eat because I figured my hostility would keep me going. I walked back and forth a few times, checking out things I'd missed or that were new since my tour back in ninth grade. There was the bench studded with old cutlery and stamped with the words "Game of Benches," which I suppose was mildly amusing in an irritating, art-school kind of way. The windowed walls of the atrium looked out onto gardens and various metal and wood art installations. There was a winding pathway that led to a shed with double doors. They were wide-open, and a couple of figures moved around inside.

I passed under the post-and-beam canopy and stood just outside the building, taking deep jealous breaths of the fresh-cut-wood scent. A boy and a girl were bent over a wooden pole.

"Pretty cool, eh?" said a voice beside me.

I looked over, expecting to see one of the other contestants or Mr. Carmichael, but instead met the gaze of a gaunt guy holding a welding mask.

"They're doing a totem pole. It's going to be amazing. I'd

like to try something that marries the wood carving and the metalwork in an interesting way," he said.

I felt envious that he spent his days thinking about interesting ways to combine wood and metal, but it was hard to resent him. The guy was too thin for his height and for the breadth of his shoulders. Pale. Kind of haunted. In fact, he looked like some of the guys in my school who are heading for trouble.

"I'm Brian," he said.

"John." For some reason I added, "I don't go here. To this school, I mean."

"Pretty soon I won't either, if I don't get my act together. That's what I'm doing here on a Saturday. Trying to get caught up so my expensive education doesn't go down the crapper and take my life along with it."

Well.

"You got behind?"

"You could say that," he said. "You visiting someone?"

"No. I'm, uh, here for a contest. We're having an orientation."

Brian waited, curious but not pushy.

I thought about lying about what kind of contest it was, but went with the truth.

"To get into the fashion program. On a scholarship," I said.

"Really," he said.

"I know I don't look like a fashion person."

"What does a fashion person look like?" he asked, half smiling.

I didn't want to sound negative, so I didn't answer.

"You look all right. You're wearing nice colors. And you've got that intense vibe all the clothes culters have."

"Clothes culters?"

"That's what we call the fashion students. They're hard-core, even for a school like this, where everyone is very intent on their thing. No one can touch the culters. Focus up the ass."

I couldn't help laughing.

"Well, I'm sort of a long shot. I'm just as interested in metalwork."

"Right on," he said. "That's my deal. If you think about it, *art* is sort of a long shot. Attending a school like this is a long shot for most people. My mother's parents have cash, and they foot the bill. As long as I don't screw it up and get kicked out. And if fashion is your bag, or metalwork, this is the place to go."

"Right."

Brian stared at me. "You know, I'm sure you're on the up-and-up, but if you're not, run away if two girls and a guy come up to you and start asking you questions. Trying to get people to tell the truth is a big thing around here. You might want to avoid it."

"Will do," I said, my mind torn between wondering what he was talking about and remembering the extensive lies I'd told in my application.

"What do you get if you win?"

"A one-year scholarship to the fashion program."

"Ah, the big scholarship. Well, if you're the lucky winner, I'll show you around the metalwork shop. In case you want to make chain mail pants or something. Keep in touch," he said. He handed me the coolest business card I've ever seen. It was a small piece of metal, super thin, with his name and number stamped into it, almost like a dog tag.

"Now that's a business card," I said.

"Latest project. Glad you like it. Cast-off bits from the shop should be put to use somehow."

He said good-bye and headed off to combine wood and

metal in new ways, and I reluctantly returned to the atrium, where the other contestants milled around, having brain-numbing conversations.

Charlie Dean came over to where I stood by myself, waiting for Carmichael to call us back. She wasn't participating in any of the conversations, which was a surprise. I'd have expected her to be talking the ass seams off everyone in sight.

After I sighed loudly for what must have been the twentieth time, she said, "You're sighing a lot. Are you okay?"

"Yes."

"I sigh a lot sometimes," she said. "It's nerves. Stress. I meditate to overcome it."

"Medicate?"

"No," she corrected. "Meditate."

"Oh." I had literally never met one person our age who meditates. Until now.

"Is that why you were late this morning? Because you meditated for too long?" I felt like getting in a dig. I don't know why.

She frowned in that way people who hate to move their faces do, but she didn't answer. That irritated me, too. So I kept going.

"I'm feeling good about this," I said. "You know, I really relate to what Carmichael has been talking about. The theory behind fashion design. I appreciate a more rigorous approach to design of all kinds. Incorporating social and historical aspects and whatnot."

Now she was frowning for real.

"You do?"

"Sure. I'm into the intellectual approach. What's the word? Cerebral? Yeah. I feel like Carmichael likes a more cerebral approach. Which is sort of my specialty."

Now I had her. She was sweating. Invisibly, but I could sense it.

"I just hope that my Charlie Deans are good enough," she said.

"Your what?"

"My looks. I call them my Charlie Deans."

Referring to her stuff that way wasn't as funny as you might think. It made her sound disturbed. Her face makeup was at least two shades lighter than her skin, and she wore dark swooshes of pink on her cheeks that extended up to her ears.

Was that kind of makeup a trend?

I wondered if she was trying to psych me out by acting vulnerable. If so, it was working. I'd been so busy lying that I hadn't even started to worry about what I would make for the fashion show. My "John Thomas-Smiths" were probably going to consist of . . . I had no clue.

I should drop out of the competition before I embarrassed myself in front of the most embarrassing people in the world. But I didn't. I may be a liar, but I'm not a quitter.

Fun Fashion Facts by John Thomas-Smith

Fashion is the most intense expression of the phenomenon of neomania, which has grown ever since the birth of capitalism. Neomania assumes that purchasing the new is the same as acquiring value. If the purchase of a new garment coincides with the wearing out of an old one, then obviously there is no fashion. If a garment is worn beyond the moment of its natural replacement, there is pauperization. Fashion flourishes on surplus, when someone buys more than he or she needs.

—STEPHEN BAYLEY

CHARLIE DEAN

DATE: MARCH 2

Days until fashion show: 63

I arrived at the atelier—*atelier!*—over eight minutes late—an eternity! I was the tiniest bit breathless because I am unused to running and have never found physical exertion fashionable and it was quite awkward but the teacher was so nice and I think I recovered well and made an excellent impression after those first few moments.

The assistants, Bijou and Tesla—their names are to *die for*—asked us to come into the Poiret room. The POIRET ROOM! (As anyone who might chance to read this will know, Paul Poiret was the *godfather* of draping and a *major* figure in fashion history.) I can't even say how much I love that the fashion wing of

Green Pastures has a Worth Room, a Westwood Room, and a Chanel Room. It shows such style and knowledge!

Once we were seated at our desks I was able to assess the other contestants. Allow Charlie Dean to *peindre un portrait*.

My fellow contestants were of all ethnicities and body types, genders and, one suspects, sexualities. We were *pure fashion* in that regard.

One could be described using one word. *Sincérité. Avec un soupçon de patchouli.* She was full figured and had long, spirally black hair. If I had to guess, I'd say her ancestors came from *Romania*, which would be so glamorous! Or maybe her heritage was *Welsh*, which would also be fantastic! Her look was witchy, if not exactly bewitching, if you'll forgive a little pun. She had a major smoky eye going on, and a vampire lippie, and her entire *maquillage* looked like she had a part-time job smudging sage at haunted houses or maybe selling curses, three for a dollar, at the corner of Haunted House and Third Street. Her name tag read "Ainslee McPhee."

It wasn't my *favorite* look, but there was a commitment behind it that I admired.

A boy called Jason Wong wore a fabulous shredded ensemble. Totally *nouveau* Berlin punk visiting LA. Loved, loved, loved.

A pale girl named Ellen was channeling Anna Wintour by way of Audrey Hepburn. *Terribly* tidy in flats, cigarette pants, and a sharp bob is how I'd characterize her look.

Some of the contestants were not *notable*. They were instead pretty or cute. Whatever you want to call it, they were inoffensive, unless you like your fashion with some distinctiveness. But I'm sure they were very nice girls and their hair was really very long and shiny, which is never a bad thing.

I'd seen at least three or four of the other contestants in the halls of R. S. Jackson, although I didn't know them personally. I wondered how they'd found out about the competition, since I'd intercepted the announcement from Mr. Oliver's mail. They must have kept track of the website. Several of them apparently congregate in the old art room on breaks, as Charles had mentioned. I had no idea they were working on fashion design in there! What a terrific surprise, although I also hoped none of them was *too* skilled.

Then there was John Thomas-Smith from Careers class. He absolutely reeked of street cred and comfortable ease in a nothing sort of outfit. Charlie Dean needs to study him, especially now that he's revealed his love of intellectual design. How does he manage to look so stylish in such mishmashed clothes? Is it connected to his intellectualism? John Thomas-Smith has excellent color sense. I was happy to see him, even though I had assumed he wouldn't be serious competition and now I fear that he might be. I want everyone to succeed in the competition, but obviously I hope I succeed the most.

There was a darling girl called Madina, who I think was Muslim. She had marvelous dark eyes and wore a *beautiful* silk head scarf. She was absolutely next level in her white denim jumpsuit with many zippers. Another girl named Jo, short for Jo-Ann, had a Joan Jett look that was beyond belief cool. Jo-Ann looked at me for a moment too long and then winked, which was so saucy and hilarious of her! So rock *et* roll in her T-shirt with the gorgeous cover image from *Moonshot* on the front. If you haven't read it, *Moonshot* is a collection of Indigenous comics. To. Die. For. Art. The cover image is particularly fabulous and of interest to all people who care about art and design. Another girl, white, with the glorious nearly translucent skin of the true redhead, wore a fabulous chiffon smock in various shades of smoke that swept around her wheelchair, transforming it into a veritable chariot when she moved! *Magnifique!* She called herself Cricket and said dry, cutting things and was generally *très chic* and funny, and her wonderful red hair had a wave the ocean itself would envy.

Mr. Carmichael, the head of the fashion design program, was absolutely the most stunning example of a well-dressed and handsome older man in his excellent gray blazer, dark jeans, beautifully cut *sel et poivre* hair, good loafers. The perfect pink shirt. Sigh. He was the best-dressed teacher I'd ever seen. Of course, he is probably much better compensated than the teachers at Jackson. I think the people who determine teacher pay should know that students, at least this student, feel more nurtured and better educated when their teachers can afford excellent clothes.

After his introductory lecture Mr. Carmichael congratulated us again on being accepted into the competition and said that our applications were "most intriguing."

"I'd like to thank Tesla Wharton and Bijou Atwater for agreeing to help out with the competition. They are two of our most gifted seniors."

I'm glad Bijou is not a competitor. She is *purest* style. Her hair is black with a white streak, and her outfit was the kind of chic that costs a lot of money and requires absolutely unerring taste. When Mr. Carmichael called her gifted, her eyes closed briefly in the most deliciously *feline* satisfaction.

I was sitting next to Jason Wong, the boy wearing the deconstructed look of shredded leather and denim. He leaned over and whispered, "Her dad funded most of this program and built the whole fashion wing."

I didn't react, but Bijou stared at us as though she'd heard the comment.

Tesla, the other assistant, had hair so pale, it was nearly

silver. She was thin and graceful, with a pale athleticism-slash-*sportif* thing going on that made her look quite *enchantée*! Like a ballet dancer on a break or maybe a gymnast on her day off.

After lunch Mr. Carmichael had us talk about our backgrounds and perspectives on fashion.

If the contest was for enthusiasm, Madina would win the top three spots. She and her family recently immigrated to Canada after fleeing a terrible war. She has five brothers and was so compelling on every level, I almost couldn't stand it. I wonder if she'll incorporate head scarves into her looks. I really must get better educated about world fashion. There is so much to learn about other traditions, and I can't wait.

Witchy Ainslee informed us she likes incense, the color green, and "island living." Her particular focus was on sustainably produced clothing and organic fabrics with a historical bent.

Beside me Jason Wong told us that he wants to be a costume designer for the movies. He said he is an avid reader and writer of horror.

When asked about his passion for fashion, John Thomas-Smith said, "A bit of everything and a lot of nothing." When Mr. Carmichael told him to go deeper, John said he sometimes resented fashion and how it pressures people to fit a mold.

"Can you unpack your critique?" asked Mr. Carmichael.

Mr. Carmichael speaks to us like we're in the third year at Yale! *J'adore!*

John looked embarrassed and said nothing, but Mr. Carmichael waited him out.

"I just think that some aspects of it are, uh, sort of bullshit."

Mr. Carmichael watched. Then he looked at the rest of us.

"And you? Do you think fashion is 'sort of bullshit'?"

"No!" said two of the identical girls together.

"Yes," said Cricket from her chair. "Obviously."

The matching, long-haired girls swiveled to stare at her. Cricket stared back from under the swoop of flame-red hair that nearly covered one eye. Her hair was so perfect for her. And that chiffon dress. It really was *extraordinaire*! Such *panache*! Next time I see her in the halls at Jackson I will go and speak to her. Maybe.

"Industrial fashion doesn't recognize that not everyone is a size zero able-bodied lemming bot," she said. "And regular people can't afford custom clothes."

"Unless they change the way they think about clothes," said Ainslee.

"The fashion world is full of thieves," said Jo-Ann. "If I see one more big-name designer label knocking off indigenous designs, I'm going to . . . pinking shear someone."

Everyone laughed, except me and John. I didn't laugh because my heart felt too full of love for my fellow competitors. I don't know why he didn't laugh.

"This competition is designed to allow you to critique fashion as well as participate in it. We want to see that you have thought deeply about designing clothes that reflect your values and that honor your models. We want to see evidence that you understand not just the fashion industry as it exists today, but where it comes from and even where it might go."

And then he gave us a *magnifique* lecture on the word "fashion." He talked about how it means to make something, to change something, that it refers to a multibillion-dollar industry and is also a synonym for "trends."

He told us he wanted us to consider the spiritual dimensions of clothing design. Now they were all gaping, except for me. Gaping is very unattractive.

Ainslee asked what Mr. Carmichael meant by "spiritual." It

was *évident* that Ainslee thinks she knows *beaucoup de* spirituality and was thinking she'd be having a conversation among equals.

"At the risk of sounding too esoteric or vague, some theologians say our spirituality can be defined as how we channel our desires," he answered. "Fashion is all about desire. Who we want to be. How we want to be seen. During this competition I want each of you to think about what your deepest desire is. How has that desire brought you to the study and execution of clothing?"

"Fear!" said Jason, the horror lover. "We live in fearful times. Clothing is armor! Also, I want to be a costume designer for horror movies."

Mr. Carmichael nodded.

"I am sickened by fast fashion," said Ainslee. "Clothing should go back to a time when it meant something."

"Tradition and elegance," said Ellen, the tidy girl. "Plus revolution."

John added nothing, but he was paying close attention.

I'll say this about the conversation. I loved it. Every word. Because I believe that fashion design is a way to release the inner dreams! *Histoire vraie!* Mr. Carmichael was being so deep, and he was asking us to be deep, too! Our designs had to be more than beautiful and well made. They also had to be spiritual. That would be no problem for me. Clothing is basically my religion.

"As I was saying," Mr. Carmichael went on, "everything we do as artists, designers, and human beings has multiple dimensions. We are looking for young designers who are going to explore the boundaries of what fashion can do and what it should do."

So this was what students learned in the Green Pastures

fashion program! They weren't just getting news and views from the latest hot stylist. They were learning the history, art, politics, economics, sociology, and philosophy of fashion. I felt my heart swell and my brain grow.

Charlie Dean HAD TO ATTEND THIS SCHOOL! There was simply no other option.

ten

MARCH 2

Mr. Carmichael ended the day by telling us about "croakie books," which are apparently these notebooks where fashion designers "document their collections of looks." He reminded us that our "mood boards," which I think are collages of inspiring pictures or something equally lame, would be due along with the croakie books the day of the fashion show. Then we were dismissed.

We had a little over two months to go away, do some research, draw a few ideas, then turn one of the drawings into an actual outfit that a model would wear in the fashion show.

Time to drop out. Not only do I dislike and disapprove of fashion and fashion people, I massively underestimated the amount of work that they do. Two months might seem like a lot of time, but I have my career as an underperforming high school student to consider. Then there's my part-time job selling soul-destroying salad. I have Barbra and Booker to hang out with, metal to cut and pound. I'm just too busy for this contest. Plus, I maxed out my skills when I filled out the application. I could *maybe* do the illustrations, but I seriously doubt my ability to sew garments that reflect my feelings about clothes and are innovative, well-made, *and* spiritual, FFS. I've never *seen* a piece of clothing that was all of those things. I'm not sure I've ever seen *anything* that was all those things. I'm also incapable of making something that would "meet the inner and outer needs of my model," partly because I have no idea how to find a model. Barbra would laugh in my face if I asked her. She hates being in the spotlight.

Barbra and Booker are going to laugh so hard when I tell them I'm dropping out after the first day. But that's okay. I am used to not being taken seriously. I barely take myself seriously.

Still, I have to admit that underneath all the resentment, I really liked being at the school. That Brian guy was interesting. He didn't seem remotely fashionable. I learned some things from Mr. Carmichael and didn't mind the other contestants as much as I thought I would. A few of them even seemed sort of cool. Cricket was pretty funny and sharp, and Jo had a stellar up-yours attitude that I admired. And Charlie Dean may be bizarre, but she's not boring.

After we were dismissed we left the atelier with slow steps. Mr. Carmichael stood at the doorway, nodding and saying each of our names as we passed. I thought I might get the cold shoulder, since I'd been fairly negative, but he was nice.

"John," he said. "Thanks for your contribution today. You brought up some interesting points."

"Sorry," I said, and I meant it. The man was trying to give us disadvantaged types a way into the school. He acted like we might have important things to say about fashion design and art, and I felt sorry I was there under false pretenses.

I stopped to use the bathroom, and when I came out I realized I'd left my sketchbook in the classroom. There wasn't much in the book other than a few notes I took during the lectures and some small drawings, but I didn't want to leave it behind. When I walked into the classroom, only the irritatingly named Tesla remained. She was picking stray pieces of paper and juice boxes off the tables.

She was basically an archetypal Salad Stop customer: thin as a child gymnast, glowing skin, excellent posture, straight teeth, distant expression. I'd only barely registered her during the day. I make a point of not seeing people like Tesla, even when I'm taking orders from them.

"This yours?" she asked, holding up my book.

Her eyes were the color of backyard pools.

Stupidly, I pointed at it, like I was identifying a suspect in a photo lineup.

"I was about to look through it," she said, almost smiling. "To see what you're capable of."

Was the girl flirting with me?

She wore a short leather jacket and baggy pants with elastic at the ankle and crazy shoes that looked like a cross between an army boot and a sandal. Her shiny blonde hair was piled on her head in a careless way that probably took a long time to get just right.

"You'd be surprised," I said.

"There's something interesting about your look. I haven't quite unpacked it," she said, echoing Mr. Carmichael.

Much as I wanted to ask her WTF she was talking about, I didn't, because I sort of liked the idea that she was thinking about me, analyzing me, "unpacking" me. As hard as I rage against not just one machine, but *all the machines*, I am not immune to the charms of the good-looking girl.

"Let me know when you figure it out," I said.

"Is that vintage Patagonia?"

I looked down at the old fleece I wore. I found it at one of those thrift store sales where, for five dollars, you get a cardboard box to fill it up with whatever you want.

Tesla moved closer to me. She was taller than I thought. She touched the collar. "Synchilla," she said. "Cool."

She smelled like fresh-cut grass.

"Are you aware that you smell like a lawn?" I asked.

"My fragrance is called Mown. I got it in New York."

My nose was full of her.

I took a step back. This conversation needed to be cut short. I needed to clear my nose. Or my head.

"I probably shouldn't say this," she said. "But if you need anything, advice or whatever, I can help. You seem like . . ."

"Like?" I said, in spite of my best intentions. Why was I sniffing this fresh-cut-grass-smelling, New York City–visiting rich girl and asking her what she thought of me? I'm such a mystery to myself sometimes. I seriously worry that I am not a good person.

"You seem interesting," she said. "Different. Most people in fashion are just so, you know, focused on fashion."

"You're not?"

"Oh, I totally am. I'm into technical wear. Sports clothes. Same-same but not."

"And I'm different how?"

"I can tell you think about other things."

She had that right.

"Well, thanks, I guess. I should go. Someone's waiting for me outside," I said.

"We can walk out together," said Tesla. I watched as she put all the paper in a recycling bin and grabbed a leather satchel. I forced myself not to stare.

Two minutes later, Tesla and I came out the front doors

of the school. Booker stood straddling his bike near the bike stand where I'd locked up my Norco. He glanced up from his phone, and when he noticed Tesla he did such a hard double take, I almost laughed.

There was no way to avoid introducing him, but I tried to make it quick.

"This is my friend Booker," I said.

"I'm Tesla," she added, and reached out her hand. He took it with something like wonder.

"So did John win the contest yet?" Booker asked.

Tesla laughed. "Not yet. But he's doing great."

Then she gave us a little wave, and we watched her stride across the road and into the parking lot. Her car wasn't, thank god, a Tesla, but it was pretty fancy.

"Dude," said Booker, staring after her. "What, who, how? You have to tell me everything about that girl."

I unlocked my bike.

"She's no one. She's just helping with the contest. I had to go back to get my notebook, so we ended up walking out together."

"Whoa," he said. "Just whoa."

"Don't get too carried away. I'm going to drop out of the contest. They want me to think about clothes. They want me to *make* clothes."

Booker watched Tesla pull out of the parking lot. I watched him watch her. When she was gone, he turned back to me.

"John," he said. "Stop trying to skip over the fact that I just met an angel who smells like fresh-cut grass. Shit like that should not be skipped over."

"Let's go. We've got to meet B at the bakery. She'll be mad if we make her wait," I said.

We rode side by side down the wide shoulder of the gently sloping road that led away from Green Pastures.

"If it doesn't work out with Destiny, I may need to grab Tessa's number from you."

"Her name's Tesla, you goof," I said. Then I changed the subject.

Reasons Fashion Is No Way to Spend Your Time

Marcus Fairs: So is fashion dead or has it just become a ridiculous parody of itself?

Li Edelkoort: It's a ridiculous and pathetic parody of what it has been. I know because I've seen fashion shows of Thierry Mugler which would have 65, 75 models for three quarters of an hour. We would be on our chairs, shouting with tears in our eyes and the whole place would go crazy. Check Thierry Mugler's old fashion shows online. You see the difference. It moved us.

Marcus Fairs: You said in your talk that fashion used to predict the future but doesn't now. Has it lost touch with what's going on in society?

Li Edelkoort: Completely.

—"IT'S THE END OF FASHION AS WE KNOW IT," *DE ZEEN MAGAZINE*

PART THREE

The Small Matter of Models

eleven

CHARLIE DEAN

HERE'S AN IDEA © CHARLIE DEAN DESIGNS:

*Find an old pair of cowboy boots and gild them with
metallic paint, cover them with studs, and carve cool designs
in the leather. Everyone should have a pair of apocalyptic
cowboy boots for days when you need to walk on the moon.*

DATE: MARCH 4

Days until fashion show: 61

I was so inspired by the workshop at Green Pastures Academy
of Art and Amazingness that I spent nearly ten hours on Sunday
working on mood boards and making notes and drawings for
my ensemble. What I came up with was absolutely stunning
and elegant. Glam, glam, glam.

I paced around my room for twenty minutes because repet-
itive action such as walking stimulates creative flow. Back and
forth, around and round. I ran my hands over the fabrics of
clothes hanging on the rolling racks. I stared at the images on
my mood boards.

And just like that I thought of the perfect model. Her name is Bronwyn and she is next level. Not just the pretty, but *raffinée, raffinée, raffinée.* She's the feature window in the Barneys of Life.

Bronwyn has tawny skin and golden hair and tiger eyes and is ultra-lean but somehow curvy and looks like the world's most exclusive and thrilling pet. My dad watches a lot of drug movies, which is not a good choice, in my *humble avis*, but *ça ne fait rien.* His favorite drug film is called *Scarface.* It's about a young man who hails from Cuba, very sweaty, like our landlord, Mr. Devlin, and highly ambitious, unlike our landlord. The young man in the movie becomes a major drug dealer and cokehead and there's a disgusting scene in a shower with a chainsaw that should have scared my dad straight years ago, but hasn't. Anyway, in *Scarface*, the drug dealer gets fantastically rich and essentially buys himself a gorgeous woman who is played by Michelle Pfeiffer, one of the world's most *élégante* actresses. He also buys an actual, literal tiger, which he keeps chained in his yard.

Leaving aside the issue of healthy relationships based on shared interests as well as illegal animal trafficking and proper care of pets, Bronwyn reminds me of both the Michelle Pfeiffer character in the movie *and* the tiger. She prowls around the hallways looking bored and detached, and her beauty makes her seem rare and unexpected in the mundane surroundings of R. S. Jackson, although her fashion sense is not good.

She knows who I am because she introduced herself to me when I'd been at R. S. Jackson for only a few weeks. No one else had bothered. I was trying to get my leather briefcase (full funky '70s, weighs about thirty-eight pounds empty) into my locker when she appeared beside me.

"Hey," she said. "Do you do your own hair?"

I had arranged my hair into my favorite style with the two wings on either side of my head. A classic look but not one to be attempted by amateurs.

"Yes."

"It suits you."

"Thank you."

"Where'd you get those threads? Around here?" she asked.

She was standing very close to me, and I was nearly overwhelmed and disoriented by the feeling I always get around the extremely beautiful. Like the secret was RIGHT THERE but also infinitely far away. What perspective would reveal the mystery? Should I examine the nose? The skin? The hair? The arch of the brow?

I will never stop trying to figure beauty out. It is life's greatest challenge and its most enduring satisfaction.

En commun with other truly stunning people, Bronwyn had imperfections, but they only added to the overall effect. A small scar on the cheek. A tiny gap between her front teeth that was to die for. Pure Lauren Hutton!

"I made this," I said, touching the fabric of my dress. Fitted, royal blue, with a narrow red belt and exactly the right red pumps and short red jacket.

"Holy crap," she exclaimed. She sounded genuinely impressed.

Everyone passing by us watched Bronwyn as she talked to me.

"I think your look is rad," she said. "But I couldn't do it."

"Oh?" I said.

"It's too out-there."

"Oh," I said. Because *en tout candor*, what else was there to say to such a comment, made so casually? Out-there? Where was *there*? How far out was it? That's the problem with the un-fashionable. They don't understand that to choose clothing in order to fit in is to die a little every day. If it was attention she was afraid of, she should know by now that for someone who looked like her there was no avoiding it. Bronwyn would draw stares until she died. The best she could do was take control of how she was perceived.

Perhaps her aversion to attention explained her outfit. Either that or Bronwyn was unequipped with style or taste. She had on a flannel shirt and leggings, the standard uniform of three-quarters of the girls at the school. Comfortable, fitting-in, thoughtless clothes. The leggings showed the butt, the flannel shirt showed the don't care, the puffy boots showed . . . well, to be honest, Charlie Dean does not understand a puffy boot any more than she understands its sibling, the Croc. These were clothes best suited for a day spent at home. Alone. In the basement.

As I stood there in the hallway I imagined Bronwyn dressed in a custom Charlie Dean gown. Bronwyn, I'd like you to meet American *Vogue*! Italian *Vogue*! British *Vogue*! ALL THE VOGUES!

One day, I thought then, I would find a way to get Bronwyn into one of my gowns. Now I had my opportunity.

When Monday morning rolled around, I had several sketches ready, as well as sample swatches, mood boards, and pages of notes about finishing details plus hair, makeup, shoes, and jewelry.

But I couldn't seem to find the best-looking girl at our school. Not a surprise, since Jackson is so huge. I checked the hallway where I'd sometimes seen her hanging out with her friends. I asked one of them if she'd seen her. The friend shrugged and said she hadn't.

"Check at noon," said a girl in a gray hoodie who was stooped over her phone. "She has volleyball on Monday mornings."

When the noon bell rang, I collected my materials and went to find Bronwyn.

This time she sat among her friends wearing the exact same ensemble she'd had on the first time I talked to her. No makeup, hair in ponytail. Zero effort and still exquisite.

"Hello," I said, trying not to feel awkward. "I'm Charlie Dean. We met last year?"

As I spoke I reminded myself not to turn statements into questions. That is not how successful people communicate. It was *un peu* tempting because Bronwyn and all of her unadventurously attired friends were sitting, legs outstretched to show off dreadful footwear, staring up at me.

"Hi?" said Bronwyn, who was unafraid to speak in question marks.

I swallowed and smoothed my jacket down my sides. I'd worn one of my favorite vintage suits: an Alberta-sky-blue blazer with pink edging and a pink wool pleated skirt with a substantial brown shoe. A total Margaret Thatcher meets Princess Diana by way of Barbara Bush number. My suit takes the Easter Egg risk, misses by the vane of a feather, and ends up pure power pastel.

"I wondered if you might like to, uh, model for me," I said, going for the direct approach.

"I'm sorry, what?" she said, not sounding friendly at all.

I ignored her friends, who were staring at me with mouths ajar.

"That time we talked you said you liked my look. So I am hoping you will wear a dress I designed for you."

"Uh, okay," she said. "That's a little random."

One of her friends giggled.

I felt myself growing less able to talk. Less able to explain myself and my noble intentions.

"I need to find a model. For the dress. It's going to be very beautiful. I need someone very special to wear it."

This was all coming out quite wrong. Diana Vreeland would have said it in a way that would make every girl in that hallway want to wear my clothes.

If I didn't have a collagen-saving policy against scrunching up my face I would have done so. Instead, I tried to stay still.

"Uh, I'm not that special," said Bronwyn stubbornly.

"Sure you are," said her friend. "*She* thinks you are, anyway."

Charlie Dean would have bet two of her favorite suits that the friend was jealous of Bronwyn's beauty.

"No, I'm not," said Bronwyn. Her face was flushed. I couldn't tell if she was talking to me or the friend.

"I have—" I held up my portfolio case. It held the drawings of the dress in which I'd imagined Bronwyn and the swatches.

"No," she said. "Thanks anyway. But I'm not really into it."

"Okay," I said. "I'm sorry." I turned to leave, barely able to make my wooden legs move.

I'd only gone a few steps when I heard one of the girls behind me speak up.

"She'd like to get you into one of her dresses, Bron."

"Shut up."

"I think she probably wants to get in there with you."

It sounded like all of them joined in the laughter.

I did not allow my posture to soften, even though it hurt to breathe. Just a little.

twelve

MARCH 5

On Tuesday night I was in the garage, sitting on a stool at my worktable, trying to draw some fashion designs. They kept coming out looking like total crap, and I kept tearing out pages, crumpling them up, and throwing them on the floor.

My grandpa walked into the shop just in time to see me hurl the book across the room, where it cracked open against the foot shear machine we'd rigged up against the back wall.

"That'll teach it," he said, when I noticed him. He walked over and slowly bent down to pick it up.

"Sorry, Gramps."

"Probably deserved it. That book'll think twice about trying something like that again."

He set it in front of me.

He doesn't do his old-timey metalwork anymore because he's got asthma and the doctor says he's inhaled enough bad stuff to last a lifetime, but he was really good. He'd work out in the backyard for hours at a time, and he made all kinds of stuff: decorative, useful. When he noticed I was interested, he decided that the backyard setup wasn't good enough for me. He bought me the new welding station and set up the whole garage for me to work in. He found me an ancient rolling bender and a bender break, and even made a foot shear from spare parts his friends donated. I've got all his old snips and scissors. Quite a few of them are too rusted or battered to be very useful, but I like having them. And he bought me new ones, too. With the big worktable and all the sculptures in various stages of completion, there's not much room in there. Definitely not enough room for my grandparents to park their car.

I knew my grandparents really couldn't afford to set me up like that, but I also loved having a fully equipped shop. I try to keep it real neat so he knows how much I appreciate it. At least, it's neat when it's not covered in crumpled paper and sketchbook parts.

"What's cooking?" he asked, holding his stained World's Best Grumpy Old Man coffee cup in front of him. Maybe because he was a shift worker for nearly forty years, he can drink coffee until right before bed and it doesn't seem to affect his sleep.

I puffed out a breath. I knew my grandma had told him about the contest, but he hadn't brought it up with me yet. That's how my grandpa is. He doesn't pry. He waits for me to be ready to talk.

"I guess Grandma told you about the contest? The one I just qualified to enter?"

"That's right. She said something about that. It's for that school up the hill there? The fancy one old man Green gave all his money to?"

Green Pastures' founder was a local farmer who got really famous for his paintings of farms when he was already fairly old. He donated all his money to start the school. Plus,

I think he also sold nearly a thousand acres of prime land.

"Yeah, well, I got into their scholarship competition," I said.

"You going to show them some of your work? Maybe we should get professional photos taken of your projects." He scanned the shelves that held some of my smaller metalwork projects. He looked at the big ones that stood around the room.

"That's just it. The contest isn't for, uh, metal sculpture. It's for fashion design."

He cocked his head. Waited for me to explain. My grandpa has eyes that see. He knows I'm not on a first-name basis with fashionability, if that's a word.

"All the contestants have to make an outfit. For a fashion show."

"Is that right?" said my grandpa. "So you want to be a fashioner?"

"I think they're called fashion designers, Gramp. But no. It's just a way to get into the school."

"That place is so damned expensive," he said. "Me and your grandmother and your mother talked about it. Wondered how we could get you in there. It just costs too much for regular working people." He sighed.

I felt a rush of relief that they had some sense of financial self-preservation and that there was a limit to how much they would do for me.

"You know, your grandmother has an old Singer machine. Never known her to use it. I think it's in the basement."

This kind of calm, thoughtful vibe is why, at his retirement party, so many people got up and said my grandpa was the best foreman they ever had. That was a good night. Him and my grandma two-stepped together like two synchronized tops, spinning around the floor. He's as present as my dad is absent. One day I'll be more like him.

"I know it's kind of screwed up to try to get in this way," I said. "Since I'm not really into fashion."

"Sometimes a person has to take the indirect path," said Gramps. "Side roads. Access routes. Alleys, even."

"Yeah, well. We'll see. So far my drawings of clothes suck," I said. I flipped a couple of pages.

The designs all looked like they belonged on superheroes who'd taken up low-end prostitution after retiring. I remembered my comments to Charlie Dean. Intellectually rigorous. I was so full of it.

"They look good to me," said my gramps. "But my glasses prescription is way the hell out of date."

Just like that, all my anger was gone.

I went to close the book, but spotted a phone number written in pencil, just inside the front cover. The name Tesla was written underneath. I closed the book. Opened it. The name and number were still there. I closed it again.

My gramps went back in the house, and I kept drawing, trying not to think about the number I'd just seen. An hour later Barbra arrived. She'd been out for dinner with her family for her little sister's birthday.

She stepped into the garage from the side door, bringing fresh night air with her.

When she kissed me, I inhaled her familiar scent.

"So?" she said. "Tell me the news of the world, Grasshopper."

Among the reasons I love my girlfriend is that she is not shy about weaving *Karate Kid* references into her sentences.

"I've figured out what they mean by a croakie book," I said. "It's spelled C-R-O-Q-U-I-S." The source of this information, a book called *Cool Fashions for Kids (Ages 8–12)*, lay open on my worktable. I began to read aloud. "'A croquis book is where a designer sketches concepts and construction details and communicates her ideas for each look.'"

I glanced at Barbra and saw she was giving me her full, if concerned, attention and continued. "'Your croquis book is your fashion diary and your fashion workbook! It will allow you to create collections that pop and sizzle and will wow your friends!'"

"Well, jeez," she said. "Popping and sizzling are critically important."

"Drawing fashion figures is way harder than you'd think. The proportions are screwy."

She sat on one of the paint-splattered chairs beside my station. "So you're going to keep going? In the competition?"

"Yeah. For now."

"That's good."

"You mean it?" I asked. Because there was something in her voice that didn't sound convincingly happy.

"Of course. Just please don't get all *fashion-y*. Or *Green Pastures-y*."

"I would never," I said, and noted again that my girl isn't big on change.

"Good. I like you the way you are." She shivered. "It's so cold in here."

"Space heater's busted."

It's a mark of Barbra's and Booker's excellence that they're willing to spend any time in the garage with me. They hang on to sheets of metal when I need them to. They put up with the noise of the spot welder, riveting, the banging of hammers against metal, and the screeching and clanging of the machines. They never complain about the essential anti-socialness of metalwork. If Barbra wanted to head into the house to warm up, that was okay with me.

"Well . . ." she said.

So we went in the house. Into my room.

B left at around nine o'clock, and I went back into the shop. I flipped through the sketchbook, pretending to just happen upon the number again. I stared at it for a long while. Then I sent a text.

> **Whoever invented fashion figures was a sadist.**

The reply was nearly instant.

> **So you found my number.**

Yes, yes. I had found the number.

Reasons to Drop Out of the Fashion Competition

When a woman says, "I have nothing to wear!" what she really means is, "There's nothing here for who I'm supposed to be today." —CAITLIN MORAN

thirteen

CHARLIE DEAN

HERE'S AN IDEA © Charlie Dean Designs:

When the world hands you lemons, make lemonade. Out of Meyer lemons! Serve that lemonade in tiny jars with a single ice cube with a leaf of pineapple mint frozen inside. Wear a frilly 1950s apron with a green parrot and a yellow pineapple over a classic housewife dress when you bring the tray around.

DATE: MARCH 7

Days until fashion show: 58

Even three days after the incident with Bronwyn I continued to feel *quelle tragique*. That is a long time for Charlie Dean to be down in *le dumps*. I make it a policy to overcome negative feelings and forget unfortunate events *tout de suite*!

But things were not ideal. My father seemed depressed, probably because Mischa hadn't come around for several days. In fact, I hadn't seen her since the morning of the workshop, when I'd finally coaxed her out of the bathroom like a tiny fawn out of a dappled grove. This was not how my dad's relationships usually went. His ladies had a tendency to stay until we had nothing left. Like giant carpenter ants.

I spend almost all my time in my room, which I have transformed to make it many times more attractive than the rest of the house. I've painted one wall and the inside of the door the exact red of the fringed Barbados tulip, in honor of Diana Vreeland, who was famous for using red in her interiors. I've painted the other three walls and the ceiling the shadowed white of silver birch bark on a January afternoon. This summer I even refinished the hardwood floors so they gleam and appear to be of higher quality than they are. Antique mirrors make the room look much bigger. There are rolling racks along two walls, and my desk, which I built myself, lines another whole wall of the room. It's a simple piece of finished wood held up by wooden brackets with a cut-down antique cane in the middle for stability. Another piece folds underneath, and when I pull it out it forms a big T. The desk is perfect for cutting and drawing patterns for my bigger creations, and I rest my fabric on it while I hand sew. A large refinished wardrobe holds my fabrics. One dressmaker's dummy stands near my best chair, and the other rests in the corner.

My room is like a little oasis of good taste in the desert of bad taste that is the rest of the house.

I stared down at the design I'd created. I was increasingly unhappy with it. Pretty? Yes. Elegant? Yes. Groundbreaking? No. I was torn. Play it safe with an impeccable gown or risk it all?

I thought about John's comments about how he liked an intellectually rigorous approach. I thought about Mr. Carmichael's lectures about fashion theory and history. I could tell at least a few of the other contestants were chance takers. It was written all over them.

Just as concerning, there was no one to wear it. I felt stumped on every level. *Merde!* I didn't have the funds to hire a professional model. I don't think there even is a modeling agency in town.

My father got home and appeared in my doorway, and I admit that I looked over his shoulder for Mischa. I couldn't decide whether I wanted to see her or not.

"Charlie girl," he said. "How you doing?"

"I'm fine."

"Good. Good. I'm glad one of us is."

"Are you okay?" I asked.

He shrugged. My dad is one of those people who, depending on the day and his state of mind, can look anywhere from twenty-five to fifty-five. He's actually thirty-six. He's handsome and rather chic, in a slightly bedraggled way. There is a reason he has no problem drawing the eye of ladies, especially those with severe problems.

"Fine," he said.

"Are you taking care of yourself?" I asked, which is code between us for are you staying clean.

"Oh yeah."

"How's Mischa?" I asked, the words out of my mouth before I had time to stop myself. I never ask about his ladies. I don't want to know.

He heaved another sigh. "I don't know, Charlie girl. Not good, I don't think."

You don't want to know about this, I told myself. Do not ask about this situation.

"Why?" I asked.

"Her ex just came back to town. I guess he's bad news. It's got her down. Me too. I miss her. She's a sweet girl."

"Ah," I said.

"She's isolating in her apartment. Afraid to go out. It's terrible. I've asked her to come over, but she's afraid. She won't let me visit in case it makes things worse. She just got out of treatment herself a few weeks ago. I'm worried about her."

Do not engage, Charlie Dean. *Do not.* You have enough problems of your own without getting involved with your father's affairs of the heart.

"Where does she live?" I asked.

"Right around the corner, basically. On Albert Street."

"Do you want me to go see her?"

My father's face cleared like a sky swept clean by a storm. He smiled, his features becoming young again.

"That would be amazing, Charlie girl. I just want to make sure she's okay."

"Give me the address. I'll go over this afternoon."

My dad was like a kid, all full of enthusiasm. He slapped his hands together and generally twinkled.

"This is great, Charlie. Just great."

Half an hour later I was on my way to Mischa's.

She lived only four blocks from us in an apartment that wasn't as grim as some of its neighbors. The building was a basic box, but it had a fresh coat of paint and hardly any shopping carts out front. My dad had given me the buzzer number for her apartment, and I pressed it, feeling slightly disoriented. To be honest, Charlie Dean was not sure what she was doing chasing after one of the ladies.

The ringer sounded many times. Then there was the hollow click of someone picking up the receiver.

"Hello?"

"Hi, Mischa. It's Charlie. Charlie Dean."

Silence.

"I just thought I'd say hi. See how you were."

"I'm fine."

"Can I come in?" I asked.

Another long pause.

"Okay. I'm in 304."

She buzzed me in, and I made my way through the orange-and-brown-wallpapered, fake-wood-paneled 1970s lobby and into the elevator. Even the dead flies in the overhead lights looked vintage.

I knocked on her door.

"Yes?" she said, as though we hadn't just spoken over the intercom.

"It's Charlie."

"Okay."

She opened the door and peered out.

I tried to smile reassuringly.

"Hi," I said, wishing I'd chosen to stay home. My store of small talk was completely exhausted.

"Do you want to come in?" she asked, looking as though she'd like nothing less than to let me inside.

"Sure."

The apartment was clean but dark and nearly empty. It smelled strongly of cigarette smoke.

"I just moved in," she said. "I didn't pay the fees on my storage locker."

If there's one thing Charlie Dean knows about, it's the role storage lockers play in the lives of those who are frequently evicted. A storage locker is basically a halfway house for people's belongings.

"It's very tidy," I said, standing in the living room/dining room that contained one lumpy couch covered with a blanket, and a large TV. A full ashtray wobbled on an overturned plastic crate on the tiny deck. The sliding door was cracked open a few inches.

"Do you want to sit down?" she said.

"Maybe we could put on a light?"

She gave a little laugh. "Sorry. I don't have any lamps yet. The overheads are so bright."

She turned, and for an instant she was silhouetted against the half-open blinds. I saw what I hadn't seen before. Mischa was beautiful.

My aversion to my father's ladies and the trouble they brought, not to mention the way they were not my mother, had blinded me to the fact. But Mischa had a marvelous profile and line to her, an elegance that wasn't obvious when she was in her jeans and leathers. She had long, slender limbs, a graceful neck.

"Will you be my model for the fashion show?" I blurted.

She frowned and tilted her head back as though trying to avoid a blow.

"Aren't models supposed to be really young and perfect? You know, fifteen and a hundred pounds?"

"We can use anyone who inspires us," I said. Then, because I felt like I had to be honest I said, "Plus, I asked this girl at school and she said no."

I thought of the laughter that had followed me down the hall after I approached Bronwyn.

"God, I feel more like a house that's about to be torn down than a model," she said.

I stared at her as something caught fire in my imagination.

"You'd be perfect," I said.

We stood awkwardly in the dim living room.

"How's your dad?" she asked.

"He's all right. I think he misses you."

"I'm just, uh, taking some time out. I've got some stuff on the personal front to deal with. I haven't been feeling well."

"Your ex," I said.

"It's all okay. He hasn't been around." She gave a little shudder. "God, he would hate me modeling, even for a high school fashion show. That's probably all the more reason to do it."

"So you'll say yes?" I asked.

"I'll stop by tomorrow or the next day. We can talk about it. You can show me your designs."

A smile transformed her pale, angular face into something glorious. She wasn't unblemished golden perfection, like Bronwyn. Her look was more complex. More fragile and on the verge of fading from one more hard blow.

As soon as I got home I set all the drawings and mood boards of the unoriginal, unexciting dress aside. I pulled the copy of *Black Friday* with its photos of abandoned malls from under a stack of glossy magazines. Some were stripped down to their rebar frames. Some were just left as is to slowly sag into the landscape, honeycombed with empty stores waiting for the consumer who never came. Flooded floors were elaborate reflective pools mirroring cracked atriums and soaring glass walkways.

These images of light cascading through shadowed interiors and escalators paused forever were the ones that made me swell with emotion, good and bad. They were remarkably, unexpectedly beautiful, just like Mischa. My thoughts went back to the gutted mall across the street from the fateful motel in Edmonton. My heart imploded, but as I flipped through the pages of the book I had to acknowledge the power of the photos. They were beautiful and sad. The concept took shape in my mind!

Back to work I went, printing out photos and doing sketches and putting samples of colors and textures and thematic connections on a new mood board.

My design would risk it all—it would take emotional and intellectual chances—it would be filled with loss, disappointment, and hope. And it would be worn by the ideal model.

fourteen

MARCH 7

Fashion is like a terrible disease transmitted through the eyes. My poor orbs were being exposed to so much fashion design that I was starting to have the same reaction I get when I see a really good painting, an interesting building, or a cool sculpture. It's this clenched feeling around my heart, like somebody's squeezing it. My hair stands on end. Who am I kidding? My hair always stands on end.

Even more baffling was the fact that Tesla, definitely *not* the type of girl who would normally pay attention to a guy like me, kept texting. It was messing me up.

In the positive column, I found the name of the style of clothing I would make if I ever get a model. It turns out that some designers specialize in "deconstructed" fashion, which is when the clothes are a mess, with the seams all shitty and unfinished and nothing fits properly. Deconstruction is apparently some big movement in art and philosophy and literature inspired by a sadistic French philosopher called Jacques Derrida, who expressed himself in the most complicated way possible so no one completely understands what he was getting at, even now. I know this because I tried reading the Wiki entry.

As a deconstructionist, I could send my model down the runway wearing a golf bag and clown shoes, and if anyone asked me to explain, I'd just say something about Issey Miyake's 1994 collection or every second collection by Rei Kawakubo, especially the one she did with the big stuffed lumps sewn onto random parts of the clothes. Genius.

Having figured out my approach, I started looking for a model. After hinting around the subject for a while and not getting anywhere, I reluctantly broke down and asked B if she'd do it. She told me to never ask her something like that again, and she was only just sort of joking.

I called Booker and asked him if his new sort-of girlfriend, Destiny, would like to be my model. He said he'd check, and three minutes later he turned me down on Destiny's behalf. Apparently she had "other things to do" that day, even though I hadn't told Booker what day the show was.

It was a pickle and a conundrum, as my gramps likes to say. During my shift at the Salad Stop after school, I thought about whom I should ask to wear my ugly clothes. I considered the problem as I served twelve kinds of organic salads to customers who should have been eating something that was not salad. I thought about it as I wiped down counters and put the expired greens and mixed salads into the organics compost bin right before closing time.

The doorbell chimed, and I cursed under my breath. Last-minute salad customers are an offense in God's eyes.

I swiped my hands down my green canvas uniform apron with the pattern of cascading lettuce leaves. The apron made me feel this borderline despair that was actually sort of invigorating. What would John Galliano or Valentino say about my life and my uniform? Nothing positive, I bet.

Four girls, all around ten years old, waited at the counter. Well, three stood at the counter. A fourth stood a few feet behind them, looking like she didn't know what the hell was going on.

"We're just closing up," I said.

"It's 5:55." A white girl with blue eyes and long, straight brown hair pulled into a tight ponytail pointed at the sign with our hours.

I sighed. What were preteens doing eating salad? Shouldn't they be eating Pizza Pockets or something like that? What was the world coming to? Was no one safe from salad?

"Yeah, okay, what can I get you?"

"I would like an apple-cider-marinated kale salad with walnuts and apples. Hold the pomegranate seeds. I think I might be allergic," said the brown-haired girl.

"You're not allergic," said the girl next to her. She had olive skin, a wide mouth, and strong features that would make her either super striking or homely in the next few years. Right now she was walking a fine line, and puberty would push her over it. "You're just not adventurous."

The strong-featured girl, all chin and nose and cheek, but mostly chin, looked at me. "*I'll* take her pomegranate seeds," she said.

"Me too," said the third, a ponytailed Asian girl. She had a pretty face and a gentle expression.

I waited for the one standing behind them to place her order.

"What about you?" I asked when she didn't speak up.

"*She's* not ordering with us," said the strong-featured girl. I decided she was not going to be attractive when she got older.

The girl with the brown hair turned and spoke over her shoulder to the fourth girl. "That's right, Esther. Don't try copying us by ordering the walnut and kale salad. With or without the pomegranate seeds."

"Exactly. You've been copying us all day. And we're really getting sick of it," said the girl whose kind and pretty face was apparently a front for an unkind and unpretty personality.

The little brats were bullying the kid right in front of me. Like I didn't exist. Like I wouldn't react. I don't know why that irritated me so much, but it did.

The girl standing behind them had wild dark curls and large eyes with dark smudges under them, like she didn't get enough sleep or was sick. She pursed her lips but didn't speak.

"We don't have any pomegranate seeds," I said. "Something wrong with the crop this year."

For the two hundredth time I wished the boss would take the seeds off the menu. Who puts a seasonal item on a permanent menu, anyway? Only someone who takes a lot of steroids and was continually giving himself mini-strokes at the gym due to overexertion.

I thought about telling the mean girls that nobody likes assholes, even young ones, but I didn't have the energy.

"Okay, so you're *not* all together?" I said. "You want to order separately?"

The brown-haired girl put her arm around the shoulders of the girls on either side of her, turning them into a single mean-girl organism. "Just us."

"Your mom said for you to buy salads for all of us," said the fourth girl in a quiet voice.

"Just because you don't have any money doesn't mean

you get to sponge off my family," said the first girl, who was clearly headed for fame and fortune as the sociopathic CEO of a Fortune 500 chemical company.

"She said—"

"Whatever, Esther. Just order after we're gone so we don't have to hear your voice anymore."

These were the scariest kids who'd ever come through the Salad Stop, and that's saying something, given that all we have here is salad.

After the ringleader paid for three salads, I told them that I'd be with them in a moment. I grabbed three corn-fiber bio-degradable takeout containers and slipped into the back and out the back door. I glanced around quickly to make sure no one was watching, then used tongs to scoop up three bunches of greens, food of the damned, out of the compost bin, and slopped them into the containers.

I carried the containers to the front of the shop, and then added the bare minimum of fixings, minus the pomegranate seeds.

I'd have done worse, but they *were* just kids, even if they were terrible people.

"Here you go," I said, handing each of the three girls a container. Kale is so fibrous that hardly anyone can tell if it's fresh or not. "Enjoy, now."

They each grinned at me. The one with all the features batted her eyes.

"Bye, now!" they said, then giggled and swaggered out in their matching Hunter boots, like they'd just vanquished an entire army of Marvel arch-villains. The door opened and closed, and the doorbell sounded a tropical birdcall, which is exactly the kind of thing that causes morale to soar among Salad Stop employees.

I looked at the girl who wasn't allowed to copy the salad order of other girls.

"Sorry about the wait. What can I get you?"

"Nothing." She gazed at the ceiling as though inspecting it for spiders, and I realized she probably had no money to order one of our god-awful, soul-destroying salads.

"No shirt, no shoes, no money, no problem. It's on me. What'll you have?"

She looked down, as though she didn't want me to see her surprise. When she looked up, there was a very small smile on her face. "I think I'd like *exactly* what they had," she said, so deadpan, I laughed out loud.

"Good for you," I said. "That's the up-yours spirit!"

With a bit of a spring in my step I went to the fridge behind me and pulled out the stuff to make her a marinated kale salad, with extra walnuts because fuck it. She deserved them.

"That's not where you got their salads," said the girl.

"Cor-rect."

A grin had spread across her face. It was sort of a funny face. Hypermobile. Like an old-school comedienne.

I pushed her salad container, stuffed to bursting, across the glass countertop.

"Thank you," she said.

"Bon appétit!"

She turned to leave the shop but hesitated at the front door.

"Everything okay?" I asked.

"They're still out there."

"Can I ask what exactly you're doing hanging out with such nasty girls?"

"Dahlia's mom is taking me out for her Moms Make the Difference volunteer commitment. We went to Cathedral Grove to look at the trees."

"Really."

"The trees were huge. But I already knew that. Quite a few people have taken me to see trees."

"Why's that?"

"Because everyone thinks disadvantaged kids need more trees."

"Oh," I said. I felt a little stab of shame. I totally would have taken a poor kid to see trees. Of course, I was and still am a fairly poor kid, and trees are free.

"My foster mom already shows me lots of trees. She bought me all new clothes for this trip."

"Oh yeah?"

I peered over the counter and saw that Esther wore the same outfit as the other three. A hoodie, patterned tights. On her feet she wore the same fancy rubber boots as the other girls.

"As soon as Dahlia and Morgan and Brittney saw me they said I was copying them."

"I've seen lots of other girls in wearing those kinds of clothes," I said, trying to make her feel better.

"I don't even *like* this outfit very much," she said, lifting her chin a bit. "Even if it *is* comfortable."

"What kind of clothes *do* you like?" I asked.

She squinted suspiciously, like I'd said something creepy.

"I don't really know. Maybe sports clothes? Sometimes, I wear my brother's basketball jersey. But it smells like sweat no matter how many times my foster mom washes it."

I thought for a second. Processing. "So are you interested in clothes?" I asked, an idea dawning in the dustiest reaches of my brain.

She crinkled her nose suspiciously.

"I'm not stranger-dangering you. I'm in this, uh, competition. A fashion competition. We have to design an outfit for someone. To win a scholarship to art school."

"You can use a kid as your model?" she said.

"Why not?"

"What would I have to do?" she asked.

"Tell me about what you like to wear. Then I guess I'd measure you and then make you something to wear in this fashion show. Do you think new clothes would make a difference? You know, in dealing with them?" Outside in the parking lot, the other three girls were getting into a shiny sport-utility vehicle.

"I don't know," she said. "They're all obsessed with modeling and stuff like that."

"Well, what say we make you a model first?"

"That," she said, all serious faced, "would put sand in their eye." She was obviously repeating something she'd heard an adult say, the way I repeat things my gramps says. I got a huge kick out of the small, hilariously sinister smile on her face.

"Here. I'll give you my number. Give it to your mom."

"Foster mom," she corrected.

"Right. I'll explain the project to her. The fashion show is in May, so we have some time."

I wrote my cell number and scribbled a note on the back of a Salad Stop card: *Dear Esther's Foster Mom: Please call about Esther taking part in a fashion competition.*

I didn't want there to be any confusion about why I was giving my number to a kid. Be just my luck to get arrested as a creeper while I was trying to cheat my way into a private school.

Outside someone honked the horn.

A lean lady in exercise clothes bustled out of the Liquor Depot with two bags full of booze.

"Thanks," said Esther. And she walked out the door in the new clothes that had failed her completely.

John Thomas-Smith's Increasingly Pointless Argument against Fashion and Fashion People

"Crinoline fires" killed 3,000 women between the late 1850s and late 1860s in England. Women would lose sense of their circumference, step too close to a fire grate, then flames would be fanned by oxygen circulating under their skirts. . . .

—ANN KINGSTON, "DEADLY VICTORIAN FASHIONS"

fifteen

CHARLIE DEAN

HERE'S AN IDEA © CHARLIE DEAN DESIGNS:

Sometimes you simply must wear a hat. And sometimes that hat is going to be very large. Embrace that moment when it comes! Think of Britain! Think of polo ponies! And whatever you do, don't forget a feather in the brim.

DATE: MARCH 10

Days until fashion show: 55

Mischa didn't show up the day after I went to see her or the day after that. I sent her three texts, and she didn't respond.

On Sunday, after I got home from a four-hour shift at the makeup counter, during which I helped numerous people who desperately needed it—why don't schools offer a mandatory course in understanding your skin tone?—I found my dad slumped in a chair in the kitchen.

At first I worried he was high, but my *père* does not linger in common areas when he's using. He likes his privacy. Thank Dior!

"Hello?" I said. "Everything okay?"

He had no book or magazine in front of him. No food. Just him and the unfortunate kitchen table.

It should be said that my father and I spend a lot of time asking each other if we're okay. It's nice, but also a little unhealthy from a codependence perspective, which I learned about during extensive attendance at Alateen in years past.

"Yup. I'm fine, Charlie. Heading out to a meeting soon."

"That's good. Taking your two-month chip?"

He nodded but didn't look excited. My father has taken quite a few chips. Perhaps the excitement has worn off. Maybe I should make him an eccentric and hilarious belt made entirely of sobriety chips. Or perhaps not.

He asked how work was, how school was going. Then he asked if I'd heard from Mischa.

"Not yet. But I'm sure she's coming over soon."

"That's good," he said. "I worry about her."

I did, too, since I needed to take her measurements so I could begin her dress. It would not be a simple project.

"So are you two . . . ?"

"I hope so. When she gets things settled. She doesn't want to get into a hassle with her ex."

I didn't know how I felt about that. Mischa was a definite improvement over most of my father's romantic leads, post–my mom. For one thing, she didn't look like a turnip left in a heavy metal band's root cellar for three years. For another, she might be the person to bring my fashion and education dreams to fruition. But I couldn't forget that my dad and relationships were not a good combination.

I went to my room and brought us out some nice crackers and a small piece of good cheese and shared them with my dad.

The food seemed to lift his spirits, and when he left for his meeting, his back was straight and his footfalls firm.

He'd been gone for about ten minutes when I heard a vehicle pull into the driveway. It says something about the state of
the vehicle's repair that I heard it over Edith Piaf singing "La
Bohème" on my computer. *Si romantique*, not to mention a re-
latable story of housing instability!

I turned the music down and looked out the window to see
whether it was Mr. Devlin. If it was him, I decided I wouldn't
answer the door. But it wasn't Mr. Devlin, it was Mischa, getting out of an old GMC camper van, an appalling beige-y
yellow with brown stripes. It was the sort of vehicle one associates with low-income seniors who have made a lot of poor life
choices.

I don't know what I thought she'd drive, but it wasn't that.

I rushed out of my room and opened the front door before
she could knock. My greeting stopped in my throat.

Mischa had a black eye.

And a fat lip.

We stared at each other.

Here is a sad fact: Charlie Dean has seen a beat-up face or
two, usually her father's. She even saw him getting beaten up
once by a gang member who had been ordered to give my father
a lesson about managing his *dettes*. (But the gangster didn't say
it in French, because he was a member of the lower-echelon
criminal underground and probably a high school dropout.)

His swollen shoulders had looked like small, round boulders
under the lurid rose-and-skull pattern of his Ed Hardy shirt.
Acne studded his neck and jawline as though the shirt was giving his skin a rash. My dad had been using hard for weeks, and
the nightmarish visit seemed like the inevitable finale. When
I saw the young gangster all I could think was that Ed Hardy
was not a designer who would stand the test of time. I was
right. Twelve years old, and I called it.

"Go to your room, Charlie," my dad had said, as though he was concerned about providing me with a wholesome environment.

"She better not call the cops," said the gang member.

"She won't," said my father.

Heart pounding, I went to my room, locked the door, and sat on my bed and tried to focus on the copy of *Vogue* my father had stolen from a laundromat for me.

The blows in the kitchen sounded like an Easter ham falling repeatedly off the counter.

It never crossed my mind to call the *gendarmerie*. Too much likelihood my dad would get arrested along with the gangster, and I'd end up in the care of the ministry again.

Don't get me wrong. I'm not against *gendarmes* or law and order! When someone robs a Charlie Dean showroom in Montreal, Toronto, Los Angeles, New York, or Paris, the authorities will be called *posthaste*.

After the front door slammed shut that terrible evening, I went to check on my father. He was bent over in his chair, holding his face in his hands.

"Get me a tea towel, would you?" he said without looking up.

He held the dark towel I'd given him to the lower half of his face and tilted his head up to slow the bleeding.

"Well, I'm glad that's over," he said, his voice muffled by the terry cloth. He sounded like a man elated after surviving a tough job interview.

Now here was Mischa with the same expression on her face. She had the same to-hell-with-it attitude. All her anxiety was gone. The worst had happened, and she'd survived it.

"Gorgeous, right?" she said. "Don't worry. It'll be okay by the time I do your fashion show."

What to say? What to do? Intervention? Wise words? Counselors? Also: she was still willing to model for me?

"Ouch," I said.

Mischa pointed a long index finger at her swollen lip as though at an exhibit.

"You mean this old thing?" she said. "I've had this forever. Since last night at least." She gave a slightly crazed-sounding laugh.

I did the only thing I could think of. I brought her into my room. It's the nicest space in our house, and I hoped it would be healing for her.

Mischa didn't sit. Instead she turned in a slow circle, like someone who found herself in a strange but wonderful neighborhood.

"Would you like some tea?" I asked.

"Sure," she said. "Wow, I had no idea it was so nice in here. If I could smell properly, I bet it smells good, too."

Bad taste in men, good manners. One can't help but think that it would have been better the other way around.

I gestured for her to sit down on the chair I'd re-covered using an old tapestry I'd found at a flea market. Someone's dog had chewed off the fringe and one corner, but there had been enough left intact to cover the seat and back of my chair. I'd upholstered the arms with a soft wool tweed in oatmeal and greige. At the foot of the chair was a small ottoman re-covered with a remnant of an old Persian carpet. The chair and the ottoman were going to look fabulous in the converted barn I planned one day to own. I would take a page from Mrs. Vreeland's book and place handwoven baskets full of hand-dyed yarn all around. It would be unutterably *charmant*.

I poured the hot water into the round glass pot. I put in a

chrysanthemum bud and watched its pink blossom unfurl like a slow-motion explosion.

"Whoa," said Mischa as she watched the tea bud transform.

I arranged our glass teacups without handles on the tray instead of looking at her. The small glass and wood container with the honey wand sat neatly on the plain wooden tray.

"My friends used to call him Demon," she said.

Her black eye made her look a lot older and a lot younger. Like half her face was a shadow of who she would one day become.

"We were never very good together," she said, holding up both ends of the conversation. "We brought out the worst in each other. But even though I have this"—she pointed vaguely at her battered face—"I think he heard me when I said we were done. That I'm moving on and he should too."

My hand hovered over the tea set.

Listening to her made me glad I am probably not destined for romance at all due to being too busy for it and not being able to afford the distraction. Diana Vreeland was married to her husband, Reed, for most of her life. But he cheated on her for years. I would happily settle for being in love with fashion.

"I'm sorry," I said, because I was. "Did you call the police?"

She ignored me.

"Is the tea ready?"

"People who hurt other people are dangerous," I said, realizing that was a less-than-incisive observation.

"I don't want to get him in trouble. I just want him to go away. I'm in recovery now. He's not."

I poured out the tea and put the container of honey on the side table next to her.

"This is by far the fanciest tea I've ever had," she said, and I could tell she was done talking about what had happened.

All I could offer Mischa was someone to talk to, an excellent cup of tea, and an extraordinary outfit. Maybe that would be enough.

I brought over the drawings for her to look at. "Here's the dress I want to make for you," I said.

Mischa stared down at the page.

"This is incredible," she said. "I don't even know how to describe what I'm seeing here. It's not exactly the kind of thing you find at the local mall."

"Funny you should say that. The inspiration is failed malls," I said.

She glanced up. "Come again?"

I showed her my copy of *Black Friday* and my mood board with printouts of photos of malls that had gone bankrupt and been abandoned. "Oh," she said, flipping back to the drawings of the dress. "I think I see it."

"Malls in particular are so interesting. You can really see their structure when there's nothing left inside. Big skylights and glass ceilings."

"Is that why the dress is all shades of white and gray and has those . . . ribs on the sides?"

"Exactly. I want to show how the dress is held up. The underlying architecture. On the overskirt I'm going to paint geometric shapes, like discarded furniture. Like this," I said, and pointed to an image showing overturned plastic chairs in a food court. I showed her the sample paintings I'd made. "I'm also going to do a pleated panel to suggest an escalator."

Take that, intellectually rigorous John Thomas-Smith! I was pushing some serious boundaries here. Risky could be Charlie Dean's middle name!

"And you know how to sew something like this? Like on a machine?"

"I'll do some on the machine to save time, but I will do a lot of it by hand."

She stared at me, and her bloodshot eye made me wince.

"Are you saying that I remind you of a bankrupt mall?"

Explaining my designs has never been easy for me, and I wasn't about to get into the personal associations with the worst moment of my life, but I tried.

"The design is about expectations. Everybody wants something from beautiful people. From beautiful women, especially. But I think they're most stunning when they refuse to give anyone anything."

"Huh," said Mischa. "I need to think about that."

She smelled like cigarette smoke. Her perfume had too much citrus.

Her gaze slid up to mine. "You are a thinker, Charlie Dean," she said. Then she looked away, long lashes fringing her cheek. Her beauty showed more wear than Bronwyn's, more fragility. She was failure and, I hoped, new beginnings. From a certain angle she looked like my mother.

"You and this gown will be magic," I said.

Mischa smiled crookedly at me to protect her swollen lip.

"I could use a little magic."

PART FOUR

*Lifesavers and
Other Garments*

CHARLIE DEAN

HERE'S AN IDEA © Charlie Dean Designs:

Take the time you need to be well dressed and properly groomed. Do not rush in matters affecting your look. Even a careless style takes focus! With this in mind, go to bed one hour earlier than usual, get up one hour earlier, and see your personal style bloom!

DATE: MARCH 11

Days until fashion show: 54

Now that I had my model and my design and was fully immersed in the competition, every other commitment in my life—and Charlie Dean has a lot of commitments!—felt like a burden. I asked my manager at Shoppers if I could get time off, and he very kindly granted it. I am, after all, the top part-time makeup salesperson at any Shoppers Drug Mart in the mid-Island region. Many are the women who no longer show facial exhaustion thanks to my skill with foundation.

R. S. Jackson Senior High was not about to grant me leave, however. And I needed to pass my courses or I wouldn't be permitted into Green Pastures with or without a scholarship. There was also college to think about. Most colleges want even the most brilliant incoming students to have a high school diploma.

All that to say that I brought my paints and drawing pads and other art supplies to school with me. At lunch, instead of going to the counseling office, I went to the old art room, now used for adult education in the evenings, so I would have enough room to spread out and work.

And Charlie Dean has to admit she was curious about what some of her competitors were up to.

"Well, hello," said Jo, the tall, imposing girl from the workshop, when I walked in carrying my portfolio.

She sat at one of the scarred tables working on what seemed to be a piece of trim. In front of her were thread, a tray of long, ivory-colored bugle beads, and scissors.

"Oh," I said. "I didn't know you went here." I'd never seen her at school before. I'd have remembered. She was absolutely striking and fierce.

"I'm in the alternative program," she said. "We have most of our classes in the portables. I need a flexible schedule because I travel all the time with the basketball team."

"I thought there was no gym here anymore," I said.

"The school still has some sports teams. We get private funding from a few businesses in town. Sit down," she said, her smile white and her dimples mesmerizing. "I won't look."

At that I blushed, but then I realized she meant at my work.

I settled myself at the other end of the long table and pulled out my watercolor pad, my brushes, and paints. I was working on various details of the gown, as well as shoes and accessories, and I've always loved the look of fashion in watercolor.

"Do you have a model?" asked Jo.

I nodded.

"Me too," she said. "But first I got shot down in flames by Bronwyn."

My head jerked up.

"You'd think I asked the girl to go steady," said Jo, biting off a thread.

I felt a strange rush of relief at her words and the casual way she spoke them.

"Me too," I breathed.

"I heard Jason Wong and Cricket asked her, too. She turned us all down like we'd offered to give her a case of the plague. Cricket was pissed."

"Yeah, I was," said a voice from the door.

I looked over to see Cricket maneuvering through the door in her chair, a big fabric bag on her lap.

"Bronwyn whatever-her-last-name-is had the opportunity to help a deserving candidate, who is not you two or Jason, win a scholarship. I doubt she's a good person. And she may even be prejudiced against fashion designers," said Cricket.

Jo laughed. "She must be wondering if she's the only tall, skinny, good-looking girl in this whole town. Too bad she's shy."

"It's a waste," said Cricket, her red hair swooping over one eye as she unpacked a piece of fabric stretched over an embroidery frame. "Beautiful people have a responsibility to allow themselves to be used by those of us who need them."

She opened a box full of thread and began to work stitches, referring now and then to a drawing.

We sat like that, working together, speaking once in a while, and I must admit that I felt so social! It was strange and exciting.

Cricket's boyfriend came in on his way to meet his improv group.

"You need to eat something," he said, putting a sandwich beside her.

"Did your little brother make it?" she asked. "Is there mud in it? Small plastic animals?"

The boyfriend, who also had fabulous hair, dark and dramatically shaped, shrugged.

"I ate one of them and survived." He looked at us.

"Do either of you know the Heimlich maneuver?"

I shook my head no, but Jo nodded yes.

"If Cricket eats a toy, please don't let her choke. But make sure she eats. Since she started this fashion competition she keeps forgetting to eat or sleep. It's worrying."

I nodded. Felt another surge of solidarity. It was good to be among people for whom fashion was everything.

"He seems nice," said Jo when he was gone.

"He is," said Cricket. "That makes one of us."

"Well, I've got to get to practice," said Jo. She closed up her containers, put everything in a case, and stood up. Charlie Dean couldn't help but notice again that Jo was *absolument statuesque*! Nearly six feet tall and *all line, line, line,* as Diana Vreeland used to say. She wore a black leather jacket and a light-wash jean with old-school Adidas.

She came to stand over me, and my breath caught in my throat.

"You don't talk much," said Jo. "But I kind of like that about you. Nice to see you again, Charlie Dean."

Finally I convinced my slack mouth to smile.

Jo turned and stalked out of the room, leaving behind waves of raucous energy like the final notes on a heavy metal song.

"I think Miss Jo likes you," said Cricket in a singsong voice.

My face burned at the thought of it. At the pleasure of it.

Then I gave my head a little shake. It was all too much to contemplate. If I had to lose the competition, I would like to lose to Jo. But I wasn't going to lose. Not to Cricket, not to Jason or John or Jo or any of the others.

No distractions. Not even gorgeous ones.

seventeen

MARCH 11

Esther's foster mom called on Monday.

When I answered and started talking in my retail voice, Barbra glanced over from where she lay curled on the bed, reading a novel. Booker looked up from the floor, where he sat having a mostly one-way text conversation with his girl-friend, Destiny.

"I'm in this competition," I told the foster mother, who introduced herself as Sheryl. "I need a model to wear the clothes I'm designing for a, uh, fashion show."

"Esther's quite excited. She said you were, and I quote, 're-ally cool.'"

The woman sounded friendly, but her voice had a hint of no-bullshit that reminded me of a teacher.

"I think Esther could use some pampering, to be honest," Sheryl said.

I stared down at the drawing I'd been working on. I was using Charlie Dean's croquis blanks, which were just naked human shapes with weird, elongated fashion proportions.

The outfits weren't exactly deconstruction. They were barely identifiable as clothing. And they definitely weren't kid-appropriate. Esther did not need to be parading around in a busted bustier and bizarre short shorts. Also: pampering? I knew less than nothing about pampering.

"Can you tell me more about the contest?" Sheryl asked.

Barbra watched me. I took some comfort from her gaze. I could do this. Fashion design is not rocket science and neither was lying about fashion design.

I explained the school and the competition. "The winner gets a scholarship to the Green Pastures fashion program."

"That's a big prize," said Sheryl. "I've heard how much that school costs. So what will she wear?"

So soon with the hard questions.

"I'm not sure. I got the impression when I met her that she's got a lot of, uh, inner excellence, and, you know . . . I thought she doesn't need to look like everyone else."

As soon as I said it I remembered Esther telling me how her foster mom had spent a bunch of money to buy her clothes and fancy rubber boots to help her look like the other kids. I'd blown it.

The stillness on the other end of the phone had its own sound. My room was dark except for the reading light Barbra had adjusted over her book, the lamp aimed at my drawing pad, and Booker's phone. I felt comforted by the presence of my friends, as well as my grandparents listening to the TV too loud in the living room.

"Amen to that," said Sheryl finally. "She is a very special young lady. I hate to see her trying to look like everyone else. But she wants to fit in. At least, sometimes."

"Totally. I get that. I'm thinking I'll do a street-style look for her."

Barbra and Booker exchanged glances, probably shocked at my use of genuine fashion jargon.

"Street style," said Sheryl. "I'm sorry. I'm not familiar with that."

"It's, like, noncommercial fashion. Sort of indie. Personal. Street style is where a lot of designers get their ideas."

"Okay. Just to be clear, I'll be there for the whole process," said Sheryl. "And if this starts heading in a direction that's not good for her, I'll shut it down."

"I totally understand," I said.

She lowered her voice. "The thing is, I think Esther does need some help with how she sees herself. Maybe this experience is coming along at the right time."

My stomach constricted around my organs. I barely even knew who I was. It was too much pressure to put on my nonexistent fashion design skills.

We made a plan for me to visit their house the following Monday afternoon. Sheryl gave me the address, and I explained that I could come by in the evening, after I finished my shift at the Salad Stop.

"You poor guy," she said, and laughed. Sheryl definitely seemed like a good bean, and that made me feel better for Esther.

When we hung up, I stared at the stack of pages of crappy, unpampering, and unhelpful designs.

"So you're going to be allowed to use the kid you met?" said Barbra. "That was her foster mom?"

"Yup," I said. "I am in it now."

"Right on," said Booker, checking his phone for the twentieth time in as many minutes. "You might end up being head designer at Gap Kids. My sister says those fancy kids' clothes cost more than regular-size clothes."

"I have no clue what I'm doing," I said. "The kid deserves someone who knows something about clothes."

Barbra nudged my knee with her foot.

"I doubt anyone else is going to discover her being bullied in a Salad Stop and ask her to model in a fashion show."

"Maybe that was her bad luck," I said.

"No way, man," said Booker. "You're going to make her something reckless and revolutionary. Change her whole life for the radder."

"Radder?" said Barbra. "Really?"

He shrugged his big shoulders. "It's like rad, but more so."

Two hours later I was staring down at a page of naked fashion figures, their spindly limbs angled into unnatural positions. It was ten thirty, and Barbra was asleep on my bed, looking perfectly neat and composed. In a minute I had to wake her up to walk her home. Booker still sat on the floor, which is his preference because like a lot of tall guys, especially ones who carry a bit of extra weight, he's got a bad back. He was leafing through some of the fashion books I'd borrowed from the library. He didn't look up when he began speaking. "Don't worry about it. You'll come up with something. If you listen, people will always tell you what they need."

That was Booker. Mr. Deep when you least expect it. Destiny was an ass for not calling him back.

I leaned my head back and stared at the shadows and the water stains on the ceiling. My grandparents' house needed a new roof. It would take me the rest of my life working at the Salad Stop to buy Gram and Gramps a new roof.

"I started this whole thing as a sort of prank, and now a disadvantaged kid is expecting me to make something cool for her to wear."

"Maybe you'll find the perfect inspiration while you're walking me home," said Barbra, her voice thick with sleep.

"Oh, B," I said. "Why wouldn't you agree to be my model? I could send you down a runway in a sleeping bag, and you'd look good."

"You know why."

She'd lifted herself onto her elbows. She smiled sleepily at me, and for an instant I could do anything. Be anyone. And it didn't matter that I was not private-school or college material or even the kind of person who was supposed to dream big.

I answered my own question. "You won't model for me because you're not into clothes and don't like being the center of attention."

"Exactly. You'll figure something out for the kid. All I ask is that you don't turn into one of those people we can't stand."

"Me?" I said. "Are you kidding?"

"I'm on the alert for goofy facial hair, suspenders, dumb caps. If I see any of that, I'll have to step in. Remind you who you are."

"John, brother, the thing you need to remember is that you always look good," said Booker. "You've got that *je ne s—* You know, that French word that means you look good."

"*Je ne sais quoi.* It means 'I don't know,' not 'you always look good.' Do me a favor and don't start using bad French. All these fashion people are heavy into the mangled French." I know enough from my grandmother, who is from New Brunswick, to know when French is being abused, but I don't know enough to speak it well myself.

The kids who attend Green Pastures all probably speak French fluently. They probably even have Parisian accents, thanks to all their annual field trips and summers spent at their second homes in the South of France. I thought of Tesla.

She looked like someone who spoke French. Flawlessly.

Barbra was sitting on the side of the bed, pulling on her boots.

"Since we're on the subject of fashion, do you think Destiny would like it if I dressed like a cowboy?" asked Booker.

"Destiny would like it if you dressed like someone who sold Ecstasy and drove a Trans Am. Scratch that. Destiny would like it if you *actually* sold Ecstasy and actually drove a Trans Am," said Barbra.

"A man who works at the Crumb for his daily bread cannot be driving Trans Ams," said Booker.

"Nor should he want to," said Barbra.

"How does an Ecstasy dealer dress, anyway?"

"Look at the Facebook photos of her last two boyfriends," I suggested.

"Harsh, John. Unnecessarily harsh," said Booker.

"Good luck, big guy," said Barbra. She knelt and gave Booker a big hug. For a smaller girl, she gives big hugs. She was bundled into her big woolen coat. I loved her in that coat. It made me want to snuggle her.

"I'll probably be gone when you get back," Booker told me. "It should be late enough for me to avoid interacting with the maternal death star."

Barbra and I walked the three blocks to her house in silence. The streets were still and dark. A car pulsing with bass passed us, and I pulled her farther onto the sidewalk, away from the road. Someone threw a beer can out the window. It clattered down wet, black pavement. Red taillights blinked out around a corner like a tiny emergency, and the can finally came to a stop against the curb.

B let go of my hand and reached down to pick it up. I felt guilty for a second, because it hadn't even occurred to me.

She set the can next to a telephone pole.

"A few cents for a bottle collector," she said.

"You're a good woman, B."

She gave me a sharp look.

"What does that mean?"

"Nothing. When I'm around you, I'm just aware of how good you are. Especially in comparison to me."

"Don't be a goof," she said.

B and I have been together for four years. Sometimes it feels like forty.

"What? It's a compliment," I said.

We'd reached her driveway, and I walked her to the door. The motion-sensor lights came on and blinded me for a second. She pulled me in close and kissed me. The light went out, and she slipped inside the house, one arm extending to wave at me briefly, like a drowning person.

I was a block away when I sent the text. I wish I could say Tesla sent it, but that would be a lie.

> **I could use some advice. Got a model but I don't know what to make for her.**

The reply came back in less than a minute.

> **Can I help?**

> **Are you allowed?**

I asked.

Like that was a big concern for me. Mr. Ethical.

While Tesla and I texted back and forth, my phone buzzed.

Buzzed again. New messages. They'd be from Barbra. She always checks to make sure that I get home okay. I ignored the beeps.

> Why not? I'm not a judge. I'm a helper. Let's get together.

> When?

> What are you doing next Monday after school?

> PD day for the teachers. No school.

> Come to Green Pastures for lunch. We'll discuss your predicament.

I kept stopping to read and respond to her texts. I was blown away by the fact that she texted the word "predicament." I was in front of my grandparents' place and had just sent Tesla a text saying I'd be there Monday at noon when I realized Booker was outside on the stoop, waiting for me. There was a big bag of chips beside him, and he dipped his hand into it steadily and relentlessly in that automatic way he snacks. Like he's completely unaware of what he's doing.

I slid my phone into my pocket.

"Hey," he said. "I'm just getting ready to leave."

"Okay," I said.

"Who were you texting?"

"B," I said, putting a guilty hand into my pocket and then taking it out.

"Really?" He wiped his salt-covered chip hand on the step and then on his jeans. "Because I was just shooting texts back and forth with her. She said you weren't responding to her texts and she worried you might have been mugged or drive-by toilet-papered or something. You were making us nervous, man."

"Maybe there's something wrong with my phone. I just sent her one saying I was home."

"Okay," he said. He got heavily to his feet and handed me the half-empty bag of salt-and-vinegar Lay's.

"Take these, okay? They're making me hate myself."

I held the bag, and he clapped me on the shoulder.

"Keep yourself right," he said.

Then he was gone.

Slogan for John Thomas-Smith's Line of Antifashion T-shirts

As beautiful as fashion imagery can be, the so-called dream that the industry projects can lead to unhealthy behaviour. According to the National Eating Disorders Association, twenty years ago, the average model weighed 8 percent less than the average woman. Today's models weigh 23 percent less. —IMRAN AMED

eighteen

CHARLIE DEAN

DATE: MARCH 16

Days until fashion show: 49

When it was time to measure Mischa on Saturday night, as we'd arranged, she didn't show up. *Quelle drag!*

I had adjusted the design and accessories to take into account some of her special requirements. We would hide old track-mark scars on her arms with long gloves, or I'd make arm sleeves that would leave bare half her biceps and shoulders, both of which are nicely toned.

I would adjust my dressmaker's forms to be her exact size

and shape. She's not as tall or as paper-thin as the ideal runway model, but she's got lovely proportions. Once I had her carefully measured, I'd cover the padded and altered forms with a muslin casing. After that, I would purchase muslin in approximately the same weight as the fabric I intended to use, drape it onto the dress form, then use the muslin to make a toile of the dress, and then use that to make the pattern. After that I would buy the fabric from . . . somewhere!

If I had every resource, as couture designers do, I would start with the fabric and work out from there. That wouldn't be possible in this case because I still didn't know where I was going to get fabric for my designs.

While I waited for Mischa, I drew details for hems and seams and made notes about finishing techniques. I read my favorite fashion blogs and reread a tattered copy of *Worn*, an alternative fashion magazine that I absolutely adore.

I finally went to bed at two thirty a.m. and was woken an hour and a half later by a commotion outside the house.

At first, I tried to pretend I didn't hear the loud knock followed by a high-pitched voice demanding to be let in.

When I could ignore it no longer, I got out of bed and crept across my room to listen against the door.

Was Mischa out there, making a racket because she was sorry about missing her appointment to be measured? Had she been out for an incredibly early jog and decided to stop by?

I nearly laughed out loud. Any time *une droguée*, which means "a drug addict" in French, jogged at four a.m., it was usually not in pursuit of health or missed beauty appointments.

There were no noises from my father's bedroom. I'd been concentrating too hard on my work to notice when he'd gone to bed. He knows to leave me alone if the door to my room is closed. He understands the artistic process.

I knew I would find another model if Mischa dropped out,

but I really hoped it wasn't her out there. Here's a drop of wisdom for the Alateen newsletter. If Mischa was high, then Mischa was no longer the person Charlie had met and liked. She would be just another one of my father's unhappy ladies. Addicts change when they use, become different people. My father had told me this, more than once.

"Don't trust me when I'm high, Charlie," he said. "My words are not worth the air they float away on when I'm using."

This was hardly news to me.

As I huddled behind my bedroom door, heart beating the rhythm of high alert, there was the creak and a shuffling noise. My father was getting out of bed and going to open the front door. I willed my breath steady.

Would there be police this time? Or just neighbors watching the action unfold? It was all so tawdry. And tiring. How was a person supposed to maintain the semblance of a beautiful, creative life when other people insisted on conducting their sordid dramas on her doorstep?

Muttering. More muttering.

Then the front door closed and footsteps padded back down the hall. One set of steps only.

I opened my door and peeked out. My father stood in the hallway in his T-shirt and track pants. Looking as normal as my father ever looks.

"Charlie girl?" he said.

"Yes?"

"Did the noise wake you up?"

"Yes. But I wasn't sleeping that hard."

"Sorry about that. The lady from across the street lost her dog. And my guess is that she may have misplaced her meds. She's going up and down the street looking for both of them."

"Oh," I said. My heart finally dropped back into its accustomed place. "It wasn't Mischa?"

"She texted me yesterday. She's in Comox this weekend. Visiting her family."

"She was supposed to come by tonight, I mean, last night, so I could take her measurements."

"She must have gotten the day wrong. She's excited about modeling for you. About the dress you're designing for her. You have a real gift, Charlie girl."

"Thanks," I said. No matter what his problems and the mistakes he's made, my dad is a nice person.

"I'm not getting high," he said, as though we'd been having a frank discussion about the matter. "I know I've been acting a little sketchy, lately. I've been worried about Mischa and I am a little sick, but not dope-sick. I don't blame you for suspecting me of chipping. But I promise I'm not. I've just got a little cold and am generally run-down."

My blood pressure dropped still further.

Here's another little tidbit about having an addict in the family for those who have not had the pleasure. Yet.

If they so much as sneeze wrong, you think they're getting high. That is, unless your commitment to ignoring the problem is total. If you're a sailor on the river Denial you could find them OD'd, surrounded by paraphernalia, and you'd attribute the situation to mild exhaustion. I lean more toward the paranoid side of things.

I thought he was probably telling the truth, but even if he wasn't, I appreciated the lie. Pretending he was clean was the next best thing to his *actually* being clean. My motto: If he's lying, he's trying. (This is an inversion of the Narcotics Anonymous saying—trying is dying—which I find unduly harsh.)

When *mon père* is in full-scale self-destruct mode, he stops caring enough to even tell me what I want to hear. That is not the mode you ever want to see your drug-affected loved one in. No *monsieur*.

We stood silently in the dark hallway for a long beat.

"That's good, Jacques," I said. "Let me know if you need anything."

"Don't you worry about me," said my dad. "You've had to do too much of that already. I'll get back on top of my game. I just need extra sleep for a few days."

My dad, in common with a lot of IV drug users, has a touch of hepatitis. It keeps his energy low and his chances of getting liver cancer high. We don't talk about it.

"I'm real proud of you, Charlie Dean," he said. "You're going to win this competition. I can't imagine any of the other candidates being a better designer than you. You really are remarkable."

It was a nice moment in the hallway with my dad there in the dark of the predawn morning.

"You going to go back to sleep?" he asked.

"Yes," I said, even though I probably wouldn't because I had too much to do.

"You work too hard. I really have no idea where you get that from." He laughed. And so did I.

"So Mischa is coming back, then? She still wants to model for me?" I said.

"Absolutely. She's gotten out of that bad thing with her ex. I think she feels like this modeling experience is going to be a major turning point in her recovery. How great is that?"

"It's really great," I said.

"You're just one of those people, Charlie Dean. You can't help but make things special."

"Good night, Dad," I said, inappropriately, since it was morning.

"Good morning, Charlie girl," he said.

nineteen

MARCH 17

My feeling that fashion and fashion people are eating my brain is getting stronger. I'm starting to notice what people have on. I'm spending precious time in my life considering whether the cut and style of their clothes suit them. Worse, my fellow contestants are everywhere.

It's awful and embarrassing and even sort of uncanny.

Today I was on my way to the scarily named Squid's Fish & Chip Shack with Booker and Barbra when I saw Charlie Dean. I figured I'd been so rude to her that she'd stay away, but no. She crossed the street and came straight toward us.

"Hi, John," she said, planting herself in our way.

"Hey."

I could feel Booker and B checking her out. B doesn't like people who make a spectacle of themselves, and Charlie Dean was a spotlit spectacle all the way from her complicated hairstyle to her polished shoes. She had on a black-and-white-checked suit, supertight and old-fashioned, and brown high heels that managed to be the opposite of sexy. This was her Sunday afternoon outfit. I wondered how she dressed on Saturday night.

"How's your look coming?" she asked. No social niceties for Charlie Dean. All business.

"Fine," I said.

"That's good," she said. I knew she wanted more details. I didn't give them to her. It helped that I didn't have any.

Barbra moved to stand closer to me, and she elbowed me in the side as she introduced herself.

"I'm Barbra," she said. "So you're another fashion contestant?"

"Yes," said Charlie Dean. "Nice to meet you." She cocked her head to the side and stared at B, who wore jeans and sneakers and an old cord jacket lined with fleece. "Your outfit is perfect for you. It accentuates so many good things."

Barbra's head reared back in surprise.

"Oh," she said. "Well, thanks."

Charlie looked at all of us. "In fact, I love everything about the three of you. Your whole look is just wonderful and effortless." A pause. "I don't do effortless myself, but I like it in other people."

Booker and B were grinning, enjoying funny and peculiar Charlie Dean.

"If you want to join some of the rest of us in the competition to work on your look at school, we meet in the old art room at noon. It's nice. But sort of intimidating." She nodded briskly. "Okay. Good-bye." And off she went down the street. She had an odd way of walking. She sort of leaned back with her torso so it looked like her hips led the way. A huge leather purse hung over her arm. Charlie Dean reminded me of a marionette.

"I love her," said Booker and B together. They slapped each other's hands.

"Let's invite her for fish and chips," said B. "I want to hear you tell her about your *look*."

"Ha, ha," I said. "You two are hilarious. You should have your own show. And that girl would eat my kidneys if it would help her win the scholarship."

"I think she's charming," said B. "She likes my look."

"She likes *our* look," said Booker. "We'll discuss it further at Squid's."

For the rest of the afternoon I did my best to pretend that everything was normal and that I wasn't meeting another girl to discuss fashion, a girl B wouldn't find nearly so funny as Charlie Dean.

twenty

CHARLIE DEAN

HERE'S AN IDEA © CHARLIE DEAN DESIGNS:

If you are in a competitive situation, wear a black body suit. It doesn't matter your size or age. Wear thin black leather gloves and frown a lot. You will win that competition. And feel like a stealthy cat burglar!

DATE: MARCH 17

Days until fashion show: 48

Mischa showed up on Sunday evening at about five o'clock, and I don't know which of us was happier to see her: me or my dad. It was wonderful to open the door together, and I feel certain we wore matching father-daughter grins. I was relieved to see her with no new injuries.

Jacques was kind and let me take her away to measure her, and she stood patiently while I took measurement after measurement.

"I'm going to have a panic attack to end all panic attacks before this thing is over, aren't I?"

"*Absolument pas!*" I said.

"Charlie?"

My dad's voice sounded from behind the door.

"You almost done? Misch and I are going to a meeting. We need to leave soon."

I opened the door, and Mischa walked out to meet Jacques. They both looked very happy and full of possibility.

It was strange to be so happy in my own home. With one of my father's ladies.

It had been great to see one of my fellow contestants on the street and have a nice talk. John and I are getting along quite well, although his calm confidence about his look makes me nervous. Everyone else is very stressed out, but he seems like he barely cares. I guess it's all part of his laid-back style. His girlfriend is so beautiful and as natural as a willow bough in a spring breeze. His friend is also fabulous. He wears his heaviness well and seems so marvelously *good-natured*.

Everything really is coming together. It's like I've always said: All good things are possible if you try hard and stay stylish.

Jacques and Mischa called out a good-bye when they left, and I copied the measurements into my computer and then began to decide what would come next. That's when I heard a vehicle pull up outside.

Were my dad and Mischa back already?

I looked out the window into the new dark of the evening and saw Mischa's van parked in the driveway. A large black truck idled in front of our small, ungraceful house.

Was our landlord driving a new vehicle? He usually drove a small gray truck. It was nowhere near the first, and we were up to date on the rent. I walked out the front door with my cell phone, ready to take a video or a photo or something to document his latest intrusion, but whoever was in the truck turned on the lights and peeled away. I caught only a glimpse of the driver under the streetlight. It wasn't Mr. Devlin.

When I went back inside, I was careful to lock the door. I went back into my room and engaged all the locks.

twenty-one

MARCH 18

When B asked what I was doing with our extra day off school, I told her I had to help my grandmother's friend move some furniture. When Booker asked if I wanted to go to the skate park that afternoon, I told him the same thing. I may be a liar, but at least I've got my story straight.

There was something surreal about going to Green Pastures for lunch. It wasn't just that the place felt like a massive monument to the unfairness of life and that every time I went there I felt like I was going through the front doors of the country club when I should have been going through the servants' entrance on my way to the dish pit. The real issue with my visit to the Land of the Severely Overprivileged was that it was a whole new shade of shady.

Not only was I lying to my girl and my best friend, I was getting one over on the other contestants. They didn't get to go to Green Pastures for lunch and/or get advice from one of Mr. Carmichael's right-hand people. I was basically flying the Hypocrite Copter for Channel 7.

I justified it by telling myself it was all for Esther. I repeated that to myself when I locked up my bike and walked over to meet Tesla, who had just come out of the front doors.

She wore a gray dress. Plain, but probably the nicest dress I've ever seen. It looked as soft and petable as a sleeping kitten. The sleeves were rolled up to her elbows, and the hem reached just below her knee and was belted at the waist. It was the sexiest thing I'd ever seen for reasons I didn't understand. I had to stop myself saying "wow" like some guy whose prom date has just come down the stairs.

"Hello," I said, and stuck out my hand. "Nice to see you."

She shook it, a bemused expression on her face.

"Well, hello," she said. "Shall I escort you to the boardroom, or would you prefer to go straight to the corner office?"

"Sorry I'm being weird. This place makes me nervous."

"Don't be."

The bell rang, and the students who started coming out of the doors looked, at first glance, like any students. Hungry. Bored. Worried. Hungry. Relieved. Hungry.

"Ready for lunch?" she asked.

"Yeah. I guess so."

The people I know usually go to the corner store or the dumpy pizza place next to the gas station for lunch. None of us goes to the cafeteria at Jackson because it specializes in some seriously unfine dining. Gray meatloaf that tastes like it was made with chunks of erasers, eerily flavorless acid-green Jell-O, lumpy potato-starch goo, and carrots that taste like leftovers from the first Iraq war. Not the one in the 2000s, but the first military coup in 1936.

I had a feeling lunch at Green Pastures would be different.

"Come on," said Tesla. With the exception of her dress, everything about her was golden and shining. Her hair, her

skin. Even her fingernails were painted gold. It was like having lunch with a Disney Princess at her fantasy magic school.
I felt plain. And hungry. And guilty. But at least I felt something other than resentful, which was a nice change.

We walked through the crowd, and I listened to random
bits of conversation.

— "I want to try that stamp-on copper sheeting."

— "I disagree with what she said about Chagall."

— "The full potential of Silly Putty hasn't been reached."

— "It's about capturing light. That's why I'm making my
own pinhole camera to document this piece."

Not long ago this kind of talk would have made me want
to punch a wall. But some crack had opened up in me, and
a sense of strange possibility was leaking in. What would it
be like to finish each class all fired up about some cool thing
you learned? It must be amazing to end each day consumed
with something other than disappointment at yourself and
the world.

No one paid attention to Tesla and me, except for a few
fashion people, identifiable by their black clothes and severe
hair. They inclined their heads at her like herons inspecting
something just under the surface of the water.

Tesla walked by without acknowledging them. "This week
the Digital Arts students are doing the menu and the cooking,"
she told me. "With the help of our regular chef, obviously."

Obviously.

Jesus.

"Every program gets to design and execute the menus for
one week each year," she continued.

"The painters always plan their menus using the color
wheel. Once they tried to get as many tones and shades of the
same color as possible. Unfortunately, the color was white.

We had rice and pasta and peeled apples and boiled eggs, white cheddar and kohlrabi."

She laughed, and I tried not to squint at all the shine radiating off her.

"So what will Digital Arts serve? Thumb drives in a mercury sauce?" I asked.

"If it's too awful we can go to the Salad Stop for lunch," she said.

I swallowed and prayed for an edible meal.

We'd reached the cafeteria. It was announced by a sign in metal letters mounted on posts that arched over the doorway.

"It's new," said Tesla, seeing that I was checking out the sign. "Very industrial, isn't it? Looks like the sign for a death metal club. Which works, I guess."

There was so much I wanted to ask. About going to a school where the students made signs like that. About why she glowed the way she did.

Instead, I followed her through the double doors, and we were greeted by a Digital Arts student dressed like a carnival barker.

"Come and get some delicious, healthful vegetable candy," he said. He had a *handlebar* mustache. Kill me now.

We were served a stack of julienned vegetables arranged to

look like Pick-Up Sticks, a little pile of white navy beans that had been dyed to look like jelly beans, and a puree of bright green "minty pea mash" served in a tiny plastic Garbage Can-dy bin. There is such a thing as too much irony and not enough food.

I figured all the items on my tray topped out at seventy calories, max. Seventy-two if I ate the plastic container.

Tesla asked a girl wearing an apron with a giant plastic lobster pinned to the front if we could have two garbage bins each. The girl said no, there weren't enough.

No wonder students from Green Pastures come to the Salad Stop every chance they got. Compared to this, one of our salads was the caloric equivalent of a hot dog and fries.

When we sat down, Tesla pointed to her pink plastic pail.

"Isn't it just so perfect that Spiegelman came up with this?"

"Mushed-up peas? I thought the Brits invented that."

"No. The Garbage Can-dy concept. Do you know Spiegelman's work?"

I thought I did but was afraid I might be wrong, so I didn't answer and pretended to be busy eating.

"He won a Pulitzer for *Maus*, but what gets me is his work on alternative comics. She denies it, but you can tell our most famous graduate was influenced by him. A little too influenced, if you ask me. Keira Pale? You know her? The graphic novelist who drew all those stories about her family? Her sister still goes to Green Pastures."

I'd heard the name. Knew there was some controversy. But until now I made a point of not caring about the dramas of the ultra-successful graduates of Green Pastures.

I ate a spoonful of pea mash. It had a texture like lightly crusted over snot but was surprisingly tasty. "He should have made them bigger," I said. "The cans, I mean."

Behind us the Digital Arts barker announced: "We have

run out of delicious, healthful vegetable candy. You will now have to eat regular cafeteria food."

A sturdy woman with two blonde braids wrapped around her head began switching out chafing dishes, removing the empties, turning on the electric heaters underneath.

"Want to go up again?" asked Tesla. "There should be chicken and rice and a vegetarian option."

"You?" I asked, ready for her to say no, she couldn't possibly, because she had to maintain her size zero figure or get thrown out of the club of people who never eat more than seventy calories per meal.

"God, yes," she said, and got about twelve times cooler in my eyes.

And we went back for scalloped potatoes and curried carrots, and I took a breaded chicken cutlet, and she had some kind of tofu dish.

"This is a weird cafeteria," I said. "But the food's good."

"Everything about Green Pastures is weird and good," she agreed. "That's why I love it."

When we were finished, she asked if I was ready to go to the fashion wing.

I glanced at her as we got up.

"Are you sure you're allowed to be doing this?" I asked. "Bringing me around. Helping me out."

"I told you, I'm just an assistant," said Tesla, moving efficiently down the hallway. "Mr. Carmichael asked if I'd help and I said yes. The scholarships are important. The school needs to be accessible to talented people whose families can't afford the tuition. It can get a little rarified around this place."

I didn't trust myself not to say something ungrateful or bitter, so I changed the subject. "And is what's her name?— Bijou?—is she all about the common folk, too?"

"Bijou's all right. Her dad is Charles Atwater and she's superrich, but she mostly uses her powers for good."

"She volunteered, too?"

"No. She's being punished. She was too harsh with some little kids when she judged their fashion show."

That I believed.

"What's Carmichael going to say if he sees me with you?"

"He won't see us," she said. "He's in Montreal this week. And anyway, I'm not going to *do* your design for you. We'll just talk about it. I'll see if there are any resources I can connect you with. Books or websites. I'm sure you know a lot already, since your application was accepted. I'm just taking an interest."

She stopped outside the atelier with its carved wooden double doors.

"There's nothing untoward going on here," she said.

Still More Inspiring Sayings for John Thomas-Smith's Bad Mood Board

The Technical Textile Markets report that "in the fashion industry, the demand for man-made fibers has doubled in the last 25 years." Since this clothing is made from synthetic materials, they do not degrade and will forever stay in the ecosystem.

— "WASTE COUTURE: ENVIRONMENTAL IMPACT OF THE CLOTHING INDUSTRY."
FROM HTTP://FASTFASHION.WEEBLY.COM/ENVIRONMENTAL-ISSUES.HTML

CHARLIE DEAN

HERE'S AN IDEA © Charlie Dean Designs:

If you're happy and you know it, clap your hands! But make sure they have been carefully moisturized, nails manicured according to your unique style, then covered in gloves as soft as angora show rabbits. Because hands, even happy clapping ones, must be protected.

DATE: MARCH 18

Days until fashion show: 47

I am careful with my money and never waste funds on anything ugly or unnecessary. Even so, I worried that my savings would not be enough to buy good fabric for my dress, which demanded the best.

I'd considered the needs of my model, gotten her measurements, sketched my design. I was ready to create the toile. But I couldn't send a muslin dress down the runway!

I'm a resident of Nanaimo, British Columbia, as opposed to

Toronto or New York or London or Paris, so my fabric shopping options are limited.

On the Monday of our teachers' professional development day, I stood in the middle of my room, surrounded by every piece of fabric and every piece of clothing I owned. Could I *Pretty in Pink* some old outfit to make my creation? No. I had a specific design to execute, and besides, Andie's dress had looked like a sack, even though I adored her can-do-with-scissors-and-satin attitude. Maybe I could find a way to turn average fabrics into my extraordinary vision, the way Gaultier did with his madcap and glamorous denim pieces? That would show the right proletariat spirit of making do and innovation.

But no. My heart was set on finding *magnifique* fabric for my *magnifique* design. I must have been moaning out loud because my father appeared in my doorway.

"Charlie girl? Everything all right?"

I could tell that he was feeling healthier and in good spirits because he and Mischa had resumed their romance. Also, he was wearing a fedora. The hat was a sign of wellness on him the way it's a sign of watching too many Britney Spears videos on other people.

"I'm fine," I said. If you have a parent who has trouble coping, it's important not to ask for things, because the non-coper parent does not deal well with added pressure. You don't want to overwhelm them by asking for money, emotional availability, or security. A lot of the kids I met at Alateen couldn't accept that concept. They wanted, insisted, *demanded* their parents act like other parents. They were setting themselves up for disappointment. Charlie Dean is here to tell the curious that not facing the facts is a recipe for *pein de cœur*, which, for anyone who does not speak French and refuses to

open Google Translate, means "heartbreak." At least, I think
it does.

Kids who demand more than parents can give are like animals throwing themselves at the bars of their cages. Very sad.
Tragic, even.

I keep all my needs on the DL, which means "down low"
for anyone who does not speak English abbreviations. My lack
of demands keeps Jacques's stress level from rising, which I believe helps him stay clean. Alateen said that I had no power
over whether or not Jacques got loaded. I agree *in principle*,
but just to be on the safe side I keep my dad's emotional plate
as clear as possible. One does what one can for the remaining
parental unit.

"Why are all your threads on the floor?"

My dad, for all his failings, appreciates that I'm highly
organized.

"I'm just trying to figure out my fabric options," I said. "For
the fashion show."

"You are going to *own* that contest. There's no chance anyone else in this town—hell, on this *island*—is half as good as
you."

He leaned against the doorway in his three-quarter-length
shearling coat, which was too warm for the spring season. I
found it for him at a thrift store in Red Deer. It was probably
worth nearly $1,000 new, but I got it for $35. I haven't told
Jacques its real value in case he tries to pawn it.

"Maybe," I said.

"Charles? Tell Papa what's wrong."

I looked at him, hands on hips. We were both wearing costumes. Mine was tweedy tomboy, his was alterna-rocker dad.
We might have been dysfunctional, but at least we were interesting to look at.

"I don't have the right fabric for my designs. The fabric is going to be expensive. I . . ."

My dad sighed.

"You a little short?"

"Only on funds and fabric selection," I said.

I glared at the fabrics piled around me and draped over every surface. I loved the jumble of colors and the textures, the shadows and the light reflecting off the various surfaces.

"Just so happens I got a little payday," he said.

I gave him a sharp look. Couldn't help it. My dad and unexpected paydays were a terrible combination. He's on long-term disability, and he earns money under the table from gigs. When he's using, he also earns money selling drugs, which he immediately uses to buy drugs for himself.

Suspicion overwhelmed my natural *politesse*. "Are you dealing?"

"No ma'am," he said, unperturbed. "It came from your mother's people."

I knew instantly it was true. He was clean. That was obvious from his behavior. Every so often a small sum of money from my mother's estate comes through. The lawyers usually divert it from us into what we've been told is a fund my mother's parents set up for me that I can have when I'm thirty. *Thirty!* I might as well be *forty* or *fifty* for all the good it will do me then. Other than that, my maternal grandparents try to pretend Jacques and I don't exist. Just like they pretended my mother didn't exist after she developed her problems. The lawyers are probably afraid that my dad will spend the money on drugs (can you *imagine* the nerve of those lawyers?!), but sometimes a payment from some dividend or share gets through. When that happens there's a fifty-fifty chance I'll see it.

"You know what, Charlie girl? We're going to go to Victoria

and get you whatever the hell material you need so you can win this competition."

Have you ever had one of those moments when your heart feels dangerously big? So big that you worry it will rupture?

"It's going to be expensive," I said. "To buy what I have in mind."

"When you are a famous fashion designer, you are going to keep me in the style to which I hope to become accustomed. I consider all matters to do with you an investment in art and talent and in the betterment of the world."

I told myself to calm down. Don't get your hopes up, Charlie Dean. Things have a way of not working out when Jacques is involved.

"We're going today," he said. "Right now. Just let me get Mischa."

I almost didn't breathe until the three of us were belted into our old Taurus and on our way to Victoria.

x   x   x

HALF THE EXCITEMENT OF GOING TO VICTORIA WAS TAKING our car over the Malahat. The twisty, narrow road can be quite dangerous thanks to speeders and inattentive drivers. Young men in huge trucks treat the Malahat like their own personal Indy 500. A person in an unreliable *véhicule*, such as our 2001 Taurus, approaches it like a bedouin tribesperson setting out across the Sahara on a lame camel. An act of faith and desperation!

There was a festive air in the car for a Monday late morning. Mischa sat up front with my dad. She wore an oversize knitted hat, the wrong shape for her head and face, but the happiness in her eyes overrode the *chapeau* style fail. In fact, she looked positively *fraîche*. Jacques wore his hat and a devil-may-care expression. I sat in the backseat, making notes and sketches, tending to my overstretched heart, and trying not to criticize my dad's driving.

Mischa was not so *circonspect*.

"God, Jack," she said. "You drive even worse on a highway than you do in town. I wouldn't have thought that was possible."

The Barr Brothers played at a reasonable volume on the old stereo. I'd made us French-press coffees to go. I hoped my dad wouldn't take offense at Mischa's comments. He might be mellow, but he could also be touchy.

"You'd better pull over and let me drive," said Mischa.

To my relief, my dad just said that would be fine with him. "It'll let me think about some things. I think a song might be coming on," he said.

Another positive sign! *Père* Dean is a good songwriter—Charlie Dean will give him that. Jacques has the soul of a poet and the habits of a member of the Velvet Underground.

He pulled over on the side of the highway, just outside of Ladysmith. Mischa moved into the driver's seat, and my father came around and got into the backseat with me.

"Do you mind, Charlie girl?" he said. "It seems very creative back here. I want to soak up some of your energy."

I nodded, and he sat quietly beside me and began making notes in his small black notebook.

In other circumstances, Charlie Dean would have asked Mischa if she had a valid driver's license. As the most mature person in the car, I thought it might be important to do a safety check. But my dad was humming his song and jotting down lyrics, and so I left it.

Even though I was just traveling with my dad and his girlfriend, I felt socially accomplished *par excellence*!

After another hour or so we were on Douglas Street, entering downtown Victoria. The traffic pressed in around us, heavy, every driver jostling for position.

"Where do we go?" asked my dad.

"It's on Pandora," I said. "The shop is called Special Occasions Fabrics and Notions."

I put the address into my phone and the GPS guided us in. "Turn right at the next light."

Mischa parked the car directly in front of the store.

"U2 parking," said my dad. "Just imagine. Bono's whole life is like this. Our trip was clearly meant to be."

We all got out and stretched.

"Do you want to come in?" I asked them.

"I don't think so," said my dad. He turned to Mischa. "In order to make up her mind, she's going to need to touch every piece of fancy material in the place at least six times. What say you and I go for lunch, Misch?"

"Perfect," she said. "We can walk from here." It was one of those marvelous March days made of spring breezes, blue skies, and new possibilities.

The three of us stood on the sidewalk outside Special Occasions, and I found myself hugging my dad. It surprised him. Charlie Dean is not much of a hugger. Then I hugged Mischa, too. It was either that or risk exploding from the excellence of it all.

"It's good, isn't it?" my dad said to me when I'd let go. "This moment."

I nodded. My dad understands some things. He even knew this was the time to answer the question I'd been afraid to ask. He whispered in my ear the upper limit I could spend, and I nearly dropped my handbag and the portfolio case.

"Are you *sure?*"

There are times when having an impulsive wild man for a father isn't the worst thing.

I spent three of the best hours of my life so far shopping. I contemplated gold floral-embroidered tulle, Swiss sequined tulle, jacquard brocades in every tone, all-over lace appliquéd with tiny, glittering stones, astonishing laser cuts featuring insects and birds, guipure laces, embroidered silk georgettes, spot organzas, sequined silk chiffons, and hand-beaded sequined meshes. Some of the fabrics were three or four hundred dollars a yard. Some were even more! I complimented the proprietor, a woman in what looked like an *actual Chanel suit*, on her astonishing selection, and she reminded me that there are two fashion colleges in the small city and a couple of well-known evening-wear designers. My good fortune seems never to end!

In addition to the *magnifique* specialty fabrics, the store carried nine kinds of silk, including a stunning silk faille grosgrain, douppioni, lamé, taffeta, and gazar. Heavens! And don't get me started on the Devoré velvet with beading.

Jacques and Mischa checked on me. The first time, they opened the door to the shop, which was small, considering the riches contained within, glanced around, and quickly backed out when they saw me talking to the young salesman, who was dressed like a modern Pilgrim, and the owner, Mrs. Lasky. We were discussing whether the metallic silver double organza with hand embroidery might be incorporated as a panel in the front of the skirt. The second time my dad and Mischa looked in, I was in deep meditation over a bolt of zibeline silk, one of duchess satin, and a breathtakingly beautiful hand-painted taffeta silk. Mischa and my dad smiled, and I could see how pleased they were for me. I can't imagine anyone has ever been as happy as Charlie Dean was right then.

After I chose the fabrics and picked out the trimmings of threads, boning, boning casing, fabric for the linings, interfacing, and fasteners, I was exhausted but thrilled. I'd managed to stay within the budget, but only barely. I texted my dad. He and Mischa must have been waiting outside because he came right in, went to the counter, and paid for my purchases, peeling bill after bill off a roll of cash, like the biggest spender at the high rollers' table. It was a lot of money. I reached into my purse to add the few hundred dollars I had saved, and he gestured me away.

"It's on me, Charlie girl. You save your hard-earned money."

"You must send us pictures, Charlie," said the salesman.

"Yes, and you have to come back soon," said Mrs. Lasky. "I would give you a job in a second."

At the salesman's concerned look she touched his shoulder. "Don't worry, Roger. I would never replace you. Unless Charlie moves here after she graduates from high school."

Roger and Mrs. Lasky waved us out.

The bags of fabric were satisfyingly heavy in each hand.

"I'm dying to see what you bought," said Mischa as we climbed back into the Taurus.

"You'll see it when the dress is ready for you to try on." I kept sliding my hands inside the bags to make sure the fabrics were all real and as exquisite to the touch as they had seemed in the store.

"The idea that you are making something just for me makes me feel . . ." She gave a little shiver. "Special, I guess. I can see why rich women pay so much for designer clothes," she said.

"Beautiful clothes should be a basic human right," I said.

I decided then that I would let Mischa keep the gown when the competition was over. I wanted her to find other places to wear it. Maybe her NA group would have a fancy dress dance?

Maybe she'd marry my dad in it! Or maybe the dress would just sit in her closet and remind her she was special.

I slept most of the way home, and so did my dad. I woke briefly as we passed through Ladysmith and saw that my dad was still sleeping. Mischa, on the other hand, was wide awake, steering us safely home.

twenty-three

MARCH 18

Tesla sent me home from Green Pastures with a stack of books and DVDs and a list of websites. She also told me a story about how punk rock style was basically invented by Malcolm McLaren and Vivienne Westwood when they dressed the Sex Pistols up as a sort of ad campaign for their store, which was called Sex. Westwood wasn't a trained designer, but she knew how to get people's attention by cutting up clothes and putting graffiti all over them and using a lot of in-your-face color schemes. The story was incredibly depressing, from an anti-authoritarian/anti-capitalist/anti-kale perspective.

Tesla told me I'd be fine, that I had good aesthetic instincts and should trust my gut. Her eyelashes were extremely long, sort of like an alpaca's. She told me that if I got stuck with my design, I should find a classic piece of clothing and adapt it, which sounded sort of like plagiarism to me. I wanted to touch her, but I didn't.

I pedaled home in a daze of guilt and confusion. When I was halfway there, Barbra called.

My supposedly trustworthy gut twisted as I set my feet down and held the phone to my ear.

"How'd it go?" she asked. "Was it mostly moving doilies and ceramic milkmaids from side table to cabinet and back again?"

For a second I didn't follow. Then I remembered the lie I told about helping my grandma's friend. I remembered that I am a liar.

"There was more to it than that. But it wasn't bad. Turns out, she sews. She's going to help me with the design for the contest."

"That's good," she said, possibly insincerely. "What are you up to now?"

"I've got a three-hour shift at the Stop. Then I'm going to see that kid who's going to be my model."

I tried not breathe in the blue smoke gusting out of an old furniture truck as it passed.

"Everything okay?" she said. "You seem kind of distant."

"I'm good," I said. "Little nervous, I guess."

I thought of Tesla striding down the halls of Green Pastures, trailing a glittering wake of specialness dust. What must that be like?

"John?" said Barbra, and I realized she'd been speaking but I had tuned out.

"Sorry. Missed that."

"Do you want me to come with you to meet the kid? I can provide moral support and snide commentary?"

I used to want calm, sardonic Barbra to go everywhere with me. I would have worn her around me like a life preserver. But at that moment all I wanted to do was to find a mirror so I could examine myself to figure out why a girl like Tesla would invite me to lunch. Why she would flirt with me and look at me with those wide aquatic eyes.

"You don't have to," I said. "It's probably going to be a shit show. Kid or her foster mom will figure out that I don't know anything about anything, and I'll get the boot."

"You're giving me too much credit," said Barbra. "I'd love to see that. I'll drive us in my mom's car."

I told her I loved her, which was the only true thing I'd said to her all day, and then I went to the Salad Stop. After I put on my apron, I went into the washroom, where I spent five minutes staring at myself in the mirror.

x x x

BARBRA AND I PULLED UP IN FRONT OF A STUCCO HOUSE. Tired and stained pink paint gave the house the color of a dying salmon. The lawn was a lumpy square of brown stubble with a few aggressive tall weeds poking up here and there. There were no plants in the flower beds.

Esther opened the door on my first knock. She had on a Chicago Bulls jersey that hung almost to her knees. Her hair was having an uprising, and her shoes looked like they'd been through sectarian violence. I loved everything about it. She looked relaxed, and I felt better about the world until I remembered that I was here to change her or at least her clothes.

"Hi!" she said, grinning. "We've been gardening."

Barbra and I exchanged a glance. The plant abuse around here looked like a long-term thing.

A black woman, probably in her thirties, hair cut close and wearing an old flowered shirt, came to stand behind Esther. She pulled off ratty garden gloves and reached for my hand.

"I'm Sheryl Robinson," she said.

I introduced myself and Barbra.

There was a moment of silence while I tried to figure out what I should do. The technical term for what I felt was "panicked paralysis."

Barbra nudged me with her elbow, and I started talking. Babbling, really.

"So we're going to do a, uh, consultation and measurements now. If you're ready. If you're done gardening."

"We garden every day," said Esther.

I must have frowned, thinking about how the place would look if they *didn't* garden every day, because Sheryl laughed.

"You wouldn't think so, would you, given the lush landscaping situation in the front? We bought the house this August. We've been renovating the inside and landscaping the backyard. Next spring we'll work on the front yard and paint the exterior."

I looked around at the living room and kitchen. The walls were freshly painted, and the furniture looked comfortable and good quality. Real art, meaning not pictures from the local decorating store, hung on the walls. I imagined Sheryl meeting the artist and deciding to buy their stuff.

"Come in," said Esther. She had herself a nice situation here, and I felt marginally better.

"I like your jersey," said Barbra.

"It was my brother's," said Esther. "He's in jail."

I flinched. The comforted feeling disappeared.

"I'm sorry to hear that," said Barbra. She gave me another quick look, but I didn't meet her eyes. Sometimes B rolls her eyes when people talk about unpleasant personal matters. I don't think she means anything by it, but it always makes me uncomfortable.

"He did a bad mistake. But he's not a bad person."

Sheryl watched us, probably to see how we'd handle Esther's revelation. "That's how it goes sometimes," said Barbra. "One mistake leads to another."

"Yeah. He looked after me. Now it's just me." She shot a look at Sheryl. "I mean, it *was* just me," she said. "Now it's us." Her voice wasn't very confident.

My thoughts circled in my head like bits of paper eddying in the wind. What *was* the right outfit for a kid who had been abandoned by her parents or had lost them somehow, whose brother was in jail, and who was experiencing high-octane bullying? Hell if I knew.

"So," Sheryl prompted.

"Right. Yeah, let's get started. I'll just get my, um, equipment," I said.

We were in the kitchen, and Barbra and Sheryl leaned against the butcher-block-topped island and watched me fumble a measuring tape out of my pocket and pull my sketchpad out of my backpack.

I stood in front of Esther and tried to look like someone who had measured hundreds of people, if not thousands.

"I live with my grandparents right now," I told her, surprising myself.

"Are they nice?"

"Really nice."

"I've been with Sheryl and Edward since July."

"That's good," I said, deciding on the spur of the moment that the outfit would not involve pants. That way I wouldn't need to take an inseam measurement. Measuring someone is borderline invasive. You have to touch them and record their physical presence in the world. It's a pretty specific way to understand someone.

I stood with my tape measure around my neck, the way

I'd seen tailors on YouTube do when they took professional measurements.

"You know," I said, "maybe it'll be faster if Barbra does the measuring and I record the numbers."

Barbra and Sheryl cocked their heads at me, like two myna birds.

"Barbra?" I said. "You ready?"

"Uh, no," she said flatly, cutting off that avenue of escape.

"Is everything okay?" asked Sheryl.

Get a grip, I told myself.

"I just thought that working together might save time. But we're in no rush, I guess."

I gingerly wrapped the tape around Esther's nonexistent bust, getting the worst out of the way immediately, and wrote down the number. Then I measured the distance from the tip of her shoulder to the end of her wrist. Waist. Hips. All in all, I took almost thirty measurements. I'd written out each in my little notebook with space to record each number, like the book said to do. The funny thing is, Esther was beaming through the whole awkward process. I couldn't say why. Maybe getting measured is like getting a massage or something.

When we were done, I stood back and tried not to fall to my knees out of relief, like an Olympic shot-putter after the throw of a lifetime. Instead, I put the tape back around my neck. Mr. Tailor Man.

"Excellent," I said.

"I'm a good size?" asked Esther.

"You are pretty much the best size," I said.

"Even though size and weight don't matter," said Sheryl.

"Exactly," I said. "But if measurements did matter, you'd have the best ones."

"That was really interesting," said Esther. "Like going to

the doctor. You're sort of like a clothes doctor."

A clothes quack, more like, but there was no need destroy the illusion.

"So now you're going to use the measurements to make me something to wear?" asked Esther.

"Yup," I replied, praying she wouldn't ask any difficult questions, such as "Will it be a dress, shirt, pants, or pillowcase with holes cut in it?"

"How are you going to do that?" she inquired, which was one of the other worst questions she could have asked.

I looked around the orderly kitchen. Dragged my gaze past Barbra, who widened her own eyes in response.

"On a sewing machine," I said slowly.

"So you just get a piece of material and start sewing? We're taking sewing at school and we have to make patterns even just to make a bag with a string at the top. You must be really good if you can just sew something without even a pattern or anything."

"Yeah," I said. "I guess I'm pretty good. Once I've got the design, I'll make a pattern. I've got this, uh, kid-size doll. I mean, a dressmaker's form. Because I want to design clothes for kids. As my specialty."

"Why?" asked Esther.

"Kids are small, so it saves fabric."

I heard Barbra make a noise, but I didn't look at her, because if I did, I'd be lost.

"It would be really fun to make clothes for babies," she said. "Then you'd really save a lot of fabric."

"For sure. But kids your age are the best."

"Some kids my age are shits," said Esther, suddenly morose. "Sorry I swore, Sheryl."

"You owe the jar a nickel," said Sheryl. "Damn." She pulled a dime out of her pocket and dropped it into a tarnished copper piggy bank on the counter. "I'll pay for both of us."

"You guys do a lot of swearing?" I asked, relieved to change the subject.

"We're all working on reducing it. Bad language is a habit, isn't it?"

"It sure is for me," I said.

"Me too," said Barbra.

"My brother said I shouldn't swear," said Esther. "But him and his friends swore a lot. I guess I learned it from them."

"You could have made a lot of money from your brother," I said. "If he paid a nickel for every swear."

"He didn't have a job," said Esther.

I cleared my throat.

"Now I have to assess your needs. Can you tell me a bit more about what you like to wear? That's your brother's jersey, right?"

Esther shrugged. She was leaning against the counter in front of Sheryl, and she seemed to shrink. "Yes." She plucked at the hilariously long red-and-black jersey.

"She wears it every day," said Sheryl. "It has a lot of sentimental value for her."

"It doesn't smell like him anymore. Except for sort of smelling like sweat."

"It's that mater—I mean, fabric," I said. "Lots of exercise clothes hang on to smells."

That was one fact about fabric that I knew for certain, since I'd been stinking up gym clothes ever since I started school.

I went on. "So you like clothes that remind you of your brother. What about yourself? Tell me what you like about yourself."

"Nothing," said Esther in a flat voice.

"Esther," said Sheryl. "Come on now."

Then something came over me. I'm not usually a speech guy. But somehow words started pouring out of me for this kid who didn't like anything about herself.

"Well, Esther," I said. "That's some *bull*shit right there." I emphasized the word "bull," just like Booker does. Without making a big deal of it, I dug into my pocket, found a quarter, showed it to her, and then dropped it into the pig. "Going to need the whole twenty-five because I'm going to be swearing quite a bit for the next little while."

Esther kept leaning awkwardly against the counter, in this house that wasn't quite her house yet. I looked at the pretty woman who wasn't quite her mother but who seemed to want to be her parent.

"I'll start by telling you what *I* like about you," I said. "From what I've seen, you have a truckload of character. I saw how you handled those little bitches at the Salad Stop. You didn't react. You didn't back down. *Rock solid*. Only the bravest, most honest people can stand up to that kind of crap."

I looked at Barbra and Sheryl. "Tally?"

"Fifteen cents," said Barbra, as though we'd practiced.

"Okay. So I like your character and your bravery and your rock-solidness. I also like your hair. It's also cool as hell. That hair has an attitude that is going to take it places. I don't know whether you plan to go along or not. But I dig what your hair has to say, and you should, too. I only wish I had your toughness when I was your age."

A small smile had crept around the edges of Esther's mouth.

"Your face is also excellent. It's not like everyone else's face, and you should be thankful for that. I don't even know what to say about your face. Cute is part of the story, but it's not the whole story.

"Barbra? Help me out here. How would you describe Esther's face?"

Barbra considered for a long moment. "I would call it striking."

"Sheryl?"

"Interesting. Thoughtful. Funny. I think it's a beautiful face."

"Yes," I said. "I agree with all that. You've got a damned amazing face."

Without being asked, Barbra pulled her change purse from her pocket, withdrew four dimes, and pushed them toward me.

"And physically?" I said. "You just couldn't be any better. I mean, there are big kids and small kids and tall kids and short kids and kids who can walk and kids who can't. They've all got something to recommend them physically. *Everyone.* Tell me about yourself, Esther. What do you recommend about your physical self? Sheryl? You can weigh in, too. Barbra? You've got eyes. What are you seeing here?"

"She's fast," said Sheryl.

"I can tell," agreed Barbra. "And her skin seems good. Got her all wrapped up tight. And it's a nice texture and color."

"I like her arms," said Sheryl.

"Look at those feet," I said. Her feet in the filthy white sneaks seemed too big for her height in a way that was really charming. "They are awesome. I have always admired a good foot."

"I like to jump," she said. "And I might be a dancer one day. Or something."

"Bam!" I yelled, and her eyes widened in alarm. "Right there! That's the shit. Barbra? How much?"

"A lot."

I dropped two more dimes in the pig.

"Okay. I'm done swearing. I *literally* can't afford to swear any more over your awesomeness, Esther. I'm out of money. It's going to be a pleasure to make an outfit for you that showcases how cool and hilarious and fast you are."

Something worked behind Esther's funny little face and Sheryl was hiding what I believe may have been a few actual tears. It was a performance, the *Swan Lake* of fashion consultations. Some tiny part of me imagined myself getting that little talk when I was her age. It would have to be enough that I got to give it to someone else.

"I'll call when it's time for you to come in for a fitting. Until then."

Without hesitating, I grabbed my backpack and nodded at Barbra. We walked out like fashion ninjas, leaving Sheryl and Esther in the quiet kitchen.

B grabbed my hand as we walked to the car. When we'd driven for five minutes, she pulled over and leaned over to kiss me.

"You, John, are amazing and full of surprises."

I basked in the afterglow of my own words, of my girlfriend's kiss, and the possibilities of style, at least theoretically.

John Thomas-Smith's Indictment against Fashion and Fashion People:

I got nothing. My anger has failed me.

twenty-four

ℰCHARLIE℀ ℰ℀DEAN℀

HERE'S AN IDEA © Charlie Dean Designs:

If a friend has made a mistake, fashion or otherwise, it's best to look at what is working and/or going right. For instance, someone may be wearing a shirt in a shade of yellow more malaria than marvelous. Aim the compliment at the fit of the pant or the color of the eye in the late-afternoon light. This is how long-lasting friendships are made. Caveat: if the bilious shirt is worn more than twice, it may be time to step in with a diplomatic word.

DATE: MARCH 23

Days until fashion show: 42

Wonderful news! John visited the art room today. I think he was influenced by my invitation, and Jason and Cricket both asked him to stop by. I have a group of friends! Of course, they are also competitors, but it is nice to be among peers at something other than a support meeting about drug-addicted parents.

I am thrilled that John came because I like having friends and he seems interesting. I have a feeling there's more to him than meets the eye! Hidden depths! It's not just his comment about intellectually rigorous design that makes me think that. There's a secret seriousness to him that I find quite compelling.

"Well, hello there," said Jo. She was working on an embroidered collar piece. I was dying, *dying* to see her whole look, but we were all being very undercover and only bringing in small pieces of our work so no one could tell what we were up to.

Jo looked absolutely gorgeous, as always. Her hair was tousled rebel goddess and her ensemble of sleeveless T-shirt and long basketball shorts that only about 2 percent of the female population could have pulled off successfully was pure fabulous elite athleteness. She'd already told me my outfit (a marvelous red suit, circa 1983) was the best thing she'd seen since the last outfit I had on. Jo is an amazing person. If Cricket is right and Jo really is flirting with me, then what does it mean that it makes perfect, wondrous sense to me? I guess I know what that means, and the knowledge is like a gift box opening in my heart. Like all gifts I receive, I will open it when the time seems auspicious.

At first I thought John was just intimidated by Jo. I suspect most people are. She's very imposing. But as Jason and Cricket and Jo asked him about his design for the competition and he avoided answering even the most basic questions, I began to suspect he was having trouble.

Ooooh la la! How interesting. Mr. Intellectually Rigorous didn't have it all wrapped up or in *le sac*, as the French like to say!

But he did sit down and listen to us talk. We discussed the latest runway shows, our favorite fabrics and periods in fashion, designers and trends and bloggers. Shapes and textures and movies and music. We always pack a lot into our discussions because we're all *starving* for good conversation. John listened so intently, it was as though he was studying us. Maybe that's how all intellectuals listen.

About half an hour after John arrived, his friend Booker, tall, broad shouldered, and wearing a big untucked plaid shirt, stuck his head into the room.

"So B was right," he said. "You are in here."

John Thomas-Smith blushed.

The big guy popped the rest of his hot dog into his mouth, and it disappeared. "We wondered where you got to after math." He looked at each of us and smiled. He had a lovely smile. Open and friendly. A fine, honest face that was maybe just a little bit hungry for . . . something.

"Just leaving," said John.

"B's waiting outside," said the big guy. "I said we shouldn't interrupt, but she said . . ." The sentence trailed off, and I could tell that he didn't want to repeat what "B" had said. Somehow, I got the impression that B didn't approve of fashion and fashion people. The way she'd looked at me when I saw them on the street suggested she was not a person who approved of deep style, which is what I have. She was the kind of *au naturel* beauty who would never work at it and so would never develop a sophisticated approach or aesthetic. That was as it should be. There can only be a few truly, deeply stylish people. Every one of us in the art room was rare and precious in that way. In the competition we would find out whether John was one of us or not.

I felt a bit sorry for him that he didn't have more support from his friends. I also wondered whether John had noticed that his best friend had a crush on his girlfriend.

twenty-five

MARCH 29

Much as I hate to admit it and would never tell B and Booker, hanging around the other contestants, shallow oddballs that they are, gave me a lot of ideas.

When I sat down at my desk, I had the same flicker of anxiety I'd felt every time I tried to come up with something for the contest. I thought about the other contestants and how they talked. They took inspiration from everything around them. I was only with them in that dingy old art room for about thirty minutes before Booker and B busted me, but in that time the other contestants, Cricket, Jo, Jason, and Charlie Dean, talked about art and culture and nature. They did it in that dippy way fashion people do, but I could tell they were using everything from video games to car designs to flowers and music to feed their imaginations. Embarrassingly, I found them sort of inspiring.

The contrast between how they talked and what they talked about and how Booker and B talked was stark. All Booker and B did was make fun of them and crack in-jokes.

I was in this space where I felt like I needed some distance from Booker and his neediness and the way he was always around and B with her sharp little remarks. Maybe I just felt guilty since I'd started lying to them. Whatever the reason, it was strange to think I felt freer sitting with the ridiculous fashion contestants in an abandoned art room than I did with the two people I was closest to.

Listening to Charlie Dean and the others reminded me, indirectly, to keep an open mind when I did my design. So I tried to do that, even though my mind is not the open kind. I sat alone in my room and imagined Esther in New York City or Paris. I thought of her going to museums like that little French girl from the picture books, Madeline, I think is her name. Esther would take the subway to the museum and skateboard back until her family's limo picked her up. Her outfit had to be sporty and kind of classic and experimental all at the same time.

The dress I came up with landed somewhere between a basketball jersey and a tennis dress. Over the knee, but not too short, so Esther could run or ride and kick any asses that needed kicking. It had a white Peter Pan collar, because I think those look sharp.

I know the description of the dress probably makes it sound shitty and plain, but it wasn't. With Esther's skinny legs and radical hair, I thought it would look just right on her. I added white stripes above the elbows and a couple of inches above the hem.

She wasn't going to look like any other kid around, especially not with the metal accessories I designed to be worn with the dress. The whole look—I apologize for using that word—would be offbeat and hilarious, just like her.

Man, coming up with the dress and the accessories felt good.

The problem now, obviously, was making the damned thing.

I asked Grams about her sewing machine.

"Oh, honey," she said, "that thing is as old as me, nearly. I don't even know if it works anymore. Just like me." She laughed at her own joke, which is something she does. If you ever want to think you're hilarious, hang out with my grams. She'll laugh at anyone's jokes, including her own.

"Can I try it?"

"Of course."

She showed me where it was stashed in the basement, and I carted it upstairs and down the hallway. It was like packing a cannon. I stood there, arms killing, back aching, trying to figure out where I should do the sewing. My workshop wasn't clean enough. So I heaved the old beast into my room and let it crash down on my desk.

"Careful, hon!" cried my Gran. "Don't hurt yourself."

I had a design. I had a sewing machine, or at least a historical antique shaped like a sewing machine. Now I needed some fabric.

I took all my money, which wasn't a lot, and went to this little sewing store near our house. Stitcher-oo's was full of bright materials stuffed into cubbyholes. Complicated blankets hung on every wall. I told the lady working in there what I was after. She informed me that Stitcher-oo's is a quilting store, which apparently is different from a regular sewing store. Who knew? To save face and out of curiosity, I poked around for a while but didn't see anything I could use, unless I wanted Esther to look like a Thanksgiving dinner table. I also noticed that all the sewing machines they had for sale were expensive. The cheapest one was over eight hundred bucks.

Even sewing was elitist!

The lady told me I should go to Fab Fabrics in the north end, a solid forty-five-minute bike ride away, and so off I went, cursing the day I'd decided to enter the competition, cursing the traffic, cursing the rain that was starting to spit down. Basically, just cursing.

When I rode into the parking lot at Fab's, which was at least ten times bigger than the quilting store, I thought for sure they'd have good material. When I saw Barbra had texted me, I didn't text back. I don't know why. Too busy cursing, I guess.

None of the books I'd read had said much about how to pick and buy fabric and thread and all that other stuff, so I figured it had to be a pretty straightforward process.

Inside, I watched the other customers and what they did, but they all looked sort of lost. Nobody smiled. Watching people look for materials was even worse than watching people go blank faced in front of a Salad Stop menu.

There were about two people working in the whole place. One stood behind the counter, running the cash register, and the other was stationed behind a long table. People brought her fabric, and she wound lengths of it off a cardboard core and cut it.

I spent a long time looking around and finally decided on some material that was the right color and heaviness. It was a nice dark blue. Then I found some white material for the stripes and collar and was happy to see it was on sale. The dress was practically made. I stepped into the lineup.

Everyone in front of me had about ten different kinds of material, and it all looked awful, like pink shiny stuff and Easter egg–colored netting and so on.

"Membership?" asked the cutting lady when it was finally my turn.

"I'm sorry. What?"

"A Fab Fabrics membership. Do you have one?"

"No. Is this like Costco or something?"

The cutter, who was probably in her early twenties, sighed. She wore an expression that I recognized on myself after I worked a long shift at the Salad Stop. It said that she had had enough of people forever. Her brown hair was pulled back and tucked into a half-assed bun, and her outfit under the apron didn't seem too stylish, considering where she worked. So far, buying fabric was significantly less fun than stealing used clothes. It was even worse than trying to draw clothes.

"You get a deal if you purchase a membership." She pulled the two bolts of material I'd picked toward herself and inspected the labels.

"This one," she said, pointing at the blue material, "will be forty percent off with a membership. And this one"—she gestured at the white—"will be sixty percent off."

"Oh, so a membership is worth it," I said.

"It's Fancy Friday, so the discounts are bigger."

"Okay, so how much is a membership?"

Another bored sigh. "A hundred dollars."

"Holy," I said. "I guess I'll pay full price, then."

"Well, if you plan to buy other stuff, it will probably be worth it."

Was this going to be a one-time deal? What if I won and got into Green Pastures? Would I be allowed to drop out of the fashion program right away and go to one of the other programs? Metal arts? Carving? I thought about Tesla moving around the atelier. Talking about clothes. Fashion. Honey hair brushing her shoulders. Maybe I would make Tesla a dress next. Or Barbra. I loved B's hair, too. But she probably wouldn't wear anything I made.

Shut up, John, I told myself. *Just shut up.*

"Sir?" asked the cutting girl.

"I'll just get this," I said.

"How much?" she asked.

"Regular price. Since I'm not getting the membership discount."

"*I mean* how much fabric would you like?"

"I'm making a dress," I told her. "For a ten-year-old."

She stared at me with a please-continue-saying-moronic-things-to-me-I-love-it look. Someone behind me in the line groaned.

"It's like sort of a medium-type dress for a regular-size kid. Like not a huge one or anything."

"Do you have a pattern?" asked the cutter, not enjoying customer servicing me at all.

"I'm going to make it. The pattern, I mean. And the dress."

"Sure you are," muttered some wiseacre behind me in the lineup.

"You're making her dress out of *upholstery*?" asked the cutter.

"Is that bad?"

"Well, it's weird," said a lady behind me. "It's going to be too heavy."

"I want it to be strong," I said. "So she can rage around in it."

"Unless she's a couch, she doesn't need to rage around in a dress made of upholstery," said another lady. "But it's sweet of you to try. Is it going to be for your sister?"

"Do yourself a favor. Buy a pattern," said a third lady.

The book full of drawings of the dress was in my backpack, but I didn't want to show it to these ladies, who knew how to buy material and make stuff.

"Right," I said. "Okay." Nowhere on the application form had it said that we *couldn't* use store-bought patterns.

I slunk away from the lineup and spent an hour looking at pattern books, but all the designs seemed sort of busted. There was nothing close to what I'd envisioned. Then came the announcement that the store would be closing in fifteen minutes. I had no pattern. No material. No clue.

I walked outside and stood back far enough so I could get a picture of the neon sign for Fab's and texted it to Tesla.

Underneath the picture I wrote:

> **So screwed.**

Less than a minute later she replied.

> **What are you doing there?**

> **Looking for material.**

> **Mission Impossible. You'd better come over.**

Then she sent me the address.

I slid the headlight onto my bike and turned on the back blinker so no one would run me over.

x x x

TESLA'S HOUSE WAS ON LONG LAKE. THERE WAS AN IRON gate and a winding driveway, the whole nine yards. Actually, the driveway seemed quite a bit more than nine yards. It was dark out, but I could see everything pretty well, since the fence and the cobbled driveway and the giant house were a chalky beige color that reflected all available light. Probably listed on swatches as Suburban Ghost.

The iron gate was open, so I walked my bike through. Solar lights made the driveway into a landing strip.

My phone lit up in my hand and buzzed.

> **Down in a second**

I stood in front of the four-car garage wondering WTF I was doing here.

Tesla appeared around the corner of the massive house.

"Hi," she said, nearly whispering. "Bring your bike around here."

Massive beige pots with small, spindly trees in them crowded the walkway. Maybe these people were allergic to color.

"You can just leave it here," said Tesla, indicating a tall wooden fence.

"Unlocked? This seems like sort of a sketchy neighborhood."

Tesla stared at me, super poised. Not laughing. Because why would she.

"Okay," I muttered, and left the bike leaning against the wooden fence.

Heat waves rose from a pool set in a poured concrete deck that extended into a green lawn that rolled down to meet the narrow finger of lake. A pool *and* a lake. Some people have all the water features. Maybe there was a river around the other side of the house.

I wondered if Tesla's family left the pool filled and heated all year round. Maybe they fed five-dollar bills into an underground heater to keep it at optimal temperature.

The door Tesla led me through was extra tall, like it had been built for a family of giants.

"Come on," she said, ushering me into a foyer the size of the one at my school, only cleaner. If I had to describe the design in one word, it would be "new." When Tesla spoke, there was an echo.

"My parents are away."

I stood on a bold black-and-white area rug.

"Just you and your parents live here?"

She nodded. "Our housekeeper used to live in, but she got married. Now she's only here during the day."

Tesla wore a gray sweatshirt-y top, hanging off one bare shoulder, and a pair of leggings. Ballet slippers. Her hair was gathered in a loose bun off to the side.

And once again, I couldn't help but notice how golden she was. How perfect. How unlike this house, which wanted to be effortlessly classy, like her, but wasn't.

"Let's go upstairs. To my workshop," she clarified.

I bent to take off my shoes, and she told me to leave them on.

I followed her through a living room with groupings of cream and brown leather furniture, art that matched the furniture, and a stone fireplace that would have looked good in a Gothic castle, and we headed up a set of stairs.

"I'm up here," she said.

We went up past a landing that probably led to an assortment of bedrooms and maybe a complete spa facility, to the third floor.

Tesla's habitat was immediately identifiable. Long worktables, mannequins, lamps, rolling racks, an ironing board, a steamer, and sewing machines.

"This is my workroom," she said.

Life-size, framed photos of female sports figures and

dancers hung on the walls. Voices came from invisible speakers. Tesla reached for a remote control. "Listening to the *StartUp*," she said. "It's a podcast about entrepreneurs. I like to listen to stories while I work. Makes me feel like I have a social life." She fiddled with a button, and an eerie wail of Radiohead replaced the voices. Then the lights dimmed.

The room was long and functional.

"Are you an athlete?" I said.

"Not really. I dance a bit. But I want to specialize in technical clothes. Yoga, ballet, running gear. And maybe board sports."

I turned in a circle. Four full-size chrome mannequins stood around the room. They wore boldly colored leotards and tights.

"Speed skating," she said. "And bobsled. I've been doing experiments with tech fabrics."

They looked like experiments with hallucinogenic color palettes, except for the one that looked like it had been dipped in mercury.

"It's cool."

Tesla smiled. I smiled back. The mutual smile-a-thon went on for too long and made my face feel tired and embarrassed.

"So you went to Fab's," she said, at last.

"I'm going to have to say it wasn't that fab," I said.

"You should have known better than to go there on Fancy Friday. Seriously. What kind of a masochist are you?"

A good question.

"So what about you? Where do you get your . . . um, materials?"

"I go with my parents to Vancouver pretty often. Sometimes we go to Toronto. Once a year we all go to New York. We've been to Paris. And I order fabric online if I have to."

"Oh," I said. "I went to Victoria last year." Again with the dickish comments.

Tesla ran a finger lightly across her temple like she was feeling for the beginnings of a headache.

"So show me what you've got."

Was I really going to show this girl whose house was as big as my whole dump of a school, a girl who went to Paris and New York on an *annual basis*, my drawings, which may or may not be total shit and confirmation that I have no taste and less talent?

Screw it. I was.

I reached into my backpack and started to talk.

"It's for this ten-year-old girl I met. She's kind of haywire. Cute but not an easy life so far. She's had to be a bit of a warrior just to, you know, survive."

Tesla's perfectly shaped eyebrows rose in expectation.

I pulled out my book like I was giving her my own beating, bloody heart.

I opened it to the page with the drawing I liked best. It showed a girl who looked like Esther, kung fu fighting, all by herself in the dress. I'd abandoned the fashion figures. Gone with my own style.

Tesla took the book from me and stared. And stared. Her eyebrows went up. Then down.

She flipped a page and looked at the accessories for a long time.

I stared at the floor, at the door. Tried to ignore the swishing noise in my ears.

I wished I was riding my bike back down that long, beige driveway, turning onto the dark street, heading away from this princess in her suburban mega attic. I needed—

"Wow," she said. "I absolutely and completely love this."

Everything stopped. My breath. The blood in my veins.

"It's like sporty ninja golfer."

Her words were the water I'd been dying for.

"It's so charming and slightly fantastical without being too *too*. You have a great eye, John. Seriously."

"Really?" I said.

"Really," she said. "Carmichael is going to love this. He's all about Juniors. And you've done something new. It's this amazing mix of street and classic. And these accessories. They are can't even."

The grin on my face was too big. Embarrassingly huge. Showing too many teeth.

"But you are never going to get the right material for this at Fab's. You need something special. The fabric for this has got to have some future tense to it."

I had no idea what that meant.

She slid herself onto a slim orange couch, kicked off her silver ballet slippers, and patted the seat beside her.

I sat next to her and started telling her about the design. She nodded, cheekbones bronzed in shadows. When I was done talking, she put up a hand as though to stop me from moving, took my sketchbook from her lap, closed it, and placed it carefully on the coffee table.

Then we were kissing. My hands were moving up under the soft fabric of her shirt over her smooth skin, and she ran her hands up my sides. My head got stuck when she pulled off my T-shirt, and we laughed.

"Look," I said, when I was free. "You don't— "

But she was kissing me again, her hands small and strong, and she smelled like fresh grass and I was pretty sure nothing was ever going to be the same.

A Halfhearted Quote against Fashion

School officials are investigating why a fashion and sewing teacher used a class lesson that made fun of girls with fat in certain places.

In teaching material titled, "How not to look fat," one page says "busty" and "booty" are "good," while anyone with back fat wearing a tight shirt looks like a "stuffed sausage." A drawing shows the words "Uh-oh" and "sad" next to a sobbing girl with back rolls. —ELLEN YAN, *NEWSDAY*

PART FIVE

It's Fitting

CHARLIE DEAN

HERE'S AN IDEA © Charlie Dean Designs:

Bored by your usual hair and makeup? Accessories getting you down? Open a book of fashion history and learn from your ancestors! In the nineteenth century people wore dead insects and birds in their hair for special occasions. You might balk at that, but a beetle hairpin might be just the ticket! If you don't have a library of fashion history books, simply ask a five-year-old for advice. Children are awake to magic. You might end up with a Tonka toy on your belt and that would be for the best.

DATE: MAY 2

Days until Fashion Show: 2

I've been neglecting my fashion journal in the service of making actual fashion! For the past month I've given everything I have to constructing my gown. It has been a time of hard work and pure magic. Nothing eventful or dramatic happened (thank Dior!) but each day was filled with important achievements and crucial milestones from figuring out how to execute the tricky elements on the bodice, adjusting the skirt so the crinoline wouldn't show through, and, most satisfying of all, making the dress fit Mischa like she was born into it.

It was good that Mischa was dating my father because she was almost always on hand for fittings. There were a lot of those. How *incroyable* to find myself grateful to have one of my father's ladies around all the time!

Not only was the construction process immensely satisfying, Charlie Dean's home life was like something out of a wholesome family drama on the W Network. Jacques and Mischa behaved in such a *normal* way. They were usually in bed and asleep by two thirty a.m. and up by eleven and even cooked some meals! With vegetables! Early in April my father mentioned that Mischa's ex-boyfriend had left town to take a job in Alberta. Many deep sighs of reliefs at *Chez Dean* at this news. With luck, the terrible ex would stay away for several months. Perhaps even forever!

Jacques and Mischa were united in recovery and went to meetings almost every night. I worked every second when I wasn't in classes. On breaks I visited some of my fellow contestants in the old art room. Not John, though. He never joined us again, even though I asked him almost every time I saw him in Careers class. I only saw Jo in the art room one more time, because she was off playing basketball. I wondered how she was going to finish her design with sports taking up so much of her time. She was playing a risky game being so balanced in her interests and activities!

The whole thing was so *fantastique* and joy filled that I almost forgot to be on guard for problems.

Now you must not misunderstand, there were difficulties. Of course there were!

I'd hoped to do as much hand sewing as possible. I wanted to show off my abilities with running stitches, slip basting, and fell stitches and everything in between. But as the time began to run short I had to machine stitch some of the simpler seams.

After the first fitting I carefully marked the corrections to the pattern. But not carefully enough, because I found small errors during the second fitting. There were puckers in the bodice, and the underarms gave me trouble.

It took longer than I'd hoped to hand hem the skirt. The appliqué seams I used on the bodice and the sequined mesh section meant to conjure the effect of broken windows was *très*, *très* complex! *Très* unforgiving! But worth every second of my time. All of that was simple compared to the boning I used to showcase the structural elements of the skirt and bodice. And don't get me started on the most technical aspect: the sculpted, asymmetrical Valentino-inspired crumb-catcher neckline, made rigid with a combination of boning, sweat, and tears. I fretted *forever* to make sure Mischa's bosom was properly covered, but the edge of the bodice neckline extended up and out at the right degree and angle.

All of this meant many nights I worked until one or two in the morning. Still, I tried not to miss school.

I wasn't even that tired because I was fueled by passion and excitement!

I took photos of every stage—the thread tracing on the garments, the various adjustments to the toile and patterns, the darts and easing, and close-ups of my stitches and intersecting seams and interfacing and backing. I documented everything and made sure my techniques were *worth* documenting! Two days before the fashion show the dress was ready for the final fitting. *Formidable!*

That Thursday, after an afternoon DJ-ing a coffee shop opening in a senior center for fifty dollars, my dad came to my room to see how things were going.

"Holy Hannah, Charlie girl," he said, stopping to stare at the dress on the form. "That is absolutely stunning."

I looked up from where I sat at my big table trying out possible hairstyles on my dummy head. The dress with its skirt draped to its full extravagant width over the pannier-and-cage corset was *impressionnant*. There is no point denying it.

Any serious student of fashion history loves crinolines and bustles, and I already had almost every style in my collection, in-

cluding a mantua, which I made myself. The mantua is *the* most theatrical skirt shape in all of fashion, and panniers are essential not only for people who ride bikes, but also to create an extravagant hip profile. I don't know about you, but I take great comfort in knowing that if I ever need a bustle, a bum roll, a French farthingale, or a massive hoop crinoline, I'm ready! Also, there's something about keeping the world at a distance with the circumference of your skirts that has *beaucoup* appeal!

"We're doing the final fitting tonight," I said. "I'm so nervous. I can't believe the show is in two days."

"Come on, Charlie," said my dad. "You've got this. I can't even get my head around your talent. How many fittings so far?"

"Four," I said. "This will be the fifth."

I'd double-checked every seam, zipper, button, and stitch. Mischa had started to get giddy every time she got into the dress. One couldn't blame her.

Tonight, during the final fitting, I would test makeup and hair and try out accessories. That way there would be no surprises on Saturday. I would spend Friday night getting everything ready, visualizing every aspect of the show. Visualizing winning.

In less than forty-eight hours Mischa and I would show the world, or at least Green Pastures, what Charlie Dean could do! We would shine!

"You want me to pick up some pizza for you girls?" asked my dad.

I felt my eyes bug out unattractively. The last thing I wanted was pizza in the same room with my gown! *Mais non!* I didn't even want pizza in the same *house*! What if someone touched the gown with a greasy finger? What if a pizza smell clung to the exquisite fabrics so Mischa walked the runway trailing *eau de* Luigi's Pizza Pies?

Non, non, non!

The dress fit Mischa like the peel on the banana, which is to say there was no room for her to develop a late-breaking pizza belly! Not that I would ever say that, of course; I don't approve of fashion's tendency to lead to eating disorders and unhealthily low body weights, even though it's true that it's easier to make clothes that look good on wand-thin bodies. That's why I focus on custom clothing: it can be adjusted to showcase any body type.

"Not for me, thanks," I said. "Too nervous."

"Got it," said my dad, who right then was as good as any dad who ever lived. "No pizza. How about a bag of apples?"

I laughed.

"Mischa can have a single apple," I said. "We'll share it."

"I thought so," he said. "Maybe I should move out until this thing is over tomorrow."

"Can I have your DJ equipment, then?" asked Mischa, coming up beside him and slipping under his arm.

"Afraid not. It forms the basis of my entire worldly savings," said Jacques. "Between that and my guitars, I am a one and one half thousandaire!"

"No wonder I'm with you," said Mischa. She wore no makeup, and her hair was in a ponytail, slightly dirty, as I'd requested for ease of styling. She had on a simple button-down shirt and looked like she attended an all-women college.

My dad kissed her on the top of her head.

"Come in," I said. "We've got to do the final adjustments on the dress, plus hair and makeup. We need to time how long to get you changed. And we'll walk you with the music."

Mischa gave a little squeal of happiness.

"Every time I come in this room I feel more like Cinderella."

"Which is funny, since you're sort of like *ma belle mère*?" I said, regretting the comment as soon as it left my mouth. I was relieved when she laughed, perhaps because she doesn't know that *belle mère* means "stepmother."

My dad retreated from my room, saying he was off to a meeting, and we got down to the serious business of back-combing, braiding, hair spraying, and putting makeup on and taking it off, and putting accessories on and adjusting them, and then, finally, Mischa stepped into the dress.

We were both quiet, assessing her reflection in the mirrors around the room.

Mischa was like a flare of incandescent elegance that some-one had set off indoors. She was an astonishment. I felt a single tear of simple, perfect joy come to my eye.

Before I could say how I felt, the doorbell sounded, followed by a knock. I wondered if my dad *had* gone and ordered take-out for us. Perhaps a small tray of crudités, sans dip? He was being such a superfather lately, anything was possible. More likely it was the landlord, come to see if there was any creeping that needed doing around the house.

"Don't move," I said, and went to see who it was.

As I began to open the door it was shoved open roughly, and I was knocked backward.

Before I could *comprendre* what was happening, a tall, hard-angled man had barged into our house. He stood, sway-ing slightly and glaring at me.

I knew instantly that I was looking at Mischa's ex and that he was high or drunk or some unlovely combination of both. His too-pretty face was red and rashy looking, the way people get from skyrocketing blood pressure and rage. He had cupid lips pulled tight across his teeth.

"Where is she?" he said.

My mind went blank.

"I told her not to make a spectacle of herself. Get all cozied up, playing like she's the mom in some happy little family."

"You need to leave," I said, hoping he didn't detect the slight waver in my voice.

From my bedroom there came a noise.

The man's head, bullet shaped, close cropped, swiveled mechanically.

I tried to put out an arm to stop him from going any farther, but he pushed me out of the way.

He was at my room in an instant, as though he had been in our house a hundred times. I reached the doorway in time to hear Mischa whisper his name.

Damon.

Damon the Demon.

"Don't you look fucking fancy," he said. "A real cherry tart, hey, Misch?"

Heat crawled over me. This man needed to get out of my room. Away from my dress. Away from my model. Away from the small oasis I'd created out of nothing but hard work and good taste.

"You need to leave," I said, entering the room. "Now."

Damon either didn't hear me or didn't care what I said.

Mischa tried to back up, but there was nowhere for her to go in a dress with a skirt the size of a VW. It was not a gown made for moving quickly or for escaping on foot.

"Get out of here," I said through gritted teeth. Instinctively, I grabbed the flat iron from the table it had been resting on. It was still plugged in. Heat from the metal plates rose up my hand and wrist.

Damon had Mischa in the corner, wedged between two rolling racks.

"So you want everyone to look at you? See what a hot slut you are?"

Mischa's made-up face had gone translucent with fear under the chalky makeup, her eyes too big.

This was like a bad dream or maybe a bad TV movie starring second-rate actors. How often had my life felt like that? Too many times to count. No more unseemliness could be allowed.

Damon, who couldn't have been more than twenty-five, was quick as a mean thought. He reached out, grabbed the bodice of the dress, and yanked. There was a tearing sound. She put her hand to her chest, and he grabbed her face by the chin. Hard. Matte white-gray sequins cascaded onto the floor in a small stream.

"Get off her!" I screamed, taking a step toward him. He backhanded me with a wild swing, and his knuckles caught me across the face. I fell, and the naked dress form, adjusted to be an exact replica of Mischa's body, came down on top of me.

I got to my knees in time to hear Mischa say, "I can't take this anymore." I saw only a billow and flap of ivory and palest steel satins coming in like a soft thundercloud, and then Damon was bent over, clutching at his crotch with both hands.

He reached again for the dress and pulled the skirt from the bodice. My beautiful neckline! My handstitched seams!

I jabbed at him with the flat iron and was surprised when he screamed and jerked away.

"Jesus!" he cried. "Crazy bitch!"

I dropped the straightener and watched in disbelief as Mischa aimed a kick at his shoulder but caught him in the head. Lucky for him the blows were softened by her massive skirts. He and Mischa went down in a swishing flurry of luxurious fabrics and sequins. One beautifully dressed girl, one drunken asshole, and one paralyzed designer.

"I called the police!" I screamed, even though I hadn't. The whole nightmare had unfolded too quickly. "They're on their way."

The next thing I knew he was up and running out the door. On his way he shoulder checked me, and I went down. Everything went black for a long second when my head bounced off the wood of my desk. When my vision cleared, he was gone and the two of us sat, stunned, in a heap of fabrics and toppled dressmaker's dummies.

"The dress," I said, as my senses started to assert themselves. "Let me see the dress."

Mischa gave me a look that I didn't care for. As though I was the crazy one.

"LET ME SEE THE DRESS."

She got slowly to her feet.

"MY DRESS!" I wailed. "HE'S RUINED MY DRESS!"

The bodice of the pale, structurally sophisticated dress was ripped all down the front. The left side of the skirt had been torn from the waistline and there was a long scratch down Mischa's face and blood trickled from one nostril.

Rectangular sequins from the bodice continued to slide onto the floor like small waterfalls when she moved. And there was blood!

"You're bleeding!" I yelled. "You're hurt. Don't move. Don't touch anything. This *cannot* be happening."

Mischa stared at me as though I was speaking complex French and not simple English.

"Are *you* okay?" asked Mischa.

I realized I had my finger in my mouth. My hand had been burned in the fracas. I held my other hand to my face. I was definitely going to have a black eye.

Silence settled over my bedroom as the adrenaline turned sludgy in my veins.

A strange chill calm came over me.

"You know, Mischa, I don't think I like him," I said.

We began to laugh in a hysterical way until I realized I was crying more than I was laughing. I hate to cry. There is nothing to be gained from it but puffy eyes.

When I was sure I was calm enough to speak, I called the police.

twenty-seven

MAY 2

Which confession should come first? The confession that I went to Tesla's most nights for over a month? The confession that she looked through her huge collection of fabrics and chose the material to make Esther's dress? The confession that she made the pattern and cut and sewed the pattern into the dress while I watched and said I was trying to learn, but was really just staring at her?

Maybe the first confession should be about how the whole time I was seeing Tesla I was telling Barbra lies about how I was busy working on the design or accessories. When I left Tesla's, I'd text B and tell her that I loved her, which I did, but not enough to stop me from seeing Tesla behind her back.

The only true thing I said to Barbra in my Month of Being a Deceptive Cheating Bastard was the part about working on the accessories, which had started to seem as important as the dress, or maybe more important. After all, I had dick-all to do with actually making the dress. Working on the extras, which is what I am calling the accessories because I hate the term "accessories," at least made me feel marginally less useless.

I started to resent both Barbra and Tesla, with their questions and their offhand remarks but mostly their questions, such as:

"What are you up to tonight?"

"Where have you been?"

"When am I going to meet your friends? You do have friends, right?"

"Who just texted you?"

Don't get me wrong. I appreciated Tesla basically making the whole dress for me. But I also felt like a door leading nowhere by the end of it and blamed her, even though it wasn't fair.

A few times I tried sewing or working on the pattern or whatever and Tesla laughed and said I should wait until I'd gotten into Green Pastures and my whole future wasn't riding on the dress looking good.

That made me mad. Not so mad that I stopped sleeping with her or told her to let me sew the dress. I'm not a complete 100 percent moron. I'm more like an 85 percent moron.

When I went to get the finished dress, the Thursday before the fashion show, Tesla met me outside. She seemed on edge.

"My parents are here," she whispered. "They just got back."

"Should I leave?"

I hadn't met her folks yet. She said they traveled a lot, and the trip they'd been on had been extended twice. I got the impression she wasn't in a big hurry for us to meet. I couldn't tell whether it was because she was embarrassed of me or them.

"No. Of course not," she said.

A voice called out behind her.

"Ah, Tessy, there you are."

I stopped and slowly turned around to see a woman with a lot of TV announcer–type blonde hair watching us. The woman wore a sweater that matched the beige house siding, tight black pants, and tall brown boots. If the cops needed a description of her, I'd have said she was about 75 percent legs, and the other 25 percent hair. Tesla's mom was hot, which made sense. Noticing that made me feel crappy about myself. Again.

"Tes-la," muttered Tesla.

"And who is this?" asked the woman.

Tesla still hadn't turned around.

"Hi, ma'am," I said, showing off my retail-honed communication skills. "I'm John."

"John. How do you do? I'm Liz Wharton, Tesla's *incredibly* embarrassing mother."

"Hello," I said.

"Nice to meet you, John."

I have very little experience of rich people. I can sometimes guess their salad preferences, but that's about it. My mind went to the movies. Tesla's mother would be the greedy type. Hitting on Tesla's boyfriends. She'd be dumb. A second wife. Maybe even a third.

"Why don't you kids come through the living room so we can say hello. Now that we're finally home from our trip to Asia, your father and I want to spend at least one or two minutes with you. We feel like we haven't seen you forever."

"Maybe because you *haven't*," said Tesla.

We followed Mrs. Wharton into the massive living room. A massive bonfire crackled in the fireplace.

My mind had already prepared me for Tesla's dad. He'd be tall and broad-shouldered. Flat-bellied and squint-eyed. His teeth would be extra square and white.

The image disintegrated when I saw a smallish man with thinning blond hair seated in what was either a small love-seat or a huge chair.

"Here's Tessy's friend," said her mom.

"Aha!" said the man. He put his book aside and stood. He was a good four or five inches shorter than Mrs. Wharton. He looked a little pouchy and tired, but happy to see Tesla.

She dutifully walked over and gave him a kiss.

"I'm John," I said when she didn't introduce me.

I put out my hand for him to shake.

"I'm Cliff Wharton. So you and Tesla are working on some sort of a project?"

"Yes, sir." I was glad my grandparents were such sticklers for the ma'ams and the sirs. No adult ever gets tired of hearing that, especially not parents and consumers of salad.

"We'd love to hear about it."

I shot a look at Tesla.

"It's for a fashion show, Daddy," said Tesla.

"You're in the fashion program, too?" he asked me.

"Uh, no, sir. Not yet. I'm trying to get in. The school, I mean."

He nodded.

"Is that right? Well, good on you. I had to claw my way into a private school. You know, I paid for almost half my tuition myself at St. Mark's, which is where I went starting in tenth grade. The rest was a scholarship. Did it with golf balls."

"Pardon me?" I said, struck by the realization that it had never crossed my mind to try to pay for Green Pastures myself.

"Started collecting them from ponds. By the time I got into St. Mark's, I had a team of people collecting for me. You would be astonished how many golf balls end up in water and how much they're worth on the resale market."

"No, sir, no idea."

"But it was worth it. St. Mark's helped get me into Stanford, and from there I went to MIT. That's where I met Liz."

They did that thing some couples do where they gaze fondly at each other.

Did they let people with cascading hair into institutes of technology? It was beginning to occur to me that I was a little too in love with stereotypes and preconceptions.

"Just two young mechanical engineers in love," said Mr. Wharton.

"Someone should make a romantic comedy," said Mrs. Wharton.

More loving stares at one another.

"Ha, ha," I said, so far out of my depth with these two that I might as well have been tied to a chunk of concrete and dropped in the middle of the ocean.

"Okay, so we'd better get to work," muttered Tesla.

"Nice to meet you, John," they called together as we left the room and headed up the stairs.

Neither of us spoke until we were in Tesla's workshop. I had about seven hundred questions and wasn't sure how to ask any of them.

"So your parents," I said, leaving a lot of room for her to fill in the blanks.

"What about them?"

"They seem nice."

"They are. They have pretty bad taste, but they're nice. They love each other. They love me. But mostly they love each other. Can we move on?"

I couldn't move on. I hardly knew anyone whose parents loved each other. It was like Tesla won the happy family sweepstakes. The Good Life Lottery. She was rich, beautiful.

Talented. Had a loving family. I knew some people's parents loved their second wives or husbands, at least for a while. Barbra's parents act like roommates who wished the other one would move out. Booker's mom doesn't even like her kids. My mom seems more like my second cousin than my mom.

"So that's crazy, eh?" I said. "Them being so nice and happy and everything. Plus all this." I swung my hand around to take in the giant workroom. The massive McMansion. The in-ground pool. The redundant lake.

"Not really. Can we not make a big deal of it?"

I sat on a yellow chair covered with some kind of swirling upholstery.

"Why don't you want to talk about it? If I had parents like yours—"

I didn't finish the statement because I didn't know *what* I'd do if I had parents like hers. I literally couldn't imagine it. Then again, I was also full of shit. My grandparents had been together for a long time, and they were pretty much peanut butter and jam together. They loved me. That should have been enough.

"I know, I know. I've got everything and you have nothing." Tesla's pale, perfect face was set in a frown.

"I never said that." But I had said it. In a thousand little remarks I'd said exactly that.

"Can we just focus on the dress? Then we have to decide about accessories and hair and music."

Tesla started running her hands down the length of the small navy dress on the dressmaker's form. "I should come to the fitting with you," she said. "Make sure it's perfect."

My nerve endings sizzled at the thought of showing up at Esther's with a different girl. The questions. Oh man, the questions.

"First tell me why you're being strange," I said.

Tesla sighed, still staring at the dress.

"I'm not being strange. Maybe I just feel bad for you," she said.

There it was. The single sentence that activated all my carefully hidden shame.

"You're *so* angry. You have no parents and you hardly seem to have any friends. It makes me feel bad. I care about you, but you seem really lost and . . ."

"And?" I said.

"You don't have a nice thing to say about anyone or anything."

For some reason, I decided this was the moment to defend my parents. Made no sense, but there it was.

"I have parents," I said stiffly. "But they're not married, and my mom and I live with my grandparents. I mean, I do, and when she's not working overseas my mom lives with them, too. Your parents aren't the only ones that travel, you know. Not every family is composed of two rich mechanical engineers with one perfect blonde daughter. In fact, I'd say most real families aren't."

She'd gone very still as she stared at the dress.

"We're not real?"

"You'd last about ten minutes in my . . . never mind."

Her face was full of confusion and—oh hell—pity?

"I don't get it," I said. "Why did you do all this—?" I waved at the dress. "Did you sleep with me because you feel *sorry* for me?"

Tesla flinched. "No. That's not— It's just that I have a lot. And you don't. I mean, you can't even sew. And I like you. You seem so . . . unhappy."

Barbra likes how I am, I thought. Then I corrected myself.

Barbra liked how I *was*. Before I started to change. Before I started to want something different for myself.

Had Tesla meant all the compliments she'd given my design? She'd always seemed sort of hungry for me. Like I was her new favorite dish. Maybe I wasn't a main course, though. More like an appetizer. A single potato chip.

"I like you, John," she repeated. "But I don't totally *get* you. It makes me sad that you're so lonely."

I'm not lonely, I wanted to yell. I've got Booker and Barbra. But Tesla hadn't heard me talk about Booker since the day she met him, and she sure as hell didn't know about Barbra. And maybe I was more lonely lately, since I'd left my integrity in a Dumpster somewhere.

"I'm not lonely," I said, then added, like a five-year-old, "*you are.*"

Tesla, hardworking, honest, ultra-advantaged Tesla, said, "Of course I'm lonely. Everyone is a little lonely, John. But I've chosen this. If I'm going to succeed in fashion, I have to work hard instead of hanging out. You don't seem like you're choosing anything. You entered this competition, but you haven't really done anything. You don't even seem to like fashion, really. Successful people, successful *artists*, are driven. They have to be."

Fully formed, hateful sentences rose up in my mind. "So now you're an artist? A yoga bra artist? A running tight artist?" But there's a limit to how much of a turd even I can be.

"Okay, well, I'd better go, then. Get myself some friends and some focus. Stop hanging around and mooching off you. Get better parents."

There may be a limit to how much of a turd I can be, but there was apparently no limit to the number of self-pitying things I could say in a row. God.

Tesla pulled the dress from the form. She folded it into a neat bundle. "I'll get you a bag for this," she said.

"Don't bother," I said, and took it from her. The dress was perfect. Much better than I'd envisioned. "I mean, thank you."

I tucked the dress under my arm and headed out of her rooms and down the stairwell to the side entrance.

John Thomas-Smith's Indictment against John Thomas-Smith:

(See everything written above)

CHARLIE DEAN

HERE'S AN IDEA © CHARLIE DEAN DESIGNS:

*Feeling down? Want to stay in bed? You may not! Summon
the strength to conjure an outfit that will propel you into
life! Your closets, even your linen closet if you decide on
a saucy little toga, will contain everything you need. Take
that outfit you have been saving for a special occasion that
never comes and lay it on your bed, which should be neatly
made. Stare at that ensemble and vow to be worthy of it.
Eat a piece of fruit. Listen to your favorite song at a bracing
volume. Shower. Do your hair. Tend to your skin. Put on
your good outfit and blow yourself a kiss in the mirror. Et
voilà! You are officially up and at 'em. You are also officially
a Charlie Dean Champion.*

DATE: MAY 2

Days until fashion show: 1 1/2

Charlie Dean is not a crier. When her mother died, she used all
the tears she'd been allotted for life. But she felt a little weepy

in the aftermath of the assault upon her person, her model, and her gown.

Two police officers came and took a report. The officers, a very young white man and an older South Asian woman, were nice at first. They took photos of our injuries and spoke efficiently into their radios. They said they'd look for Mischa's awful ex-boyfriend. The term "APB" may have been used. There were compliments on the stylishness of my room and exclamations over the gown, battered as it was.

I heard Mischa tell them that she thought Damon might be high. They asked what he used and she said whatever, but mostly pharmaceuticals.

The male officer asked if the drugs he took were prescribed, and she said some of them were.

That's when Jacques came home. The officers looked at him, and their attitude changed. Suspicion crept into their questions.

It is true that my father looks as though he has spent some time exploring the dark underbelly of life. But it was still a shock when they began asking *him* if the assault might be drug related.

"You got anything stashed around here?" asked the woman, all business and no more concern for me or Mischa or compliments on my gown.

"Having problems with your suppliers? Come up short for your connection?" asked the young man officer.

I saw them notice the track marks on Mischa's arms. I watched her beauty fade in their eyes. What remained was only damage.

My father told them he was clean, and I could hear him trying to keep his voice even. He said he didn't know what was going on or what had happened. But there was dreadful *défaite* in his tone and in the slump of his shoulders.

"Yeah, well, we'll look into it," said the female officer in a tone that said we had been placed at the bottom of the priority list. If there had been an All Points Bulletin put out on Damon, it was probably revoked as soon as they drove off. Turned into a No Points Bulletin.

The aftermath was *si triste*! I could see my father and Mischa felt ashamed in the way only addicts do. And I felt ashamed the way the children of addicts do. I hate to criticize, but those police officers did almost as much damage as Damon.

Jacques and Mischa sat at the kitchen table. She was back in her slightly trashy civilian clothes of a T-shirt and jeans. He stared down at his hands. The pair of them looked at once very old and very young. After ten minutes or so, my dad got up and went into his bedroom. I had to fight back worry that he'd slip out and score at the first opportunity. *Les drogués* are not good at handling the stress, as I have mentioned before. But I knew from long experience that if he decided to get high, there was nothing I could do to stop him. And anyway, I was too tired. Much too tired. Tend to yourself, Charlie Dean. Tend to yourself.

Mischa came into my room and sat, unmoving, in my good chair.

"I'm sorry," she said. "This is my fault."

My mind was dull, but I tried to remember what the website I'd looked up had said about how victims of violence often take the blame on themselves.

"It's not your fault. You thinking it is, that's part of the problem," I said.

I wanted to bring conviction to my words, but all the sleepless nights had caught up with me, hollowed me out, and all the bad feelings I worked hard to keep out rushed into the void.

It's funny how one bad thing can remind you of unrelated

bad things. If you're not careful, the bad can take over until it's all you see.

I found out about my mother when I was in fourth grade. To call where we were living a home is overstating it. We were staying in room 16 at the Wild Rose Motor Inn on the outskirts of Edmonton. The motel was across from a mall, and behind the mall was my school, and I was allowed to walk to and from school by myself. My routine was to go through the mall on my way home and look at all the lovely things in the stores.

That day I carried a red tin lunch bucket that my mom and I had chosen from a novelty store because it exactly matched my red patent leather Mary Janes. On my way through I stopped in front of the window of La Vie en Rose. The mannequin wore a pink teddy with feather trim and a long candy-striped pink-and-white satin robe. I took in every detail so I could tell my mother about it. My mom and I loved to talk about the clothes we saw, even though we both preferred the clothes my mom made.

I hurried out of the mall, excited and a little afraid to get back to number 16. If my mom wasn't doing well, I had to be very quiet. If she and my dad were both not doing well, I had to pretend I was invisible so I wouldn't see or hear anything. They'd been using then for a couple of years at that point, and in those days, my dad was healthier than my mom. He kept things from getting too bad.

If my mom was feeling well, I would lie on the bed beside her and we'd talk, which meant that she would ask me questions and I'd answer. She liked to wear her pink marabou slides in bed, which I thought was very glamorous of her. I loved to stare at her pink-feather-tickled toes, and my shiny red shoes or blue boots or yellow sneakers.

Sometimes I forget the hard times and think that afternoon

on my way home to the Wild Rose Motor Inn was the last perfectly happy moment in my life. But it wasn't totally happy. Not if I'm honest.

I was on the other side of the four-lane highway, waiting for the light to change, when I noticed the ambulance parked in front of the motel across the road. My heart seemed to shrivel in my chest. There were two police cars parked behind the ambulance. When the light turned green, I couldn't make myself walk quickly. A car honked at me when I was still in the intersection when the lights went yellow and then red. As I got closer, the silently flashing lights of the emergency vehicles reminded me of a TV with the sound turned off.

When I was still twenty yards away I began to pray, even though I'd never been to church except once with my mom to look at a stained-glass window.

Please let the ambulance be at one of the other rooms.

Please let the police be there for someone else.

Please let everything be okay.

Please let my parents be fine.

Please let nothing bad happen that has not already happened. Please don't let things get even worse.

The praying stopped when I saw my dad seated in a chair outside our room. The door to our room was open and I could tell there were people inside. Other guests had come out of their rooms to watch, like gophers poking their heads out of holes. Two police officers stood in front of my dad, and he stared at his feet. Maybe Jacques had hurt himself. Maybe it was nothing serious. There were often ambulances and police cars outside of the motels we stayed in. But they weren't there for my parents. My parents were careful, they said. They promised to be careful.

I had on a yellow dress with a faint rabbit print. My mother had sewn the dress for me before she and my dad sold the sewing machine. The dress had a white eyelet frill at the bottom, and I'd been proud to wear it to school, even though the other kids were all in jeans and it was not warm enough. It was a day-brightening dress. That's what my mother had said when I showed it to her that morning, and she was right. I got many compliments on it that afternoon, at the mall, and later at the motel from adults who didn't know what else to say to me.

My dad lurched to his feet when he saw me.

"Where's Mom?" I said, looking past him.

"I'm sorry, Charlie," he said.

"Mom!" I screamed, and tried to run past him, past the police, past the people watching. "Mom."

My dad stopped me and pulled me to him, squishing my face into his hard, concave stomach.

"She's gone, Charlie. We lost her," he said.

A hole opened up in me so big, it threatened to take everything with it. It was impossible that my mother wasn't waiting inside for me. That she wouldn't lie with me anymore, asking me questions, that we wouldn't talk about pink lingerie and pretty hair colors and things that were so beautiful, we could just die. That's what we did when she was well. When she wasn't sick or high.

A police officer whose uniform shirt was too small for his stomach asked if I was okay.

"I was just at the mall," I said.

"You walked back here by yourself? Are you in school?"

"Yes. It's okay. I'm used to it."

"I'm so sorry," said the police officer. "Your dress and shoes are really nice. I can tell your mom liked to dress you up."

"Thank you. We really like clothes."

I don't remember anything else until another man, a social

worker, made me sit with him in his car. He asked if anyone was hurting me at home. He asked if I ever saw my parents doing drugs.

I said no. Of course I said no. I knew my parents did drugs, but they did them in the bathroom with the door closed. Drugs is what they did while I read books and drew pictures and watched TV. But I would never have said that to anyone. Never.

The social worker tried to distract me when the paramedics carried my mom's body to the ambulance on the stretcher. She was all covered up, so I couldn't see if she had on her pink-feathered slippers. The last I saw of her was the ambulance pulling away, those silent lights still flashing on a dingy fall afternoon in Alberta. Across the highway the mall was busy. People going in and out. Looking at all the pretty things. I wanted to tell my mom about the display at La Vie en Rose. I wanted to hear her exclaim, "Oh my god, Charlie Dean. Couldn't you just die over that candy cane stripe?"

When my mother died for real, and not just from loving beauty, she took half of me with her. But the half she left is very strong. That's what the counselor I saw when I lived with my first foster family said to me. That counselor said I was resilient, and then she explained to me what that meant. It means being flexible and springing back into the right shape after being compressed, and it also means recovering after something bad happens.

That counselor was right. I am resilient.

There is not much else to say about it. My mother was the one who taught me to sew, and we made clothes, and she laughed and laughed, and sometimes she was the prettiest of all the mothers. Other times she was the ugliest of all the mothers, and I wished she wasn't my mother at all.

I learned from Alateen and from my dad that she didn't mean to leave us. She was sick.

She was also selfish.

I was in foster care for six months after she died. That's how long it took my dad to prove that he could care for me properly.

The one good thing that happened when I was in foster care was that I met Diana Vreeland—in the pages of her memoir, *D.V.*, which somebody left in a vacation cabin that I visited with my foster family. While that family hiked and swam, I sat on the deck in my dresses and read that book. Mrs. Vreeland taught me how to see. From Diana Vreeland I learned that style and taste and a point of view are more important than being beautiful. Those things are essential, along with resilience.

I thought about all of this back in my bedroom after the assault. My mind was lazy, sluggish, and I tried to think of what to say to Mischa. I felt sick every time I glimpsed my battered, glorious gown. It hung like a crime scene on its hanger.

Mischa sat slumped in the good chair. Her posture was so bad, I began to cry, still maintaining my own excellent, perfectly upright posture.

"Charlie?" said Mischa.

"Yes," I said, keeping my voice very steady. If there had to be tears, they weren't going to be the snotty variety. I would maintain a level of poise.

"Are you okay?" she asked.

"Yes," I said, tears leaking down my face.

"You're kind of freaking me out right now."

"I'm sorry," I said. "This will pass."

My tears had one unintended positive benefit. They caused Mischa to sit up straight.

"I mean, I'm down with people crying. It's just . . . you. You don't seem very *natural* at it."

"Thank you," I said as another hot tear slid down my face. "I'm sure it will be over soon."

"It's going to be okay," she said. "You can fix the dress. Don't let him ruin this for you. For us."

I stared at her through hot eyes. I should have been shoring up *her* flagging spirits. I was the encourager. The cheerer. Mischa was out Charlie Deaning me!

Two more tears slid down my face. I extracted the soft yellow handkerchief peeking from the breast pocket of my green suit and dabbed at them.

"I think I'm nearly done," I said.

"Seriously. You just need to sew the dress back up and we're good to go."

I didn't respond. Repairing the sequined sections and the torn seams and fabric would take more time than I had.

Another tear ran down my nose and plopped onto my lap, where the moisture soaked into the wool blend.

I maintained my fine posture and continued crying while Mischa got up and went to speak to my dad. Twenty minutes later she came back to my room.

"Okay. So I'm going to go to bed now. This has been a hard day. Jack is rattled, too. Are you sure you're okay?"

I nodded again, still unable to speak, relieved that the tears were beginning to slow.

"See you in the morning," she said.

It was another fifteen minutes before I finally moved. I got up and stood in front of the damaged dress.

"Charlie Dean," I told myself. "That is enough. Get it in gear."

And so I did. An hour later my dad softly knocked on my door.

"Charlie?" he asked. And I was relieved to see that he seemed calmer. He hadn't used the incident as an excuse to get high.

The most chic thing is self-sufficiency. So that's what I showed Jacques.

"I've got a few things to finish up," I said, thinking of the damaged beading, the rips and tears in my beautiful gown. "Nothing an all-nighter won't fix."

Jacques looked relieved.

"God, you're something, Charlie Dean. It's like you're another species. A super-capable species."

"Thank you," I said. And I got to work.

twenty-nine

MAY 3

Barbra and Booker came with me when I took the dress and accessories over for a fitting the day before the show. It was probably unprofessional to bring even one friend, never mind two, but I was feeling kind of cracked down the middle.

We rode our bikes because Barbra couldn't get her mom's car.

There wasn't a lot of conversation on the way, and I was grateful for that. But when we dismounted in Esther's driveway and Booker started chaining his bike to the fence, Barbra grabbed my bike by the handlebars.

"How are you?" she whispered.

I could barely meet her eyes.

"I've been really busy."

"I'm excited to see this dress."

"My grandma's friend helped."

"Did she make the whole thing?" asked Barbra, who really does have a confrontational edge to her sometimes.

"No, she just showed me what to do."

"She must be an amazing sewer."

"Seamstress," I corrected. "Or dressmaker."

Barbra made a wry face. "Well, pardon me."

"No, I was just . . . never mind." I was just being the kind of excellent guy who corrects other people even though his whole life is a giant lie.

The front door opened, and Esther came running out of the house. With her dandelion head of curls, skinny legs, and big white shoes she looked like a cartoon.

She skidded to a stop about five feet from us.

Sheryl stood in the doorway, smiling.

"Is it ready?" Esther breathed. "My fashion outfit?"

I nodded and forgot all about the guilt and the sense of impending doom.

Barbra and I locked our bikes to Booker's and followed Esther and Sheryl into the house.

Esther's foster father waited in the kitchen, a white guy, early middle-aged, in a plaid shirt. He was trim and balding and had an honest face, like a game warden.

"I'm Edward," he said. "Nice to meet you, John and Barbra and . . . ?"

Booker stuck out his hand. "Booker. Moral supporter!"

Edward shook the outstretched hand.

"We're all really excited about this. We think Esther looks amazing all the time, but it's cool that she inspired an actual designer."

He shook my hand, and for a second, I felt like I really was a proper designer and a decent boyfriend and righteous friend.

"So, Esther," I said, putting the backpack on the kitchen table and taking out the dress, which I'd wrapped in brown paper, "you go put this on. We'll make sure it fits like it's supposed to. I made some other stuff for you. To go with the outfit."

Esther twined one leg around the other, as though to stop herself from racing off in all directions.

When I glanced at her, Barbra smiled.

"Okay," said Esther, her eyes huge.

Sheryl took the brown-paper package from the table and grabbed Esther's hand.

"Let's do this," she said.

Not even a minute later a piercing squeal came from whatever room they'd disappeared into.

"It's sooooo coooool!" cried Esther.

Barbra grabbed my hand. She was with me now. Booker gently punched my shoulder. Edward grinned, big relieved smile on his open face.

A minute later Esther bounded into the room, and the dress was, if I do say so myself, perfect. Sporty and fierce and cute as hell on her.

"That looks awesome," said Edward, who had the dad-type comments down cold.

"I love it!" said Esther, turning in a circle.

"It's perfect on her," said Barbra seriously. "The fit. The material, all of it." That made me feel like King Turd of Septic Mountain and also like Thor.

She was right. The dress fit Esther perfectly. It made her look every inch the oddball gorgeous kid, every inch funny, completely different, and completely herself. She could skateboard in it, go to a museum, graduate, kill it at a fifth-grade dance. She didn't look like a kid trying to be a twenty-year-old swimsuit model. She looked exactly like herself and no one else, which is what good clothes can do for a person.

"So you like it?" I said.

"Yes," she said. "It's like my brother's jersey. But it fits me, and it looks so cool. I love how it smells like grass."

"Grass?" said Barbra.

"Like a lawn right after it gets cut," said Esther, lifting an arm and taking a deep sniff at the inside of the elbow of the three-quarter-length sleeve.

To avoid meeting anyone's eye, I dug around in the backpack.

"Let's talk accessories," I said. "And discuss how things will work on Saturday."

While Sheryl and Edward and Esther stood watching, I pulled out the various packages containing the things I'd welded and woven and soldered. I was more excited about them than the dress, since I actually made them. But before I could show them off, Booker said he had to go.

"How can you stand to miss this?" said Barbra.

"I can't stand it," he said shortly.

He said good-bye and left without looking at me.

x x x

AFTER THE FITTING, B AND I WENT BACK TO HER HOUSE. WE had an hour before her parents were due back, and while we lay in her bed I thought about how comfortably and neatly we fit. This was my girl. I made a mistake with Tesla. It didn't even feel real, what I'd done. That was another life. Another version of me.

"You are the bomb, B," I said. "The dynamite, the *plastique*. You are whatever nukes are made of."

"Do I have to be a bomb?" she said. "Can't I be a firework?"

"A firework is just a decorator bomb," I said. "I'm the luckiest of all the basically unlucky guys."

"Well, you're the luckiest guy in this house," she said.

"Luckiest guy on this street?"

"I'll give you that. I've met the neighbors. They are not a lucky people. Especially that guy who lives on the corner. He has a face like a wanted poster. It would suck so bad to go through life with that face. But all that luck will run out if my dad comes home and finds you in my room."

B's folks probably know we're sleeping together, but they would prefer not to *know* know, which I get.

Maybe what people don't *know* know won't hurt them. I rolled over to the side of the bed, and felt around for my underwear and jeans.

Barbra leaned on one elbow, watching me.

"I have a fear," she said.

I turned to look at her.

"You're going to win this competition and then you're going to start wearing your hair all trendy. Or you'll get one of those square-faced watches and red suspenders and a surfboard that you never ride, and I won't know you anymore."

"I promise no man buns and only round-faced watches. And anyway, who do you know who's like that? Have you met someone new while I was so busy?"

She rolled onto her back. "I looked up street style. Read some street-style fashion blogs. You mentioned that was the look you were going for in the competition. A lot of the street-style guys have ridiculous hair. And square watches. Especially in LA. Do you think we're going to end up in LA when you're a famous designer? I'm never getting plastic surgery."

"B, I am very unlikely to win this competition. Even if I do, I'm not going to be a designer. The best-case scenario for me is probably a job at the mill. Or maybe I'll get my very own Salad Stop franchise someday."

She turned onto her side and stared at me. "I think you're better at fashion than you or anyone else realized. You seem to be able to create a whole different reality with clothes. It's kind of freaky."

Her long legs poked out of the sheets. Her feet were thin and pretty and she never wore nail polish on her toes, just like she never wore makeup or curled her hair. She didn't approve of vanity. I wondered if she knew how lucky she was to be basically satisfied with herself. I wasn't satisfied with one thing about myself or anyone else. Except maybe my grandparents.

I jumped to my feet and bent over to give her a kiss. Then I left, feeling more chipper than I had any right to.

X   X   X

BOOKER WAS WAITING ON THE FRONT STEPS OF MY GRAND-parents' house. He had a Mountain Dew sitting between his big skate shoes, made clownish by the orange laces. He took a big drink when I walked up.

"Want to come in?" I asked him when I reached the stairs.

"You want to tell me what you're doing?" he asked. "Who sewed that dress?"

"My gram's friend. The one who sews. I told you."

"If I go inside and ask your gram about her friend who sews and I call that friend, your story's going to check out?"

I felt nothing at his threat.

"Do whatever you want."

"So this friend of your grandma's has fancy perfume that smells like grass?"

I shrugged.

"I don't know. I never noticed her perfume. She's in her sixties."

"Come on, man. You've been hooking up with that girl, haven't you? The one from Green Pastures. B deserves so much better. If I could find a girl a tenth as amazing as B, I would count myself the luckiest bastard alive."

There had been too much talk about luckiness today.

"Maybe ease up on the neediness and the snacks, and you'll find a nice girlfriend who'll stick around."

"Screw you, man. This isn't about me. I don't get you. This contest has turned you into the kind of asshole you've been complaining about for years. Look at your jeans. Since when do you wear skinny jeans?"

A few days after I started seeing Tesla I'd gotten myself a pair of skinny jeans out of the donation bin. I told myself it didn't matter because they were basically stolen.

"That's your problem? You don't like my clothes? B's worried I'm going to get a man bun and a square-faced watch. How much time do you guys spend talking about all the things that might go wrong with me? Or things that are already wrong with me?"

Booker wasn't going to let me distract him. And he was right. I *was* wearing skinny jeans because I thought Tesla would like them and because they seemed like the kind of thing someone who went to Green Pastures would wear. They hung down my ass and weren't even that comfortable.

"You need to tell B. She deserves the truth. It makes me sick to think about her being so supportive, and you pay her back by screwing around with some little piece from a private school."

Don't call Tesla a piece, I wanted to say but didn't. And B hadn't been supportive. Not really, with her cracks about the school and what a joke it was for me to apply. Sometimes I thought Barbra and Booker didn't want anything to change.

Didn't want anything to ever get better. Barbra didn't want me to succeed.

Booker stared, red faced.

"You're ripping my guts out, man. I hope this thing is worth it. A *fashion show*. For a *fashion show* you did this."

"For art school," I corrected. And silently added, *and because I want a future*. But that wasn't right either. I didn't sleep with Tesla and lie to my girlfriend and my best friend because I wanted a future. I did it because I wanted what I wanted.

"Look, nothing—"

"Don't," he said. "Just don't. If you are too much of a coward to tell B, I'll do it."

"You'd like that, wouldn't you," I said lamely. "It's the chance you've been waiting for all this time."

He didn't dignify that with a response. He got up and pushed past me, tall and wide and unstoppable.

He was nearly running when he grabbed his bike, jumped on it, and started pedaling.

"You," he yelled when he was halfway down the block, "are breaking my heart, man."

Too tired to troll my own journal.   —JOHN THOMAS-SMITH

CHARLIE DEAN

HERE'S AN IDEA © CHARLIE DEAN DESIGNS:

Why not make every second count from a looking-fantastique perspective? Whether your job is arresting people, curing arthritis, or collecting garbage there's nothing to stop you from doing it stylishly! A police officer can pay careful attention to polished shoes and a hairstyle that looks sharp with a cap. A scientist can wear a saucy ensemble under her/his lab coat for when that Nobel committee comes calling. And the hero who collects garbage should wear wonderful muscles, tousled hair under the hard hat, plus perhaps a little scarf/bandanna appropriate for skin tone.

DATE: MAY 4

Days until fashion show: 0

Charlie Dean rallied. She pulled herself up by the bias tapes and went to work! She did not go to school on Friday because she needed every second to salvage the dress.

As my *premier pas*, I contemplated the damage done, and naturally I thought of Japan. The Japanese have a highly evolved sense of design, at least as sophisticated as that of the French. Most relevant to our case was *kintsugi*. This is a method of repairing an object and drawing attention to the broken places. In the case of pottery, *kintsugi* involves filling in the cracks with lacquer dusted with gold, silver, or platinum. The troubled history of the object becomes part of its beauty. Can you even stand the perfection of that solution? It's part of the philosophy of *wabi-sabi*, which is the Japanese appreciation for the flawed or imperfect. It's too much, really. When I have finally mastered *le français*, I may begin to study *le japonois*.

The damage to my gown was not as bad as it had at first appeared. Some seams needed to be repaired, and because I wouldn't be able to fix the sequined section of the bodice, I decided to *kintsugi* it. This meant using a large fabric insert on the right side.

The repairs, if done well, would enhance my theme of the beauty to be found in neglected, forgotten, and injured places and people.

I tied off all the threads so no more sequins fell off. The sequined parts of the bodice were meant to suggest glittering, broken windows in an abandoned mall. I took apart the lining so I could get at the inside of the bodice. I pinned muslin into the damaged place, marked it, cut it, and basted it in place. Then I cut and sewed together several strips of pale metallic silks in silver and steel, taking the Pucci metallic mini bandage dress as my inspiration.

I laid the insert pattern over the stripes and cut it out. Then I sewed the metallic striped insert into the dress bodice and re-stitched the lining. *Et voilà! Ooh la la!* The section of gleaming stripes suggested not only *kintsugi* but also luxurious bandages wrapping the ribs beneath the glamorous gown! Layers of dis-tress *healed by fashion*!

The dress was, if anything, even more beautiful and fasci-nating than it had been.

We, meaning the fashion show candidates, had been told that we could get into the dressing room at eleven a.m. to prep our models. The show started at one p.m. I was sure *someone* would be at the school long before eleven. I would arrive early and convince them to let me and Mischa in. That would give us an advantage, which is what one must seek in any competi-tive situation.

Several times over the course of the day and the evening, I called the number the police had left and checked whether they'd found Mischa's terrible ex. When I called the last time, the male officer asked why I was still up, which was not his business and was condescending. He informed me they had not found Damon, and his tone told me they didn't expect to. My only consolation was that Damon had seemed on his last legs on Thursday night. He was probably due for a big crash that would keep him down for days.

I finished all of my preparations at three thirty Saturday morning and allowed my gaze to rest upon the dress for a long while.

I went to bed, slept lightly but peacefully, got up at seven a.m., and prepared to meet the day that would change my life.

I packed the dress into a garment bag of my own design, and put the shoes, makeup, and hair supplies in a huge, hard-sided rolling case. I collapsed the crinoline and panniers and put them into a huge fabric bag. My outfit for the day, a highly structured little number, totally chic, 100 percent my own design, was laid out on the worktable, awaiting me. I'd burned a CD with the music and had saved it onto my iPad as well.

Then I sat in my meditation area. It was so peaceful in that moment, I could scarcely believe that less than forty-eight hours earlier a man had barged in, attacked Mischa and me, torn my gown, and tried to destroy my dreams. How beautifully and efficiently I'd recovered from that *contretemps*! Charlie Dean was resilience itself.

We would all get past this. Me, Mischa, my father. Even the awful ex. He had been burned in the fracas, which had probably taught him not to throw his weight around.

I set my timer for twenty minutes, rang my bell, and breathed.

Then I showered, assembled my coif, hid the bruise around my eye with a dramatic makeup application, ate a piece of fruit, put a handful of nuts into a darling little tin container, and put two bottles of mineral water in the Marc Jacobs bag I'd found at a thrift store in Red Deer.

My father says that I behave like a thirty-two-year-old who went to an Ivy League college rather than a sixteen-year-old living in reduced circumstances. I say it sounds like those Ivy Leaguers have the right idea about how to live!

At eight I knocked on my father's door to wake Mischa, and at nine the two of us were on our way in her van.

thirty-one

MAY 4

Yeah, I considered bailing. I tried to come up with a bullet-proof excuse that would justify the fourth-inning dropout. But I couldn't do that to Esther.

No kid has ever been more stoked to wear anything than she was to wear the dress I'd designed, if not made.

I spent the night before the show alone in the garage, working on the metal accessories. I ignored my phone except for a text I sent to Brian, the guy I met at Green Pastures, the metal-work guy who'd been halfway encouraging and whose metal business tag I still had.

I sent him a photo of the throwing star I'd made for Esther's madwoman hair.

He texted right back.

> Shuriken. Wicked. What's it for? Ninja rumble later?

It's for the fashion show.

Teachers will enjoy confiscating that.

Any idea how to attach something like that to a hairclip? Any idea where to get a hairclip?

Let me check with my sister.

A pause of not quite five minutes.

Score! I can give you one of hers.

We made arrangements for him to drop it off. It turned out he lived about fifteen minutes away.

When he knocked on the door, he looked healthier than he had the last time I saw him. Bigger. More color in his face.

Bites went after Brian with only about half his usual nastiness. His schnauzer face quivered with outrage, but he kept his teeth to himself as he jumped up and tried to jam his nose into Brian's crotch.

"Nice dog," said Brian mildly.

"Bites. Quit."

Growling and grumbling until he was sure we understood we were not the boss of him, Bites stalked off to lie irritably on his bed.

"Sorry. He's got some borderline sociopathic tendencies," I said.

"Don't we all."

We walked past the living room, and Brian waved at my grandparents, who were watching TV. They waved back, smiling in that blissed-out way they do when they get in front of a screen.

We headed into the garage.

"Holy. This is a helluva setup," he said. "I wasn't expecting this."

"Yeah, my gramps is an old-school metal guy. But he got me set up with all the newer stuff."

"Laser cutter, spot welder, bending machine. You don't need art school."

I shrugged. I would have liked to be around people interested in the same things. Booker and B hung out in the shop sometimes, but it wasn't any fun for them.

I walked to the big worktable and showed the throwing star.

He pulled a hair clip out of the pocket of his hoodie. "I don't think this makes the most of that star. Maybe you should do something else with it. Get a little more innovative. You've got the skills and the setup here. Why not make a statement? Green Pastures is all about the grand gesture. Save subtlety for college."

"You think?"

"Yup." Then Brian looked around and nodded. "We've got a good shop at school, but it's not better than this."

"Yeah. I'm lucky."

Brian began to inspect the metal sculptures on the floor and the smaller pieces that lined the walls. He looked up at the welded killer whale skeleton hanging from the ceiling, the crouching goblin being scary in the corner, the violent unicorn. My stuff mostly just collects dust, or it would if my grandpa didn't come out and blow everything off with his

little motorcycle blower every couple of weeks. Gramps is
convinced they're all great works of art.

All I know is that when I do my metalwork, everything else
disappears. It's as much fun to visualize the sculptures as it
is to figure out how to make them. There's something about
turning steel rods and sheet metal into art that feels powerful. Takes all my brainpower and all my physical strength.
Metal is fair. I guess that's best way to put it. Plus, I can make
my own weapons, which is cool.

"This one is excellent," said Brian, pointing at a knee-
high bull. It was made of interlocking metal panels on a wire
frame. It had come out well, I thought. Booker said it was
his favorite thing I'd done. Barbra's favorite thing was the
chained, barking dog.

I liked the pair of giant hands in chicken wire. It had taken
me a long time to get them just right.

"Thanks."

"If it was a straight metalwork scholarship competition,
you'd get in for sure."

I half laughed.

"Too late for me," I said. "Fashion is my last chance at the
place."

Brian held up the giant wire hands in his own two hands.
They sat on an oval platform.

"These are really cool," he said. "Can you move the
fingers?"

I nodded and bent one. "Yeah, but you have to be careful."

"Make sure you send pictures of all this stuff with your application for art college."

It was strange to hear him talk like me going to college was
a given.

Brian put the hands back on the shelf and started inspecting the wolf and serpent locked in an epic metal battle in the corner.

"Cool," he muttered.

"I cheated on my girl. With one of the girls in the fashion program," I said.

He inspected the battling creatures, but I could tell he was listening.

"I don't know why I did it. I guess I just wanted to be in that world for a while. And I was kind of shocked that the girl, the fashion one, was even interested in me."

Brian, whose last name I didn't know, was like some monk confessor standing in my garage. He kept his gaze on my metalwork sculptures.

"I have to tell my girlfriend. Her name is Barbra. We've been together since eighth grade."

Why was I telling this guy all of this stuff? Probably because he didn't ask questions. Also because he came right over to help me weld a throwing star onto a hair clip on a Friday night, even though we both probably knew I could do it myself.

"I guess I need to tell both of them. Deal with the consequences. I can't keep this up. The lies. My girlfriend is going to hate me. I already hate me."

"It's hard," he said. "I've been there. In the neighborhood, at least."

"Cheating on someone?"

"Getting caught up in lies and bullshit. Making a mess. Letting down people who care about me."

"I don't know how to tell her. Them."

Brian replaced the battling creatures onto the metal shelf.

"Do it in the way that causes the least harm to the people you screwed. So to speak."

"So to speak," I said.

Neither of us laughed.

Then we spent twenty minutes talking about welding and metalwork, and I came up with a better idea for using the throwing star.

John Thomas-Smith's Inspiring Saying
for the Mood Board:

_____.

PART SIX

Putting on a Show

CHARLIE DEAN

HERE'S AN IDEA © Charlie Dean Designs:

Looking for beauty means looking past, over, and through the ugly. Luckily, there's beauty almost everywhere, so you won't go blind.

DATE: MAY 4

Days until fashion show: 0

We pulled into the empty parking lot at 9:12 a.m. Mischa's face was drawn and pale, and the scratch on her face looked inflamed. When I was not saying positive and encouraging things, I tried to think of what foundation and concealer combination I'd use to hide it. Then again, perhaps the damage to her skin, like the damage to the bodice of her dress, should be accentuated rather than hidden for dramatic effect? I'd have to experiment. Good thing we were *de bonne heure*!

Mischa parked so the van faced the school.

The two of us stared straight ahead. I leaned in from my

gauche but comfortable leather passenger seat. In front of us Green Pastures beckoned, bathed by spring morning light.

"What time did you say the show starts?" asked Mischa, stifling a huge, jaw-cracking yawn.

"One," I said, and wondered how she could forget such an important detail.

"It's going to take us that long to get ready?" asked Mischa. "We could have gotten more sleep."

"You can sleep while I do your hair and makeup," I said.

Mischa sighed. Yawned again.

"You stay here. I'm going to knock on doors to find someone to let us in."

"There are no other cars in this parking lot."

"It's a very good school. I bet they have someone on-site twenty-four hours a day."

I pulled back the side door on the van and walked quickly up to the front doors and tried them. Locked. I rapped the door with my knuckles. No answer. I did the same at a side door, near the office. Nothing. I went all the way around the entire school, knocking on doors, getting no response.

The school was much larger than it appeared. I tried the wide double doors on the Carving Shed without luck and looked in the windows of each pod. All dark. All empty.

By the time I was back in front of the school, I had to admit defeat, at least temporarily. If there *was* a caretaker inside, she was asleep in a closet. *Merde!* Oh well, we'd be first in when someone finally showed up, which was sure to be soon.

I made my way back across the empty parking lot to the van. Mischa wasn't in the driver's seat. She must have gone into the back of the van to relax. It was like an old person's living room back there, with two small seats and a table that turned into a bed, cupboards, and another bench seat against one wall.

There was even an old TV installed in one corner. It was an absurd but cozy vehicle, even if the medical-supply-blue shade of the carpet and furnishings caused my eyes to experience low-grade depression.

I slid the side door open and climbed in, ready to tell Mischa we'd have to wait. What I saw in the van made the words die in my throat.

Mischa was pressed against the far bench seat. Damon bent over her. He had her trapped between his arms, which were braced against the walls of the van. I caught sight of something shiny and metal in his right hand.

Mischa saw me, and her eyes were massive and terrified, like those of a horse in a burning barn. Damon was slow to turn around. When he did, I saw that he was in much worse shape than he'd been two nights ago. Eyes bloodshot, a ferocious burn across his face, culminating in a big white blister on the bridge of his nose. And high. Damon looked so very high.

He started to say something, his words coming out slurred but intense. He'd knocked over my rolling case. My dress! Had the monster gone after my dress again? The garment bag had been knocked to the floor.

A siren seemed to go off in my head. UNACCEPTABLE! UNACCEPTABLE!

Before I knew what he had in his hand, or understood what he was saying, I was on the move. Charlie Dean had finally been pushed too far.

I reached him before he or I knew what was happening. Whatever I said was more of a wail than a warning. Because really! Enough was enough when it came to this abusive and astonishingly thoughtless and vicious creature composed entirely of BAD TASTE.

My speed startled both of us, and he stumbled back, caught

a foot on some edge of the furniture crowding the van, and went down, wacking the side of his head against the little table. I was on him like a wild animal, and he struck out, but Mischa kicked at him and he rolled to get away from her feet. It felt like there were fifteen of us in that van.

The next thing I knew I was kneeling on his back, enjoying the feeling of my knees digging into his stupid ribs. I felt one crack beneath me and was glad.

"Hold him!" I said, huffing and puffing.

Mischa grabbed at an arm, but he'd gone limp.

"Get me my bag!" I panted.

Mischa reached for a bag and shoved it at me.

"Not that one. That one is hairpieces. The big one!"

She snatched the biggest bag from the floor of the van and pushed it toward me. I plunged my hand inside and pulled out a roll of binding tape, too full of adrenaline to consider what I was doing.

I wrapped the cotton twill around and around his wrists. He still didn't struggle. I tied it off, panting.

"Don't let him move!" I gasped. "I'm getting the double-sided!"

"Charlie?" said Mischa, as I dove into the bag, grabbed a roll of adhesive, and started wrapping it around his already bound wrists. Then I did the same to his ankles.

"Charlie? What are you doing?" asked Mischa. She sat on the floor of the van, legs splayed in front of her, staring.

Damon stirred under me but didn't speak or try to get up.

"He's fine!" I said. "This is all totally fine."

His wrists were encased in a half inch of cotton twill and a layer of sticky tape I'd wrapped around and between them. So were his ankles.

"Okay," I said, panting from exertion. "Good."

"I'll call the police," said Mischa, uncertainty in her voice. I eased off his back and tried to catch my breath.

I thought of how they'd looked at her when we'd called before. Their long stares at her track marks. How they'd treated my father.

Then I thought of the show.

What were the chances they'd be done talking to us in time for me to get Mischa ready and show my looks?

Nil! The chances were nil! If we called the police, they would want to interview us. They'd want to take evidence. Statements. Not only would I not be the first one in the dressing room, I wouldn't have time to dress Mischa, do her hair or her makeup at all. We might not even be done in time for Mischa to walk.

This . . . creature could not be allowed to destroy my future.

"No," I said. "We'll call later."

Mischa gawked at me.

"What are you talking about?" said Mischa.

I didn't answer.

"Charlie?"

"Crazy bitch," said Damon into the carpet.

"We're not calling the police right now," I said. "I don't have the time. We have a fashion show to do. We've got hair and makeup. We don't have time for police interviews. I am not missing this."

Mischa's mouth hung open as she stared. If she didn't have such good bone structure, she would have looked very unappealing.

"The police might just let him go again. Then we'll have missed the fashion show for nothing. My future is riding on this afternoon."

"You're going to pay for this, you dumb cow. You attacked me," said Damon.

"I defended us. And my gown. We'll call the police when the show is over. Tell them we just captured him. They don't need to know we got him a few hours earlier. They won't believe anything he says. We'll keep him in here. Gag him so he doesn't make noise. It's just for a few hours. He can sober up while he's waiting. Think about his behavior, consider how he might turn his life around and get onto a more positive and creative path."

Damon tried to thrash around but it was a halfhearted effort.

"Charlie Dean, that's kidnapping!" said Mischa.

"It's self-defense. And effective time management. He brought this on himself."

"Fuuuu— " said Damon, attempting to smash his feet down on the floor several times like an overtired flopping tuna, before I sat on them.

"I think we've heard and seen enough out of you," I said. "It's time for you to be quiet."

"Oh my god. This is starting to seem like one of those movies where somebody ends up in a wood chipper," said Mischa.

Damon gave a cry of distress.

"Don't be ridiculous," I said. "Think of it as a time-out. For someone with extremely bad manners. Find me his phone."

Mischa hesitantly reached into his pocket and pulled it out, inspected it.

"It's dead."

"Good," I said. "He doesn't need to be distracted by phone calls right now. And don't you be afraid of him. He's done hurting people."

A few minutes later, we'd flopped Damon over and moved him so his back was against one of the single seats, which we swiveled around to face the back of the van. I wrapped the tape around his torso to fasten him securely to the chair. His feet were tied to the leg of the table in front of him. His bound wrists were hog-tied to his legs so he couldn't slam them against anything.

I put a muslin gag in his mouth. He tried to head butt me, but I evaded him and he stopped struggling.

I bent over him, keeping far enough back that he wouldn't be able to try another head butt. My hair had come loose in the fracas, and I didn't need a broken bone in my face to go with the black eye.

"Are you comfortable?" I asked.

He stared at me with his bloodred eyes. Blinked slowly.

"Do you need the bathroom? Nod if you do."

He shook his head slowly.

"We'll check on you frequently to make sure you're okay. This is your chance to sleep off whatever you've been taking. The police will come and get you in a few hours. It'll be better for you if you're sober when they come. Otherwise you might get injured during your arrest. Maybe even shot."

"Mmmmmmfffff," said Damon.

"Do you feel like you need to throw up?"

He glared.

"Good," I said. "You'll be fine. And remember, you have brought this on yourself."

"I think I'm having a panic attack," said Mischa. I told her to bend over and breathe slowly.

Damon sagged against his restraints.

"That's right," I said. "Get some sleep. This will be over soon."

"This is so screwed up," said Mischa.

I leveled my sternest gaze at her.

"Really?" I said. "You feel bad? He assaults you multiple times. Assaults me and attacks my clothes. And *you* feel bad?"

She looked down.

I reminded myself that it is not helpful to get angry with the domestic abuse survivor and tried to change my tone. "It's not surprising you feel that way. You must push that aside. This is for his own good and for ours. You're moving on. We all are. Even him."

"Mmmmfff," said Damon.

"What if someone hears him?" asked Mischa. "We're so going to jail for kidnapping."

"It's not kidnapping. It's storage. Move the van to the back of the lot, facing front."

She nodded, her face pale and perfect but for the angry red streak down her right cheek.

"Do you have something we can put in the front window?"

Another nod. "There's a privacy screen."

"Perfect. We'll put that up. Does the TV work?"

"I think so," said Mischa. "Everything in here has been charged up."

"Great!" I said, trying to convey cheeriness and positivity. Because really, what other choice was there?

"Don't worry. Everything will be fine," I said.

When we'd tucked the van away, the three of us sat in silence. Mischa was motionless on a bench seat, Damon on the floor. I stared out the windshield. A small van pulled around to the side of the school at about ten minutes after ten. A woman got out and went to the door. I spread the privacy screen across the windshield, gathered my model and my gown and accessories, and we were off.

thirty-three

MAY 4

I'm pretty sure I'm the only one who pulled up to Green Pastures on a bike that morning. I got there at 11:20, the dress in my backpack, accessories hanging in bags off my handlebars.

There were quite a few vehicles in the parking lot already. I guess I could have showed up earlier, but then I'd have had to be there for longer.

I locked my bike and stared at the front doors of the school.

My life felt like a cracked vase about to fall off a tall table.

Fashion people are completely focused on how things look. It's like they operate via a feedback loop: look a certain way and you will be that way. If you were a certain way, you should look the part. Maybe there was something to that theory.

Before the contest I thought I was too deep to care about clothes, but maybe I was just sort of lazy and didn't know myself.

I'd tried for a respectable outfit for the big day to at least show Mr. Carmichael and the committee that I was grateful that I got to take part. I wore a shirt with a collar and a sweater. Clean jeans. My newest sneakers. I told myself I wasn't dressed up for Tesla, but that factored in.

I was getting ready to open the doors when a thin girl with hair mounded up into a helmet shape came out of the school, moving fast.

"Hey," I said.

She stopped abruptly, her eyes widening. Up close I could see she was in her twenties, at least. Maybe older. She wore a plastic cape around her shoulders, and her face was painted off-white. There was a jagged red scratch down one cheek. Up close I could see that some of the hair was fake and dark ribbons and jewels were woven into it.

She moved her head stiffly, like she was afraid the arrangement of hair might fall over or collapse like a soufflé.

Keys jangled in her hand.

She made a face at me—I have no idea what it meant—and kept moving into the parking lot.

I could sympathize.

I took a deep breath and went inside. When I reached the dressing room, I could tell right off that everyone else had been there for a while. It was all laughing, talking, music, excitement, vanity lights, and mirrors. Clouds of chemicals and perfume that had something to do with hairdressing hung in the air.

Bijou and Tesla walked toward me.

I didn't know whether to look at Tesla or not.

She'd put her hair up in a smooth silvery twist and wore a white blouse and neat black pants and flat shoes. She reminded me of someone who worked in a high-end art gallery. Not that I've ever *been* in a high-end art gallery, but I've seen enough movies to have a general idea.

She veered away before they reached me, saying something I couldn't hear to Bijou. Bijou showed me to my station and took my music. My station had a chair that could be raised and lowered with a foot pump. In front of it was a brightly lit mirror. The screens on either side and the rolling rack at the back made it feel semiprivate.

I hung the dress on the rack, where it looked very small and simple, put the accessories on the counter, and waited. I'd told Esther to come at eleven forty-five.

At eleven thirty Bijou and Tesla called us all into the hallway, where Mr. Carmichael waited.

He told us the order—I was near the start, which suited me fine, and Charlie Dean was in the middle—and then he and Bijou and Tesla brought us out onto the stage and pointed to where the committee of judges would be sitting. There were chairs set out for the audience. A lot of chairs. Who was going to sit in them? Who'd want to voluntarily sit through something like this?

Carmichael reminded us that our models work "both sides of the runway" and that they should pause to show off "all angles of the looks to the judges."

"Tesla?" he said. "Can you please demo?"

Tesla climbed the stairs and took a position at the end of the runway, looking completely at ease. Then she walked along the long platform, pausing several times to turn this way and that until she hit the end and came back, pausing for longer in front of the judges' chairs.

Damn, she was three kinds of something.

We stood in a ragged group at the far end of the runway, and as she passed us her gaze caught mine, and I felt something tear when she looked away.

"After all the models have walked, they will come back

onstage and take a bow. Then the contestants and models are invited to take refreshments and celebrate with family and friends while the judges deliberate. Tesla and Bijou will collect your croquis books and design materials now."

Before we trooped back into the dressing rooms, and the contestants gathered up our drawings and whatnot to hand in, Carmichael reminded us to put our names on everything. He finished with a warning.

"The show will start on time, and we will not hold the show for anyone who is not ready. You will lose your turn. And *that* will be *that*."

Maybe I'd get lucky and Esther would be a couple of hours late.

thirty-four

ℭHARLIE
DEAN

HERE'S AN IDEA © CHARLIE DEAN DESIGNS:

There is fashion even among thieves. Kidnappers are sweaty, desperate creatures. Armed robbers are often sloppy. But jewel thieves are style itself in black turtlenecks and nicely fitted trous. No matter what crime you commit, always dress like the jewel thief.

DATE: MAY 4

It is hard to stay focused on the positive when you have kidnapped someone, even if it is for the good of all concerned. The situation was kind of like a Russian constructivist sports ensemble.

It was not the perfect fit for anyone, but at least it was simple and effective and made the most of *les options limité.*

There were eleven of us in the show. I feel certain Charlie Dean was the only one holding *un enlèvement victime* while preparing her model. It was something of a distraction, but I overcame it as I did all things.

One size
fits all.   Badly.

When the janitor let us in, I led Mischa to the dark dressing room and we took the station farthest from the door so that we could have some much needed privacy, not only to get her ready, but also so we could consult about our prisoner who was really more of a guest, if you think about it without excess *emotionalité*. He should have been glad. Every moment in the van was one not in the custody of the *gendarme*, who do not approve of intoxicated and abusive ex-boyfriends of vulnerable women. They would not be giving him any leather seats to lean against or a nice cathode-ray TV to watch.

When I had Mischa settled, I got to work, and in spite of the rather unusual circumstances and her nervous nature, Mischa settled down as I undertook her demanding hair and makeup.

At ten forty-five Mr. Carmichael's assistants showed up.

"How did you get in?" asked Bijou, poking her head into my station.

At first I didn't answer, because I was weaving a ribbon into Mischa's hair and dared not look away.

"How long have you been in here?" asked Tesla.

Mischa told them we'd just been inside for a few minutes.

One of them may have muttered an unkind remark about taking advantage, but I couldn't be sure, nor was it of concern to me under the circumstances.

Soon the other contestants began to arrive. One brought speakers, and soon the room was filled with music and the soft murmur of voices and giggles.

It was an exciting atmosphere of style and fashion. When I was sure Mischa's hair was safely and securely arranged—it was as imposing as I'd hoped, the coif of an Elizabethan queen!—and I had her foundation on, I asked her to check on our guest and make sure he was in no distress. Charlie Dean has seen a lot of addicts under the influence in her day and was sure he'd be fine, but it was best to be safe.

"He's probably sleeping. But still, don't get too close," I whispered. "Think of your hair."

Mischa stared into the mirror at her dramatic *coiffure*. She gave a small moan like a door with rusty hinges. "I hate him, but I don't hate him this much."

"Give it time," I said. "You will."

Mischa was gone for so long, I considered going to check on her. I walked out of my station and surveyed the other stations. I considered looking for my art room friends—were they friends? I hoped so—but didn't want to be rebuffed in such a competitive atmosphere.

I felt a flush of excitement at the thought of seeing Jo. She was going to show something wonderful, I knew. Moments before I gave in to temptation and went to look for her, Mischa came back and climbed into the chair.

"He's fine," she whispered. "Sleeping."

Then her gaze settled on her own reflection.

"This does look amazing," she said, and smiled.

I loved seeing the smile on her worried face. I couldn't wait for other people to see Mischa's beauty brought into focus by my vision for her. Then my thoughts returned to Jo. I'd feel badly for her when I won, but there could only be one scholarship winner.

As though my thoughts were a summons, Jo appeared behind us.

"There you are," she said. "What time did you get here? You were first, weren't you?"

Jo was the business in a leather jacket rolled to the elbows, tight leather pants, and a white shirt with white and red and black pattern printed across half of it.

"Phenomenal work, Charlie," she said, assessing Mischa's hair. "You're going to kill it. But not as hard as me."

Our eyes met in the mirror, and if I hadn't been wearing my trademark bold blusher, she would have seen the red move up my neck and onto my face.

Perhaps Charlie Dean *would* make a few moments for dating before her fashion empire was completely established.

Jo came into my work area and leaned in close to me, her face serious.

"Do you have a black eye?" she asked.

I took a step back.

"No. I mean, it's just a small bruise. It's nothing."

She frowned. "Do I need to set somebody straight?"

My blush turned into burning embers.

"No. I ran into—"

"We fell," said Mischa. She pointed at the scratch on her face. She lied easily. Convincingly. Like an addict. "I was on a step stool while she adjusted something on the dress. I took a wrong step, knocked her down. She scratched me. It was quite the clown show."

Jo watched us carefully.

"Huh," she said.

I smiled. "Yes. It was dumb."

"Be careful today," said Jo. She stared at me, hard. Then she was gone.

Dazed, I went back to work on the finishing touches of Mischa's makeup.

"Well, that girl is as hot as two forest fires meeting on a windy day," said Mischa, the boldness of her words sounding a little out of character.

I didn't answer.

"She was *flirting* with you," said Mischa. "Big-time."

A small giggle may have escaped me. *Très embarrassant!* The two of us sounded so foolish. And young. It was very nice, all things considered.

I shook my head to clear it. This was how things went wrong. The designer became distracted. Between the fashion show and Jo and our guest in the van, I had more than enough to concentrate on.

The thought seemed to occur to both of us at once, and we went quiet.

This will all work out, I told myself. The fashion show will proceed. I will win. We will ask the police to collect our guest, who will get the help and correctives he needs. And all will be well.

I would not let doubt creep in now.

And so Charlie Dean proceeded. When Mischa's makeup was complete and before I helped her into the dress, I took my turn to run outside and check on our guest. If one must detain someone for their own good, it's important to do so responsibly.

thirty-five

MAY 4

When B appeared at the entrance to my station, I could tell
Booker hadn't told her yet. She gave me a little wave, and I tried
to smile at her. The plan had been for her to stay out in the audience with my grandparents. But here she was. Backstage.

I glanced around to see if Tesla was in sight. She wasn't,
thank the sweet baby Jesus. This was not the place or the time
for that conversation. For one thing, I had a headache that
would have knocked over a steer thanks to all the chemicals
in the air. For another, I am a coward.

Esther swung her skinny legs in the chair. I'd explained
how she was supposed to walk the runway, and she said she
was nervous but ready. Sheryl and Edward stood on either
side of her.

"Okay," I said to Esther's foster parents, loud enough for
B to hear. "I think family and friends should head for their
seats in the audience soon. The show will start in about thirty
minutes. I'll shoot you guys a text if we need anything or if
Esther needs you."

"Okay," said Sheryl. She bent low to whisper into Esther's ear. "We can't wait to see you out onstage. You are going to be amazing. Because you are amazing already."

"Just amazing," echoed Edward, who'd gone a little pale.

Edward and Sheryl tore themselves away after reassuring Esther a few more times that they'd be "right outside" and "only a text away."

Barbra waited at the back of my station and said hello to them as they passed. Then she came to stand beside me, Esther in the chair between us. In the mirror we looked like a portrait of an inappropriately young family.

"Can I help with anything?" she said. "I mean, with anything that's not hair, clothes, or makeup?"

"That's okay."

She looked at the metal pieces arrayed on the counter.

"These are terrific," she said. "I get those. But the rest of this scene . . ." She rolled her eyes to show what she thought about fashion and this fashion show. "I guess some people don't know that Settlers of Catan exists. Or books."

It kind of killed me that she had to say that right then.

Esther watched us.

"Are *you* going to do her makeup?" asked B.

"We're going to leave her face natural."

"Good decision."

"I hate makeup," said Esther.

"Me too," said Barbra.

There was another second of silence. Some strange new impatience grew in me, but I tried not to let it show. B didn't deserve that.

"Well, I'll be out there watching. And cheering. Or cringing. Whichever seems appropriate."

"Thanks."

"Have you talked to Booker?" she asked suddenly. "He's been dodging my texts. And my calls. I hope everything's okay. We were supposed to come here together. He was so excited for today. Even though you said he wasn't allowed near the models." She met Esther's eyes in the mirror. "I mean the *older* models."

Esther grinned.

"I don't know where he is," I said. My stomach was a rock tumbler.

"Okay. I'm sure he'll be here soon. We'll be waiting. And watching."

Barbra leaned in to kiss me. When she drew away, I saw Tesla watching us from the back of my station.

When Tesla began to walk toward us, my brain scrambled for an explanation. An escape route. But all the doors were shut and locked.

"Is this your girlfriend, John?" Tesla asked.

My mouth was full of broken ashtray.

"I am," said Barbra. Understanding dawned on her face in stages. It was very hard to watch. She did not smile at Tesla, because Barbra's not a liar.

"I'm Barbra," she said. "And you are . . . ?"

"No one," said Tesla.

Esther watched all of this taking place in the mirror. The kid missed nothing.

"Ten minutes to showtime," said Tesla, her voice hollow. Then she walked out.

Barbra stared at me like I'd just unexpectedly kicked her in the shin.

"That girl smells like a mowed lawn." Pause. "You probably should have aired the dress out, you idiot."

Then she turned and left.

I closed my eyes for a minute, puffed out the breath I'd been holding, and got back to work making sure the ruff and head-dress were secure on the frame I'd made to rest on Esther's shoulders, tucked inside the dress. It was surprisingly heavy, and I wanted to be sure she felt comfortable moving.

When I was sure it wouldn't fall over, I pumped the lever on the chair to lower it. Esther still had to hop to get down.

"You look cool," I said.

"Ninja private school fairy," said Esther. "That's what Barbra called it."

"B's got a way with the words."

Esther peered up at me, her face and wild cloud of curls framed by the web of wires that turned into hands that held a throwing star. It had been surprisingly easy to combine the star with the Elizabethan-style wire ruff and the hands. Wire is so malleable. Forgiving, even.

"You're in big trouble, aren't you?" said Esther.

Around us the other designers were rushing to help their models into their outfits, adjusting hems and accessories, poking worriedly at hairdos.

"You could say that. I've made some mistakes recently."

"My brother always liked too many girls, too. He liked *all* the girls. They were sort of like TV to him. Or video games."

"That's not how I—"

"My brother really, *really* liked video games."

"Girls aren't like video games. Or TV. Let's go line up," I said.

ℒCHARLIEℛ
ℒDEANℛ

> **HERE'S AN IDEA** © CHARLIE DEAN DESIGNS:
>
> *When a situation calls for panic, resist the urge. Instead,*
> *focus on something you can control. Check your hair and*
> *clothing. Are you neat and presentable? Stylish? If so,*
> *remember that you can handle anything and panic is gauche.*

DATE: MAY 4

When everyone was dressed and ready, time was called and
Tesla and Bijou led us down a hallway and we assembled in
the backstage area that led out to the atelier's stage. Our guest
was safe. When I went out to check on him, he was still sleeping soundly. No problems. This was all going to work out. My
concerns alleviated, I was able to be fully present in the moment. And what a moment it was, there backstage among my
fellow contestants. I looked around and gave *un souffle*, or a
gasp as it is known in English. It was like standing in the midst
of a flock of peacocks, which is something I have not yet had
the opportunity to do. In fact, it was like standing among a

flock of peacocks from space, which is something I will probably never have the opportunity to do! All the ensembles were
astonishing and creative.

Who could have imagined so much talent in my peers? Not
even Charlie Dean, and I'm an optimist.

We'd been instructed to whisper until the first model was
called and not to speak at all while the show was on.

It all felt so fantastically *backstage*. Total theater! It helped
me to forget that we had a man tied up in a van in the parking lot. I kept having to be very firm with Mischa to prevent
her from running and hiding in the bathroom, which she was
threatening to do as her anxiety mounted. Models are *exacte-
ment* as difficult as you've heard.

We stood waiting. In her pale, architectural gown Mischa
was a small storm made entirely of nerves and *élan*. Wind
whistled quickly between her clenched teeth, thanks to her unfolding panic attack. I put a hand on her arm to steady her and
also to steady myself. We were on the verge of pulling this off.
Of showing everyone what I can do. AGAINST ALL ODDS was
the motto *du jour*!

Twice I caught Jo looking my way. Twice our eyes met, and I
felt my heart lurch. I couldn't see her model through the crowd
of people backstage—only a sliver of rich brown fabric.

"Mr. Carmichael is introducing the competition, thanking
the sponsors, and telling the audience a little bit about our program," Tesla reported in a quiet voice.

"Are the people out there?" asked Madina, the adorable girl
in the head scarf.

"Full house," said Bijou. "And we put out a hundred and
twenty-five seats."

Mischa's breaths quickened.

"Sips of air," I instructed. "Don't hyperventilate. All you

need to do is walk. You are a very good walker. You've been doing it for years." Of course, she hadn't been doing it in sky-high heels the way she would be this afternoon. I'd considered putting her in flats to help steady her and because with the full skirts no one would see her footwear, but that would have changed the way the hem swept the floor. No, high, high heels it had to be.

"Jacques will be right there. Probably in the front row. And you're ready. And you are a testament to all things gorgeous."

"Right," she said. "Oh my God, I'm so nervous."

I craned my head to see what Jo's model was wearing, but again the small crowd prevented me from getting a good look.

Applause sounded from beyond the door, and then music came on, introduced by what sounded like a hunting bugle. The music itself was operatic and martial, like a call to battle for some ancient, windswept peoples who were on a first-name basis with elves and trolls. I half expected the sounds of muskets exploding and the clattering hooves of war horses.

Tesla pointed at one of the contestants with long, flat-ironed hair, who turned to us and gave us all a nod, before turning her model to show off her look. The candidate had game!

The model, a stunning androgynous individual, wore a one-shoulder bodice formed of what looked like Kevlar. Somehow, the designer, so unremarkable in her own self-presentation, had made an utterly striking ensemble. The bodice fit like a second skin. The single strap was attached with Velcro and so were both sides of the bodice. The model wore tight pants with ballistic-type padding at the knees and great tall boots, and on their back was a *genuine quiver of arrows*. Glorious *high fashion* arrows, with fletching and vanes in gleaming shades of greens, blacks, and wine. It was a superhero outfit for the ages. One could wear it to the hottest club, to the end of times, or to a battle in ancient times. Sexy on anyone with the lean muscle mass to pull it off.

Bravo, candidate with no name! *Bravo!*

The model, fierce and nervy, walked through the door to the runway that Bijou held open. Two seconds later the applause, glorious applause, sounded. I was clapping, too, with all my might, but silently, so as not to distract.

I am a *highly* competitive person, but my heart was soaring for the contestant with the name I couldn't remember. Fashion is so full of these moments. Small wonder it is my life.

The music thundered and shook as the model walked, which took not quite two minutes, including pauses, and it faded when the model returned, triumphant, giddy, to us. The long-haired designer and her model fell into an embrace.

Then it was the turn of the witchy, deep-forest-dwelling Ainslee, she of the long curly hair and flowing garb.

The music swelled, and Ainslee whispered something to her model, a full-figured girl, who wore her hair in a complication of braids so *magnifique*, it would take four mathematicians to undo them.

The model, a natural beauty *avec* the sweetest freckles and dewiest skin, wore a modified *cotehardie*-inspired garment in *parti* colors. Four A-line panels, one side new-leaf green with a faint embroidery pattern of leaves and vines, the other a soft arbutus-bark red. Simple white streamers wrapped around the biceps and fell nearly to the floor. Traditionally, a cotehardie was a dress, but this one was a coat, open but cinched at the waist with what looked like a woven willow belt. Made of boiled wool, the coat was simple, but it beautifully accentuated the model's generous figure. When she turned to the left, the garment appeared entirely green. When she turned right, it was red. The lines were so beautiful, so suggestive. Underneath she wore an extraordinary silvery leotard and boots up to *here*! The garb was purest fairy, and even though it was red and green, there was nothing of Christmas about it. It was the season of fall and of spring in the forest. Very *historical*, of course, but that was the point. Ainslee had outdone herself.

Why wasn't *everyone* wearing cotehardie coats to every dance and occasion? Of course, the people who take part in medieval fairs and so forth might do so, but this wasn't recreation or mimicry. This was reinvention. The coat dress was as timeless as simplicity itself.

I may begin to wear a cotehardie everywhere. Enough with the suits! Bring on the cotehardie!

Ainslee's model held a single white rat in her hands. It peeked out from the cage of her fingers.

"Ewww," said someone near me.

But I loved it. Loved it, loved it, *loved* it. Unreservedly. Wholeheartedly.

The girl opened her hand and the rat cat-walked, if you'll allow the expression, up her arm and settled onto her shoulder. Then the door to the stage opened, and she walked into a swell of monumental music.

"Music's a brave choice," said Cricket, who sat near me in her chair, as her model, a tall, gorgeous boy, shifted from foot to foot beside her.

"Wolves in the Throne Room," said Jason Wong. "'Woodland Cathedral.'"

"Enchantingly moody," I said as the applause competed with the swelling music and indistinguishable chants.

"Goes well with the rat," said Cricket, swiping the beautiful red wave of hair out of her eyes.

Two minutes later Ainslee's model was back, and it was time for John Thomas-Smith's look. He'd been standing between us and his tiny model. When Bijou gestured at them, the girl, a child really, not more than ten or eleven, emerged from behind him, and Charlie Dean didn't even know what to do, and still doesn't. There may even have been some irregular beats of *mon cœur*.

The girl wore a dress of midnight navy. The sort you could dash about in, having adventures. The fabric, unusual and synthetic, looked substantial but soft, like something a selkie might wear before she turned into a deep-sea scuba diver on the hunt for rare black pearls. The dress ended just above the knee, and there were sporty little white stripes around the sleeves and above the hem. The description doesn't do it justice. There was just something so astonishingly *right* about how it looked on the girl, especially with the little white Peter Pan collar. Once my eye had taken in the unexpected perfection of the fit and style of the dress, I was knocked out cold by the accessories.

"She's got little nunchucks around her wrists," said Cricket. "So cute! And inappropriate for a kid. I love it."

Most astonishing of all was the headdress-cum-ruff the girl wore. The piece was made of fine woven metal. It fanned out around her neck and rose up from behind her head. Then the lacy metal turned into two woven wire hands, fingers splayed. Between the three-dimensional thumbs was a metal star, sharp as a sliver, lethal, witty.

"That's a throwing star," said Mischa, forgetting to have her panic attack for the moment.

The combination of things— preppy, modern little dress and baroque headdress sculpture—should not have worked. But somehow it did. The child looked like an unchained spirit of the night. Powerful, mischievous, and capable of anything.

If this was intellectually rigorous design, I was all in favor of it! I felt a surge of affection and admiration for John Thomas-Smith. He was a worthy rival. I shot another glance at Jo and saw her nodding her approval. Beside her I caught a glimpse of her model and a beaded frontispiece and a long, intricately embroidered, highly dramatic sheer coat. Slayed! Charlie Dean was already slayed by Jo's work.

John's child model smiled at us, curtsied, and headed into her music, which was appropriately strange. Some kind of bizarre dance music narrated by the world's scariest storyteller. It sounded like a children's book being read aloud in hell's lunatic asylum. *La perfection.*

John stood rigidly staring at the floor as the applause rose and fell and rose and fell. I noticed Tesla watching him, her face unreadable.

Next would be Madina. Her model was her mother, who looked absolutely stunning waiting backstage in an elaborate hijab. The outer scarf was scarlet. You have *never* seen such a rich red. A braided golden rope wrapped around her skull like a crown.

She wore a beautifully tailored gold blouse, tucked into an impossibly elegant, high-waisted red skirt. Madina's mother had a waist so slim and fabulous in the skirt that Charlie Dean wanted to start a petition to put up a statue of her in the town square. I loved that I'd expected Madina to do more of a hip-hop street look infused with tradition, but instead she went full class and grace for the mature woman.

Madina smiled so hugely at us that every single one of us had to smile back.

Her mother beamed at her daughter and swung a coat over her shoulder.

It was made with a silk brocade, ultra-luxurious, in reds and golds against a dark blue background. In a stroke of mad genius, the shoulder yoke was indigo denim, giving it the impossibly wealthy horsewoman vibe. I was immediately transported to a fabulous, spare-no-expense ranch. Arabian horses everywhere. Racing around, tails bannering in the wind. The coat would be exactly right there. Glamor and taste to burn.

I couldn't help it. I had to clap again, but quietly, barely touching my hands together.

J'adore Madina!

John's model skipped backstage, her music faded, and after ten seconds, Madina's began. French rap music! I'd gotten part of my guess right. Again, the applause from the audience was mighty, and I wished I could be at a fashion show FOR THE REST OF MY LIFE!

Cricket readied her model, wheeling around him in her chair. Knitwear! His chunky cardigan sweater was obviously handmade, extremely adventurous in a burned orange color with asymmetrical front closure. He wore a massive chocolate scarf over it, also hand-knitted, beautiful against his dark face.

Ooh la la! And the checked woolen pants in green and brown *killed*. Something told me Cricket had woven the fabric for those heavy, classic trous with a marvelous, cheeky hand-embroidered front pocket. That Cricket! Not just funny and sardonic, but so skilled. The music that surged was Gaelic, marvelous and jaunty, and her model was the best-dressed fisherman home after a long, dangerous trip, as he headed to the runway.

He came back and bent down to hug Cricket. I almost couldn't stand how wonderful it was.

Jason's model headed out. Mischa would go next.

I looked to her, grabbed her hand, and turned her around to face the assembled designers and models. Then I raised her arm, like she'd just tied for the championship fight. My fellow competitors clapped silently for my gown, and I exulted. Yes, I did. This was all going to work out.

thirty-seven

MAY 4

Esther and I headed down the hallway to the stage door to wait with the others. I made sure I was angled so I didn't have to make eye contact with Tesla.

The models went out, one at a time, and with each, some of my numbness washed away. The outfits were incredible. To think that people, especially *these* people, had invented and sewn these clothes. To think that I ever thought there was anything lightweight or easy or unimportant about making *anything*, much less actual clothes for actual living people to wear.

When it was Esther's turn, I bent down so we were eye level.

"You are going to be so awesome."

In return she gave me a pale smile.

"You too," she said.

And then she was gone into the dark circus music of Wax Tailor's "Heart Stop" from *Dusty Rainbow from the Dark.* I picked the song partly because Esther reminds me of the girl in the cover art, and because Wax Tailor is a French band, and fashion people have big love for things that are French. The song was exactly strange enough for Esther, and I forgot everything for the few minutes she was out there. It was bliss.

She came back, rolling with the applause.

Her face was lit up like there was a star pulsing behind her head, and I gave her a hug. I caught a glimpse of another model heading out.

Before I could check who it was, Esther grabbed my hand. Hers was surprisingly strong for its size.

"Come on," she said. "I want to see the other people."

We ran down the hall, around the corner, and through the doors into the darkened atelier. The stage rose above the audience, who sat on either side in rows.

A guy in a bulky sweater, very rich looking, was walking off the stage. Two seconds later Jason Wong's model hit the runway. Jason's model was a skinny, older guy. He wore a bottle-green suit, majorly badass. The music was some redneck-cowboy song about a guy not being as good as he once was. The mix of music, model, and suit was a trip. The suit made the guy looked like a degenerate gambler whose luck had finally turned right side up, the way he always knew it would. I decided that if by some miracle I actually graduated from high school, I would spend everything I had to get Jason Wong to make me a suit.

When the model guy, who wasn't young or handsome, just kind of weathered and real, stopped in front of the judges, half the people on that side of the room stood up and applauded.

The guy walked backstage, and the lights went down for a ten-second beat, and then slowly came up again as a woman's voice came over the sound system, whispering, then wailing, something about a disease.

Esther and I edged up to a corner that offered the best view of the stage. The rest of the models and designers had the same idea and crowded in around us.

Charlie Dean's model hit the stage just as the singer stopped and the music exploded.

Everyone in the place jumped.

The dress was like the exposed infrastructure of a broken dream. It was white and gray. The neckline jutted out and tilted across the model's chest like she was climbing out of a ruined building. The skirt reminded me of a collapsing scaffolding under a sheer layer painted with shadows and light in graphic patterns. It made the dress look even more like a structure, which I think was the point. The model, the one I'd seen out in the parking lot earlier, still had a bright red scratch down her cheek, and her hair was shaped into a dramatic mound on her head.

One section of the bodice shone with dull sequins, and there was a section on her left side where the sequined section was cut away to show what looked like bandages of satin bands in dull silvers.

There was a piece of narrowly pleated fabric that extended out the side of the skirt, almost like a set of stairs. The dress was completely righteous, as Booker would have said. It was probably one of the most interesting things I'd seen since I started this quest to win the scholarship. Even though it wasn't practical, it was inspiring, somehow. I wondered how I'd ever looked at Charlie Dean and not seen that she was extraordinary.

The audience started clapping as soon as the model appeared, and the applause got louder when the dress came closer.

I couldn't imagine the skill that had gone into sewing something like that dress.

"That is so beautiful," said Esther, loud enough that I could hear her over the music.

The model made her way uncertainly down the runway in her huge, radical gown, pausing to turn this way and that. Her eyes were huge and black in her pale, painted face, and she swayed almost imperceptibly. Her eye shadow extended to her temples like a shadow blindfold. The cement-colored satin gloves she wore were dirty, which added to the effect.

She stopped in front of the committee. When Carmichael nodded, she headed offstage, the singer growling and howl-

ing something about strange hellos. I almost can't express the feeling I had right then.

The clapping kept going, and I knew I wasn't ever, ever going to look at my oddball classmate in her strange suits the same way again. Charlie Dean was definitely some kind of genius.

I think we were all sort of stunned as the music faded, and we waited for the next model.

The room was silent for several long beats, then a flute sounded, followed by a loon's call, as haunting and surprising as any noise in the world. Then came a deep announcer's voice.

"The loon is also called the Great Northern Diver, because of its ability to dive and swim long distances underwater," intoned the announcer. I recognized that it was one of those old CBC Hinterland Who's Who PSAs about Canadian wildlife that we'd watched in some old biology class. Then the voice was overtaken by drums and chanting and a deep grungy electric beat that turned the place upside down.

"That's A Tribe Called Red," said Esther. "We got to go see them last year. They're my favorite."

The model came onstage covered in a see-through coat, embroidered all over. She shrugged it off to reveal a beautiful brown dress, so dark it was almost black, with a beaded section at the chest. It was seriously every kind of excellent. The skirt was split down the side from the hip to reveal an ivory silk panel printed with a series of birds, loons I think they were, in different poses. The model held up her fists and danced as she walked, and the audience clapped in time.

Goddamn. That was the most seriously rock-and-roll piece of art. Contemporary and classic and sharp as hell.

Fashion. Who knew?

CHARLIE DEAN

HERE'S AN IDEA © Charlie Dean Designs:

When things get very bad, think of Dior and his New Look. He was vilified for changing the face of fashion. Sometimes visionaries face extreme opposition.

DATE: MAY 4

We'd done it. I'd shown my work to an appreciative audience. Mischa had been wonderful. We'd pulled it off! "I need to go to the bathroom," said Mischa. "My anxiety."

"Wait until after we take our bow," I said. "Then we'll get you out of the dress, and you can go."

Mischa groaned but didn't object, and the other contestants and their models returned backstage. I supposed they'd snuck into the atelier to watch. We complimented one another and laughed with relief and joy, and it was the best moment of my life.

Did I think of our guest in this moment? No. I did not. My brain was full and so was my heart.

After an indeterminate amount of time of standing around with the others, part of the fashion-mad crowd, half-ecstatic, half-exhausted, Bijou came in and told us to prepare to take our bows. It may have just been my imagination, but she may have looked at me with new respect. I think everyone did. Of course, I was looking at all of them with new respect, too.

We got into a line beside our models. When Tesla gestured, I took Mischa's right hand, and we walked out in front of all the people. Oh, it was a moment to remember *pour toujours*!

The lights were brilliant onstage, but I could see Jacques in the third row, smiling up at us, like someone waiting for a casting call for a commercial featuring older hipsters. He smiled and smiled and looked from side to side to make sure everyone was looking at us. *C'était adorable!*

We bowed to the audience on one side, and then the audience on the other side, and they all stood and gave the standing ovation I've been waiting for my entire life. There were tears. Many of them mine; some of them on the faces of my fellow designers, our models, and our supporters in the audience. I got to see Jo's spectacular gown with its exquisite handwork and thought perhaps she would win because it was so marvelous, and maybe it would be enough to have had this moment even if I didn't win. We lined up on the stage to clap for one another and for the wonder of the moment and nodded to the committee.

And then we filed off the stage, high on fashion.

I helped Mischa out of her dress, and she got back into her jeans and T-shirt and rushed off to the bathroom. That's one way we are different. I never want to get out of beautiful clothes and back into a jean or, god forbid, a sweatpant. I headed with the other designers and models to the atelier, where we would visit with the audience and have drinks and snacks while the judges considered which of us would have a new life.

I knew I should check on our guest, but I wanted just a bit more time in a world where problems like Mischa's ex-boyfriend didn't exist.

Mingling in the atelier, post-show, was like being a celebrity. Of course friends and families said how brilliant we were and how amazing our looks had been. But at least half the audience was made up of strangers: the principal of Green Pastures, Mr. Manhas, students, people from the community, and of course the mysterious and all-powerful committee members.

People asked all sorts of questions about our influences and techniques.

We were taken so seriously. It was marvelous! *Marvelous!*

Jacques came over and hugged me very hard.

"Charlie girl, you nailed it. And Mischa"—he turned to look for her—"wore the heck out of that dress."

"She's in the bathroom," I told him.

He leaned in. "I already told you, but this experience has meant the world to her. I really think it changed the way she sees herself."

Out of the corner of my eye I saw John standing with his young model and her parents, then the three of them went to talk to someone else, and he stood alone. Before I could go over and congratulate him, he was joined by two older people, probably his grandparents. They said a few words and left.

Then he was alone again.

Where was his exquisite, *au naturel* girlfriend? Where was that big guy he hangs around with all the time?

My gaze traveled the room and found Jo. Who was staring at *moi!* *Mon dieu!* She was surrounded by at least ten people of all ages. The family of Jo was out in full force!

Before I could gather my courage to go to her and say hello, we were asked to gather together to hear the winner announced.

I'd tried to push thoughts of winning and losing from my mind, but now they were back with a vengeance, and I felt sick and a bit faint.

My dad must have noticed, because he sat me in a chair and kept his hand on my shoulder. When Mr. Carmichael began to speak, Jacques's grip tightened and I flinched.

"Sorry, Charlie girl," he whispered. "This is intense."

No need to tell me that.

There is such a thing as wanting something too much.

"I congratulate all of our designers and would like to thank their families and friends for supporting them in this competition."

We all clapped very hard, but my hands felt like ice that might shatter, so I stopped.

"The vision, execution, and the written justifications you have submitted to this competition are absolutely extraordinary. I speak for all the committee members when I say I never dreamed that we would see this caliber of work."

More applause.

A student rushed into the room, ran straight to Mr. Manhas, who sat with the other committee members, and began speaking quickly. The head of Green Pastures lurched out of his seat, and Mr. Carmichael faltered in his remarks.

Mr. Manhas rushed out of the room, indicating the student should follow him. The other judges didn't know what to do.

"There seems to be a—" said Mr. Carmichael.

Another student burst into the atelier. "*Someone died in the bathroom!*" she screamed.

My dad's hand turned into a hawk's talon on my shoulder, then he was gone, racing for the door.

I went after him. The leaden feeling in my stomach didn't stop me from running so fast, my feet barely touched the ground.

The hallway was a blur of lockers, and skylights flashed by overhead, marked by bursts of clear light. Then I was pushing my way into the girls' bathroom, past two students who stood, their phones in their hands.

Mr. Manhas was on his knees beside Mischa, who lay in a handicapped stall, her legs splayed in front of her, her head lolled to the side. Her lips were a gray-blue that matched the shadow mask we'd painted across her half-slit eyes.

"Misch!" said my father, falling to his knees.

I didn't approach. I didn't speak.

"Did someone call the ambulance?" asked Mr. Manhas.

"Yes, sir," said a pale girl.

"Is she dead?" asked a boy.

Someone held on to my arm, hard, but I was only barely aware of it.

"She's breathing," said Mr. Manhas. He turned to my dad. "Her name is Mischa?"

My dad nodded.

"Mischa," said Mr. Manhas in a loud voice. "We've called 911. Can you speak?"

Mischa lay inert as a sandbag.

"Mischa," said the principal, even louder. "I need you to speak to me."

He began rubbing his knuckles over her upper chest.

"I need everyone who is not faculty or an adult to leave. Now. Please, all students wait in the atelier. Someone go to meet paramedics and escort them in."

People behind us began to edge out of the bathroom.

"Do you have any idea what she took?" Mr. Manhas asked my father. And in the middle of my shock and fear, I felt ashamed that he knew to ask my dad that. Oh, Jacques.

"No," said my dad. "I've been clean for months now. Her too."

Then I thought of Damon. His bag of drugs. Mischa checking on him in the van. Alone.

"I think," I said, my voice faltering, "I might know. Where she got them. Maybe we can figure out what she took."

"They'll need that information," said Mr. Manhas. "Go with her," he told my dad.

And then Jacques and at least two other Green Pastures faculty members were following me out to Mischa's van.

I opened the door. Damon slept deeply, held up by his bindings. He snored softly behind his gag.

I saw the scene from others' eyes. It didn't look good. Not at all.

"Charlie," whispered my dad, "what's *happening* here? Who the hell is this guy?"

"It's Demon'. I mean, Damon. Mischa's ex. He came after us again this morning. So we, uh, detained him. He had drugs on him somewhere. I think Mischa must have gotten into them."

"Better pray it's not fentanyl," said my dad, scrambling over to the bench seat and beginning to pat Damon down. "How long has he been like this? How long have you girls had him . . . like this? Come on, Charlie . . ." His voice was pleading, and it trailed off when he realized there wasn't anything I could tell him that would make this better.

"He's only been here since right before the show. We were going to call the police to come and get him. After. We were just letting him sleep. Until then."

"Why didn't you call the police as soon as you saw him?" asked my dad.

I shook my head, trying to clear my thoughts. "We just . . . the police would have . . . I wanted to do the show. It was just for a few hours. I couldn't miss the show."

Stressed as I was, I knew I'd made a terrible mistake. My decision had been bad. Extremely bad. Kidnapping bad.

"Call the police," I heard someone say.

My dad knelt in front of Damon and dug through his pockets. When he opened his jacket pocket, he found a Baggie with an assortment of smaller Baggies inside. He dug a finger around inside, inspecting.

"Patches," he said. "Some Oxys. I'm almost sure these patches are fentanyl. Maybe it's morphine. Fuck, Mischa."

The sirens were already approaching. Probably for Mischa. Soon they would sound for me.

Two teachers from Green Pastures asked my dad to step aside and keep an eye on me.

Then they climbed into the van and began untying Damon. One took off his gag.

"Are you okay?" one asked, shaking him awake.

"What's his name?" another inquired of me.

"Damon. Damon the Demon," I said, all of a sudden too tired to give anyone any more of my explanations.

Instead, I stood stiffly while the paramedics carried Damon, wobble legged, barely awake, out of the van. Two police cars roared into the parking lot, followed soon after by a plainclothes-cop's vehicle. All had lights flashing. None of the officers who emerged were the ones we'd talked to two nights before.

I was marched on tin solider legs to the police car. I pretended not to see Mischa's unmoving body being loaded into the ambulance.

thirty-nine

MAY 4

When the announcement about the winner got derailed because Charlie's model OD'd in the girls' bathroom, things
got strangely clear for me. Clearer still when Charlie was arrested for kidnapping.

I realized, weird as it might sound, that me and my rage
were such a load of shit.

I'd thought Charlie Dean was a shallow twit. Her and her
precious suits and her mannered way of speaking seemed
like a joke. Then I saw her dress, and it was epic and beautiful. And I saw her dad, a skinny, sketchy-looking dude, and
her model, who'd nearly done herself in. And then it was dis-
covered that Charlie and her model had kept some guy tied
up in a van for reasons no one understood.

It was surreal, especially coming after that fashion show,
which was about ten times more intense than I could have
imagined.

I got hit with this unexpected understanding of how lucky
I was. For real. Like, if my mom hadn't done me the favor of

leaving me with grandparents for most of my life, maybe I would have turned into a Charlie Dean. Not that that would have been the worst thing. But turning into Charlie Dean would have been the best-case scenario. If I'd been given the truly tough situation, I'd probably be enjoying the services of the nearest juvenile detention center or in rehab or whatever.

I stood with everyone else and watched the paramedics carry off the girl who OD'd. She had an oxygen mask over her face, so she was still alive.

Mr. Manhas, the Green Pastures principal, came out of the bathroom looking haunted.

There were police everywhere.

One of them went to Mr. Manhas and said there was a problem outside. Mr. Manhas followed the cops out.

We milled around until finally a woman who introduced herself as Mrs. Landau, the vice principal, asked us all to head back to the atelier.

We walked down the hallway in an afternoon that had turned bright with a different kind of energy. From special-occasion rush to post-crisis buzz.

The lights were up, and the parents and students and designers and audience members fluttered around like moths not sure where to land. I was on my own because my grandparents had to go to a medical appointment right after the show, and Barbra had walked out. Booker hadn't shown up at all.

"Please," said Mrs. Landau. "I'd like to ask everyone to take a seat."

Slowly most people did, but those of us who'd been in the show stood bunched up near the door. Charlie Dean wasn't with us.

"This has been an emotional afternoon. From the superb

display of talent and hard work to the frightening emergency with a young person to the, uh, situation outside. My understanding is that the young lady is stable and likely to recover. I don't have complete information on the other situation. The police are handling it. But in light of what has happened, it doesn't feel appropriate to continue our celebration or to announce the results of the competition."

I didn't care too much, since I didn't have a chance. But the faces of the other competitors were like masks someone left on the lawn after a costume party.

There were a few grumbles, but it sounded more like people releasing stress than complaining.

"We will notify all competitors when it's time to announce the competition results. I must warn you that in light of what has happened here, we cannot say for sure that the competition will continue as planned. The sponsor of the competition may choose to reevaluate his support. In the meantime, I would like to thank all the young designers, the models, family, friends, and supporters for an inspiring afternoon. Please join me for a moment of silence to wish the young person who has had this unfortunate emergency a speedy and thorough recovery."

The silence held for a full minute.

When it was over, and Mrs. Landau had left the stage, I didn't move for another minute. Perspective. It was all about perspective.

I was going to have a year and a bit left of high school to think about why I had no friends left and why some people have a lot and some people have shit-all.

When I blinked and came out of my trance, Esther and Sheryl and Edward were waiting for me.

Sheryl and Edward stood on either side of Esther like they

were prepared to full-body tackle any traumatic experience that might be heading her way.

"I just wanted to say that I hope you win," said Esther. "If there's a winner."

"Thanks," I said. "You'll be the first to know. And thanks, Esther. You were really good. I want you to have the dress."

I handed the small bundle over with both hands. She took it and stared at me with a grave expression.

"Don't be sad," she said. "No matter what happens."

"I won't," I lied.

Then they left.

forty

CHARLIE DEAN

HERE'S AN IDEA © CHARLIE DEAN DESIGNS:

When you are asked about your look or your interior design, as you surely will be, keep your answers short and simple. Someone says: "Why have you used a wagon wheel for an outdoor clothes dryer?" Answer: "Because cowboys."

DATE: MAY 11

Days after fashion show: 7

Naturally, there was some explaining to do. And so I explained, leaving nothing out. I kept my answers direct and to the point. The police were very intrusive, as I have always known them to be.

When I'd been at the station for more than an hour, waiting for a lawyer who specializes in defending young people, the two officers who'd taken our complaint on Thursday night, the ones who hadn't taken us seriously when they realized my dad and Mischa were addicts, came in. They joined the questioning and then went outside with the other officers, who had started to look like a blur of officialdom rather than individuals. When the first officers came back, their tone was more understanding.

Perhaps they'd read our report from Thursday night. Maybe it was my black eye, or the long scratch down Mischa's face. Maybe it was the many previous reports that had been filed about Mischa and her ex-boyfriend.

Before, there had been talk of kidnapping charges. Drug-trafficking charges. Now there were confirming details of previous assaults. Questions about what I'd seen. What I'd heard.

I was at the police station for many hours. It was surprisingly not that bad. Officers and support staff kept coming in to have a look at me, probably because I'm one of the more stylish *apprehendées* they'd had.

Late Saturday evening they let me go. Maybe Damon declined to press charges because he didn't want to go to court for assaulting Mischa, attacking me and my dresses, and stealing drugs from a terminally ill relative. He would be answering to some of that, but not in relation to being a kidnapping victim. Thank Dior!

When they released me to Jacques, they treated us like guests who'd overstayed our welcome rather than criminals. Perhaps they were resentful about the paperwork, but one can't be sure.

I was told I might have to appear in court and might be mandated into counseling as an alternative to facing kidnapping charges. I have already decided what to wear to court. A Gaultier-esque Breton-striped top with a black suit would be witty and appropriate. Demon was also going to have to undergo anger management and day treatment for substance abuse.

But I've gotten ahead of myself. What about the results of the competition into which I poured my very heart and soul, all of my dad's finances, and all my skill and every last hope for my future?

I did not go to the announcement because I was not welcome at Green Pastures. The vice principal told us that when she called on Monday. Jacques, who took the call, said she sounded sorry. About everything.

She told my dad to tell me not to give up on my dreams even though I was disqualified from the contest. That was sweet of her, though unnecessary. Her call was followed by one from Mr. Oliver, the counselor at R. S. Jackson. Mr. Oliver said he'd been informed by someone at Green Pastures that I might need an appointment. He said he had one available in two weeks and asked if that would work for me. He sounded very tired. He said that he knew a little bit about what had happened at the fashion show. He said I should work on "getting some perspective." He added that maybe the lesson was that fashion could not "come first." Easy for him to say.

In spite of everything, I dressed nicely on the day of the announcement. After all, it would be an incredibly special day for *someone*. I wore my own recreation of a World War II–style olive suit with rust trim. It is chic, chic, *chic*. A splash of martial glamor with two fingers of nipped waist and absolutely perfect tailoring. To look at that suit is to stand on a long, breezy runway, nose full of aviation fuel fumes, surrounded by big silver planes and pilots in bomber jackets with goggles! *Ooh la la!*

The jacket features geometric rust flap pockets at the chest and the hip and the skirt ends in two rust bands. The jacket closure is a single large rust button. To die for.

I wore it to sit in my room and stare at the dress I'd made

for Mischa. We hadn't seen her since she got out of the hospital, which is why I was so surprised when my dad knocked on my door.

"Charlie girl," he said. "There's someone here to see you."

Mischa stood beside him, looking smaller, paler, but her eyes were clear and she was steady on her feet.

"Hey, Charlie Dean."

"Hi," I said.

My dad patted her on the shoulder, and she came into my room and sat down.

"Love the suit. You look really cool. Like you're in *The Great Gatsby* or something."

"Twenty years too early," I said. "The look is forties."

"I love that you know that," said Mischa. "It's enough to make me want to go back to school."

"Are you coming back?" I asked. The "to us" went unspoken.

"I'm waiting to get into a women's treatment program in Vancouver," she said. "I'm sorry that my . . . that Damon screwed everything up for you."

At that I stopped. Stared at her.

"I'm sorry that you ever went out with someone like that."

The slight smile left her face.

"I think I'm done with that. From now on, only nice guys. Possibly no guys for a while."

"Good," I said. "Because a second kidnapping charge would make it hard for me to get into college."

She laughed. And when it was time to go, I picked up the dress on its hanger, and with the wide skirts hanging over my arm, handed it to Mischa.

"I can't take this," she said.

"I made it just for you. You should have it."

She stroked the sumptuous fabric and ran a finger along the rigid neckline.

"Can you keep it for me until I come back?"

I nodded.

"Good-bye, Mischa," I said.

"Good-bye, Charlie Dean. You are an amazing designer."

"Thank you. You are going to be an amazing person."

Then she was gone.

forty-one

Mr. Carmichael asked us to sit down in a semicircle of chairs that had been set up at the end of the atelier. He, Mr. Manhas, Miss Landau, and the other two committee members sat behind a table.

"Thank you for joining us, and we're sorry for the delay in announcing the winner. We were, however, grateful to have more time to peruse the croquis and mood boards and design materials you submitted. I must tell you again that we were tremendously moved by your entries. By the creativity and depth of your visions."

Moved to call the police, I thought, curious about whether he was going to mention Charlie Dean and what happened at the end of the competition.

It was hard not to be flattered by his words, even though I didn't really belong. And he was right. My fellow fashion competitors had blown my mind. I'd even surprised myself. That's why I came. I wanted to pay my respects to whoever won.

Everyone but me was nearly rigid with excitement. With hope. That was the only bad part of this. Only one of them could win the scholarship. You'll notice I didn't say *us*. It was really more of a *them* situation.

Parents clutched their kids' shoulders. Friends gripped each other's hands.

I hadn't told my grandparents about this afternoon. When they asked what happened at the contest, I told them I didn't win. They were disappointed, but they said what they always say when I fail or at least don't succeed. "We never worry about you, John. You're going places. You're going to be the first one in this family."

Basically, my grandparents are delusional.

"Every one of you has talent and potential," said Mr. Carmichael. The other committee members nodded. "And I wish we had eleven"—odd hesitation—"I mean, ten scholarships to hand out." Then he made a funny face, like someone had poked him in the ribs. So Charlie Dean was disqualified. *That's* why she wasn't here. I hadn't seen her at school in the past week. This was probably why. Somehow, part of me thought they'd make an exception. Her dress had been so amazing. But I guess schools have to take ODs and kidnappings and whatnot into consideration when considering future pupils.

I could practically feel people holding their breath.

"You have all waited long enough. We were looking for exceptional young designers with personal and distinctive visions as well as technical and artistic abilities. You all more than demonstrated those things. However, there can only be one winner. I'm pleased to announce that the recipient of the scholarship to Green Pastures' fashion program will be Jo-Ann Wyse."

The good-looking, tall girl in jeans and a silver leather jacket turned to her parents, aunties, uncles, siblings, and cousins. Her parents were near tears, some of the kids screamed, but Jo just smiled, cool as hell.

The nearest contestants reached out tentatively to pat Jo's shoulder, but when she gave them a look, they backed off.

"Just kidding," she said. "Bring it in." Then she hugged them. Cricket in her chair, Jason Wong, the girls who look the same, Ainslee, Madina, and the rest. I was glad they crowded around her because then I didn't have to see the disappointment on their faces.

"Congratulations. You have won a one-year scholarship to the fashion program at Green Pastures Academy of Art and Applied Design."

I joined everyone in clapping, and Jo went to the front to get a certificate from Mr. Carmichael, and her family smiled and smiled and wiped tears from their faces.

I was glad for her. She is a major talent.

Jo took the certificate from Mr. Carmichael's hand and shook the hands of the other judges, who congratulated her.

Then Mr. Carmichael told the rest of us about all the aspects of Jo's designs that had factored into their decision, her thoughtful use of indigenous design, custom-work, combined with contemporary materials and motifs and an innovative sensibility.

And while I agreed with whatever he said, I couldn't help thinking about Charlie Dean, who should also have been in the room.

"We ask you to join us in thanking Mr. Charles Atwater, who not only donated the funds for the fashion program, including the atelier in which we now sit, but also finances many of our special programs. We have him to thank for sponsoring this competition and this scholarship."

We applauded because that was pretty generous. Probably the scholarship was a tax write-off or something, but it was still nice.

"When Mr. Atwater saw the astonishingly high quality of the work submitted for this competition, he contacted me to ask if there was something we could do for *all* of the competitors."

Another silence slammed down on the room.

Goddamn, I thought. Every day is like Christmas Meets Winning the Lottery Day at this place.

"Mr. Manhas and I put our heads together, and I'm pleased to tell you that Mr. Atwater and a few other donors will be funding a four-week summer fashion intensive for the students who took part in the fashion show. It will run from July fifteenth to August fifteenth and be free for those who have taken part in this competition. We'll open it up to other young designers, who will have to pay a modest tuition. We will bring in the best teachers and mentors. All participants will receive assistance with college applications and help preparing portfolios at the end of the session."

Now people in the audience were really clutching one another. More tears. The girl with the head scarf, Madina, was being hugged by all her brothers, and her dad and her mother carefully wiped tears from her eyes.

Carmichael was referring to Bijou's dad, a tan guy with a just-off-the-golf-course/private-plane vibe. Bijou was gazing at him with pride.

It's funny, but the only thing I could think was that Charlie Dean should be allowed to attend the summer school. Hell, she should be allowed to *teach* the summer school. I barely knew her, but I knew that fashion was her whole deal. That gave the whole announcement a bitter aftertaste. Maybe because I'm still a somewhat bitter guy.

So when everything broke up, I walked over to where Mr. Carmichael stood with Bijou's dad.

"Excuse me, sir," I said to Carmichael. "I just wanted to say something about the girl who got kicked out."

I had their complete attention.

"I don't know her that well, but she goes to my school. And I bet if you talk to her in person, you'll find out that she . . . that things got out of hand, but it wasn't her fault. At least not completely. Fashion is her"—I tried to think of the word—"air? water? That guy they had in the van, he was a serious doucheb— Sorry, I mean he's seriously bad news. I just hope you'll consider letting her go to the summer school. She can have my spot."

Mr. Carmichael and Mr. Atwater watched me.

"You don't want to attend, John?" asked Mr. Carmichael.

"To be honest, fashion isn't my thing, although I have a lot more appreciation for it now. I just wanted to go to this school. But Charlie Dean, she's hard-core. She kind of got me interested in spite of myself."

"She sounds like Bijou," said Mr. Atwater. "I can only imagine what she'd do without fashion. Or what she'd do to anyone who got in her way." He gave a rich-guy-nougaty chuckle.

"I hope you'll let Charlie Dean attend. Even if she screwed up. I guess that's what I'm saying," I said.

Mr. Carmichael looked at Mr. Atwater, who raised his eyebrows a fraction.

"I will speak with Miss Dean," said Mr. Carmichael. "In the meantime, I appreciate you speaking up for her. I agree that her commitment to fashion seems serious."

"Her dress," said Mr. Atwater, "was quite remarkable."

"It is. She is," I said. "And that dress definitely was." And then I thanked them both for the opportunity to participate.

I turned to leave and saw Tesla standing near the door. I stopped, thought about going over to speak to her, but she shook her head and I kept going. When I got outside, my eyes were a little prickly. I probably need glasses or something.

forty-two

❧CHARLIE❧
❧DEAN❧

JUNE 14

Days after competition: 41

It was a shock when Mr. Carmichael invited me to meet with him *otoko wa hito ni* (which is Japanese for person to person, or man to man) at the Green Pastures Academy of Making Dreams Come True! (I'm so grateful that I'm going to be able to learn Japanese just like I'm learning French, thanks to Google Translate. The world is impossibly full of educational opportunities!) I don't know what caused him to reach out. I don't know why he asked if he could read this diary.

Because I have nothing but the utmost respect for Mr. Carmichael, who is a magnificent teacher and fashion person, I gave this book to him. He learned about my childhood, my parents' struggles with drugs and with basic functioning, my mom's death. He learned that fashion is everything to me and why I thought that dress was the right one for Mischa. He learned how and why I became a kidnapper and why abandoned malls and derelict buildings have something to teach us about beauty and damage.

When I first handed him this journal, back in May, right after the results of the competition were announced, I felt sick and exposed. But then I didn't care because this book is the truth. On Wednesday he invited me to come and see him after school on Friday. He said it was chaos with the end of term, but to come anyway. He asked me to bring him my drawings and designs in progress. During that Friday-afternoon meeting, he gave this book back to me and said nothing about what was inside, which I appreciated. We talked about new designers we liked and old ones we loved. He told me how it was when he grew up in a small town in New Brunswick, one of the few kids of color, one of the only fashionable people in a town that didn't care.

He told me how fashion kept him alive.

He invited me to see him the next two Fridays in a row and then, when school was nearly out for the year, he invited me to join the summer fashion intensive with the other candidates. Well, I nearly didn't cope with the excitement!

Mr. Carmichael suggested I encourage John to come to the summer program, too. Since the fashion show John and I have had coffee a couple of times. We have good laughs about working retail. The Salad Stop sounds delicious but also like a hard place to work. My job at the makeup counter at Shoppers is much better. The clients there *need* me. But John doesn't want to come to the summer intensive. He says he's got a lot going on in his metalworking shop and won't have time, and I think he's putting together a portfolio for art college.

Still, I've promised Mr. Carmichael I'll keep working on John!

At Mr. Carmichael's suggestion, I also did something truly phenomenal.

I started an official Fashion Design Club! We meet at R. S. Jackson, and the club is open to the fashionably oriented from every high school in town! We only had time to meet once before exams started, but we have big plans for next year. Almost everyone from the competition came to the first meeting after school, and even some new people showed up, maybe because they wanted to see whom I would kidnap next. They soon forgot about that and were swept away by the power of creating style!

Jo is a member and, just as an aside, we have gone on five dates now and I think we're officially seeing each other. This is an epic and marvelous and ultra-romantic story deserving of its own journal that I will never share with anyone because it is simply too wonderful and precious to me.

Cricket and Jason are secretary and treasurer. Madina came from her school in the north end, Ainslee even came over from Gabriola, where she is homeschooled, and Ellen, the girl who looks sort of like Audrey Hepburn and who doesn't really speak, and the girls who look the same showed up. Everyone! We worked on designs together, shared fashion books and magazines. We have plans to watch New York Fashion Week on a laptop together, and study all the big designers' shows next year. Mr. Carmichael has promised to come and give us a guest lecture on menswear in September. The only one who didn't come was John, even though he was invited.

I think his heart is broken. His girlfriend is now his ex-girlfriend. I saw her holding hands with that big, handsome guy who used to be his best friend. No surprise there. I have never seen a human being look happier than that best friend of his. Except perhaps me every time I think about fashion club and summer school!

Poor John. The next time we have coffee I'm going to ask

him to make a metal bodice for me. I think it will do him good.

I suppose I ought to say something about the home situation. My dad had a small relapse shortly after the show and is currently on methadone. He is attending his meetings; he has not sold everything we own or met a new, inappropriate lady, which is a relief. We are nearly a Hallmark household!

A few days after she dropped by to see us, Mischa left for Vancouver. Then my dad heard that she left her treatment program and disappeared. I have no idea where she is, but I wish her well and I will keep the Mall of Reborn Dreams dress for her until she comes back. The dress may be the capstone piece of my Resilience Rising Collection™.

To conclude this style diary, here's something that every young person, fashionable or not, growing up in a difficult family needs to know: keep it together. It will eventually be over. You will turn seventeen or eighteen, and you can move out and start your own life. You do not need to take on the problems of your progenitors. Find something that makes your heart sing and your brain expand, and let it carry you past all the ugliness and over the low spots. Oh, it's not easy. Certainly not. You will make mistakes, but you will overcome.

As Jo has gotten to know me better, she says she's worried that if I'm not careful, I'll turn into one of those brittle people who will smash into a thousand pieces if someone hits me just the right way. She's so direct! It's exhilarating! But she's not correct. People thought the same thing about Diana Vreeland, and look at the amazing life she had.

I am strong. And I am stylish beyond all measure.

Allow me to leave you with a final thought:

So are you.

With love,

Charlie Dean

acknowledgments

I would like to thank the fashion design college I briefly attended for helping me to appreciate the artistry and skill that goes into creating clothing and for helping me to understand that I did not have what it takes to be a fashion designer.

Thanks to my mother, who helped pay for that rather costly misadventure. She let me start buying my own clothes when I was ten and hardly said a thing when I headed off to school in yet another unseemly get-up.

Many people helped bring this book into being. I'm particularly grateful to my wonderful editors, Kendra Levin, Lynne Missen, and Sharyn November, and my agent, Hilary McMahon. Thanks to production editor Janet Pascal, cover designer Danielle Calotta, designer Dana Li, art director and interior designer Kate Renner, and copyeditor Tricia Callahan. Admiration and gratitude also to the wonderfully talented illustrator, Soleil Ignacio. Deep thanks also to Ken Wright for his support of this book.

I send every good thought to the people who test read the manuscript: Bill Juby, Susin Nielsen, Andrew Gray, Serah-Marie McMahon, Robin Stevenson, Sara Davidson, and Stephanie Dubinsky. You all made it better. Extra special thanks the various people who gave me technical advice on making clothes and metal art: Anne Adema and Jason Gress and his metalworking students and Jason Ritter. Extra, extra special thanks to my husband, Jim, for everything, always.

Thanks to anyone who has designed or made a piece of clothing I've loved to wear or have admired from afar. Fashion, for all its problems, has always felt like one of the great pleasures in life.